or

rsion

the Mississippi bulldog she is, she keeps on trying; her error-filled efforts bring plausibility to a magical mystery tour of Scandinavia."

—Harriet Klausner

5 Stars: "This book rocks .... When High Steppers begin to die mysteriously and the ship's Captain keeps trying to cover it up, it's up to Sidney to find out what is going on. [The solution] involves a mysterious red bag, people who aren't who they claim to be and High Steppers getting in the way. This book is fabulous!"

—Paula Mitchell's Reviews

Shore
Excursion

Shore Excursion

7/18/2013

MARIE MOORE

CAMEL PRESS

Seattle, WA

CAMEL
PRESS

Camel Press
PO Box 70515
Seattle, WA 98127

For more information go to: www.camelpress.com
www.mariemooremysteries.com

Cover design by Sabrina Sun

Shore Excursion
Copyright © 2012 by Marie Moore

ISBN: 978-1-60381-874-2 (Trade Paper)
ISBN: 978-1-60381-875-9 (eBook)

Library of Congress Control Number: 2011945214

Printed in the United States of America

Acknowledgments

The thank-you list for a debut novel is of necessity very long because all the bits that comprise the imagination of the writer have been molded to a greater or lesser degree by so many terrific people. Then, once a book is finished, the more difficult task of bringing it into the hands of the reader begins, a task made far more daunting when the novelist is new to the business and dependent on the kindness, generosity and patience of a whole new set of friends.

I can never thank each one enough.

The publication of *Shore Excursion* and the further adventures of Sidney Marsh would never have happened without the tireless efforts of my patient and skilled agents, Victoria Marini and Jane Gelfman, and would have been completely impossible if my dear friend Kathryn Altman had not recommended my book and me to Jane in the first place. My sincere thanks also go to Catherine Treadgold, Publisher at Camel Press, not only for her work in the editing, production and promotion of this book, but also for her faith and advocacy of me and Sidney from the acquisition process forward.

For their endless reading, re-reading, advice, criticism,

support and love I want to thank my precious daughters, Marie and Susanna, my brother Leslie and mother, Doris, and also Teri Tobias, Beverly Massey, Frances Gresham, Linda Seale, Diane Hawks, Grace McLaren, and Everette Stubbs, wise counsel, faithful cheering squad, and good keepers of The Secret.

And, of course, my deepest gratitude will always and ever be to my husband, Rook, for without his love, encouragement, and support, the publication of *Shore Excursion* would only be this little dream that I once had and not a book at all.

For Rook

1

Heading home from work on Monday afternoon I had that creepy-crawly feeling, like I had walked through a spider's web and had invisible threads sticking to my face.

Ever get that feeling? Like maybe someone is watching you?

Ever worry about being followed?

Ever think—while you're walking down the sidewalk in your own neighborhood, minding your own business—that someone big and bad might just grab you or snatch you into the nearest alley?

Ever wonder if you're going nuts?

That's how I felt all that week before I left for my cruise. Jumpy. Real jumpy.

I was noticing sounds I hadn't really noticed before, staring at people on the street, listening for steps behind me, wondering if delivery guys were as harmless as they seemed.

Jumpy. Real jumpy.

I'm sure folks in my hometown would say that it's normal, even smart to feel that way if you are a single girl and living alone in any big city, let alone New York City. But I had never felt that way before. I had never been afraid before that week.

No, *afraid* is not the right word. Not afraid, exactly, more like uneasy. Creeped out. You know what I mean.

Jumpy.

⊁

The odd thing about the homeless guy who stumbled into me after work on Tuesday at the Prince Street station was that the man didn't look homeless at all, just rumpled and weary. I'm sure I looked the same to him.

Leaving the agency, I'd walked past some furniture store windows on the way to the train and almost didn't recognize my reflection in the display mirrors. Wild black hair, blowing in the wind, swirled around a pale, pale face above a black cowl-neck sweater. Pretty spooky. My makeup was a mess by the day's end and the smudged mascara under my eyes made them look even bigger than usual. I tried to wipe it off with my finger but it wouldn't budge so I gave up and hurried down into the subway. So much for the claims of the "smudge-proof" makeup!

It had been a long day. A million phone calls; then I power-shopped through lunch, snagging some great silver shoes and a knockout of a dress on a half-off sale, the only one left on the rack in a size 6. I ran into one of my clients, Miss Ruth Shadrach, at Macy's One Day Sale. She was buying some nylon nightgowns and a little red traincase for our trip.

I was tired, standing on the platform waiting for the express train, clutching my packages. I wasn't exactly on top of my game. I wasn't alone. The uptown platform was jammed with tired commuters.

Peering over the heads of some Chinese ladies, I thought I saw the lights of the train coming. That was when the man bumped into me. He was big, almost a head taller than I am, and I'm 5'8".

He was muttering something—I guessed some sort of apology—but I couldn't hear over the shrieking noise of the approaching train. The mass of people surged forward even as the train stopped, and in the mad rush to board I lost sight of him.

It was only later—when I saw that same shabby guy on the street at the park near my building, making his nest with all these cardboard sheets and little plastic bundles—that I knew he was homeless.

It was two days later—when I met him again in Union Square and then later on my street—that pity changed to fear. He stared at me and shouted, waving his arm, trying to stop me, as I hurried into my entryway. I was grateful—not for the first time—for the extravagance of a doorman building. I looked out from the window of my castle, drawbridge up, but the doorman had done his job.

The homeless man with the gutter-gravy-colored eyes was gone.

♓

I told my super about the homeless man between wash-loads in the basement Thursday night. He dismissed my concerns with an elegant Polish shrug.

"It is because you are from the south of the United States. From a small willage. You do not understand what it is to live in New York. I have fifteen years in this country. When you have fifteen years, you will know how it is in New York, and you will not be afraid. Or maybe you will be more afraid. I do not know. You understand?"

I did not understand. But then, there's not much of Janusz's worldview that I do understand.

Janusz is a good man. He has a round, round head with round blue eyes, and an impossible haircut. He can lift anything—probably even a refrigerator—by himself, and fix just about anything when he wants to, which is not very often. Crumbling plaster, locks, washing machines, window air conditioners, the furnace, anything. He has a courtly manner of speaking except when he is screaming in Polish at his helper, Pieter. Pieter does all the nasty stuff in the building ... takes out the trash, unstops toilets, mops the basement, kills rats. Pieter leads a dog's life.

I fed seven quarters into the dryer, scraped the lint off the trap, cursed all of the cat people in the building, and pressed the start button. The monster roared to life, blotting out all but shouted conversation.

Waving goodbye to Janusz, I hiked back up the steps to 4F. We have an erratic elevator, so when I don't have a load, it's quicker to take the stairs. In the spooky stairwell my thoughts returned to my dumpster-diving friend.

Homeless people are a fact of life in New York. New York City spends vast amounts of money to house and feed them, and tons of private charities and religious groups do their best to help, but it is never enough. More people live in New York's homeless shelters than the entire population of my home town, and that number doesn't include the hard cases who live on the street.

New Yorkers begin to recognize the regulars in their neighborhoods: the guy who sleeps on the church steps, the Asian woman on the sidewalk near the Duane Reade drugstore, the mutterer on the corner. You can spot the transients who drift out of town in late summer when the weather turns cold farther north. You know which ones deliberately choose a cardboard sheet on the street over a warm bed and a sermon— the same ones who balk when told to go to the shelters even on record-cold days of winter, who linger in the subway entrances until the transit cops move them out. You sense the difference between the drugged, the alcoholic, and the desperate. You know that some are basically good people who just caught a few bad breaks or ran out of luck. You know that some are cons and others are sick, or mean, or just plain nuts. And you also know, deep inside you, that there are those who are very dangerous.

I didn't know which category my new pal fell into, but I knew that I was afraid of him.

♓

On Friday at work I was too busy getting ready for my old folks' cruise to Scandinavia and Russia to think about creepy feelings or the homeless man or Janusz or anything else except nametags and dining preferences and shore excursions.

I am a travel agent, a dying breed. I was amazingly lucky to be hired for the summer after my freshman year of college by a New York agency, Itchy Feet Travel (IFT). My friends couldn't believe I was actually headed to work in Manhattan. I never looked back. I fell in love with the travel business and New York and managed to talk Itchy into a permanent job as a frontline agent.

"You are *what*?" my mother said, during the fateful phone call to Mississippi that August. "You're really staying in New York, giving up college and sorority rush and everything to work for a travel agency? I can't believe it. I don't know what your father will say. Sidney Lanier Marsh, are you *crazy*?"

Maybe. But I worked hard, took all the training I could get, and was soon promoted to a special group agent, a job I have now held for almost six years. I'm not getting rich, that's for sure, unless you count getting to travel the whole world for free.

For the last several trips, I have been in charge of a group called the High Steppers. Don't be put off by the name. This is not some dance troupe trying to knock off the Rockettes. The High Steppers are senior citizens, God love them, and I am their shepherd. My colleague and best friend, Jay Wilson, is the co-leader on most of my trips.

He and I both totally realize that travel agents may be going the way of the dinosaur because precious few of us managed to survive the airlines' decision to stop paying us for selling their tickets. When that happened, travel agencies took a big hit. Those big boys did a job on us and on the traveling public as well.

Before then, agents were paid on commission by vendors … airlines, cruise lines, hotels, etc. Their work was free to the customer. No charge. No fees. And your agent worked super hard to find you the best deal for your money, the best possible trip for *you*.

Then some evil person at the airlines decided to make more money by cutting out the travel agent. No more big commission checks to pay! Bigger profits for them! They sold the public on the idea that getting great deals was easy, that no one needed an agent at all when they could easily book a trip for themselves on their home computer. Really? Do you think your little desktop is seeing all that is out there? Do you really think that a do-it-yourself E-ticket is better than a full service, experienced, *free* travel advisor?

But enough of that. I hear enough bitterness from my former compadres—now selling insurance or bras or whatever—to waste time wallowing in the inequities of life. I'm just glad I still have a job.

"Mrs. Weiss is on line four, again," Roz's intercom voice interrupted. "She wants to know what she should wear for the Roman Toga Party. You want I should tell her?"

I love travel. Period. And, fortunately, I get to travel to places I could never afford, because I don't mind shepherding senior citizens around the world. It's my job, and I love it. I like old folks, they like me, and I make just enough to afford my rent. Barely, but that's New York.

The agency that I work for, Itchy Feet Travel, is in Nolita. When I first moved to Manhattan I had to learn all about stuff like Soho, Noho, Tribeca and Nolita just to find my way around. Soho means SOuth of HOuston Street. For all you Texans in the Big Apple, that's HOW—rhymes with COW—ston. Nolita is short for NOrth of Little ITAly. You get the idea. My personal favorite is in Brooklyn; Dumbo, meaning Down

Under the Manhattan Bridge Overpass.

Itchy Feet handles mostly leisure travel, a lot of groups, and still has a fair amount of corporate business. Most of the people who work here are good—*very* good—and very experienced. I am, too. I can fare a Buddhist monk to Sri Lanka and back with three stopovers before you can say veg meal, and without once calling the help desk. What I'm saying is, this is not some mall deal staffed with bubbleheads. We are *good*, sugar.

That Friday afternoon I was finalizing the details of the High Steppers Scandinavian cruise. With all the phone calls and interruptions, it took me almost until closing to get their travel bags assembled. My guys love their travel bags. Bright pink, with High Steppers and the Itchy Feet Travel logo printed on the plastic, the bags hold all their travel documents and pills and gel pads, with room left over for all that other stuff they claim they have to have with them. I love those loud bags, too, because it makes it easier to spot strays.

"I'm outta here, Roz. See you on the fifteenth."

"Good luck with them High Steppers, hon. I gotta tell ya, I wouldn't trade jobs with you for nothing!"

♓

After work I took the downtown R train to Canal Street to deliver travel docs to Charlie and Amy Wu, loyal members of the High Steppers, and two of the agency's best clients.

Personal delivery of documents is not usually my job, but these people are special. Besides being really good customers of our agency, they own a terrific Cantonese restaurant on Mott Street called Lotus, and also a Chinese import business that sells silk and other high-end fabrics along with teak and mahogany furniture, all at great prices. I bought the coolest stuff in my apartment at Wu's.

I pushed my way through the crowded street, heading east on Canal toward Mott, checking out the latest designer knockoffs hanging from hooks in the stalls lining the street as I went.

Skinny little women minding pushcarts filled with counterfeit DVDs and CDs jockeyed for space on the sidewalk with muscular vendors of fake Rolex and Cartier watches.

Lookouts on the street watched carefully for the trademark infringement cops, chattering steadily into cell phones, their heads swiveling back and forth like meerkats.

The word goes out at the first sign of the police, and you can hear corrugated metal stall doors slamming down all over Chinatown. Some merchants even tape up "For Rent" signs as if the stall is vacant.

It's rumored that secret passages through the backs of the little stores and all underground in Chinatown connect the whole maze, providing quick escape for merchants of illegal goods, drugs, money and people. They say that some of those tunnels go back to the days of Tammany Hall. Some things don't change, do they?

I stopped to price a handsome black leather bag with brass hardware and a distinctive designer logo. It looked so close to the real thing that I wondered if it was real, maybe stolen.

"How much?" I asked a small nervous man who was constantly watching the street.

"Fifty dollar, last price."

"Fifty dollars!" I repeated, "Fifty dollars? Too much. What about twenty?"

"Fifty dollar. Last price," he insisted. "Very nice. Very good bag, you look."

He opened the bag for inspection, and I knew that my guess was probably correct. The inside really did look real, with logo lining and intricate stitching. Besides, they will always bargain for the fakes, but never for the hot ones.

"You not like this one? Come, come in here, come quick. I have others you like, very beautiful, but not cheap. Good bag not cheap. You look. You see. Look quick. I make you best price."

He pushed open a section of the pegboard wall, revealing a dim passageway stuffed with purses, and motioned for me to enter.

"Come quick, come quick. Very nice, you like."

Now, I love to shop. All Southern women love to shop. It's in our blood, inherited and instinctive, then honed by our mothers, just as kittens learn to catch mice. But I couldn't stop. Too late. Too much to do.

"No, thanks," I said smiling, backing out. "Not today. I'm sorry. Maybe some other time."

⯈

Charlie Wu was in the kitchen of Lotus when I arrived, and I was ushered through the swinging doors by the smiling hostess—Charlie's niece, Mei Mei.

There are lots of different smells in Chinatown, some of them not so pleasant, but the aromas wafting from the pots and pans in Charlie's kitchen smelled terrific.

Charlie's wife Amy—a slim, tiny woman with a great sense of style—manages their import business. Charlie—also slim, tiny, and impeccably dressed—runs Lotus. It's hard to know how they can stay so trim working around all that wonderful food.

I have a cousin who eats everything in sight, and when I was a teenager, if I really pigged out, my mother would make dire predictions about my eating and her girth. I wear a 6, okay? But if I worked at Lotus, I'm pretty sure I'd be bigger than Ethelline.

Charlie thanked me for the delivery, and he must have seen the hunger on my face, because he offered me a meal. I hated to pass his offer up, but I really needed to get home. It was getting late, I had calls to make, and I had barely started packing.

Waving goodbye, I pushed my way back up to Canal, ducked

into the subway, swiped my Metrocard, and headed back uptown on the R.

♓

At about 8 p.m. I stopped in at Kim's bodega near my apartment for a few fantastically priced toiletries and a hot pastrami on rye with brown mustard and a Kosher pickle.

Why a Vietnamese man can make the best pastrami sandwich in all Manhattan is beyond me. I only knew that, having worked through lunch, and after turning down Charlie Wu's offer, I was totally ready for the pastrami. And for the cold, creamy cheesecake that I bought to top it off.

"You eat all this, you get soooo fat!" he jeered, staring at my rear. "Hahahaha!"

Kim thinks he is a real funny guy. He loves to make remarks about my appetite and my shape. But for the sake of his food, I'll put up with his mouth.

In reward for his humor, I paid with plastic. Kim hates that, because not only does he have to pay the card people a fee, he also has to report the transaction to his newly-adopted Uncle Sam instead of slipping the cash in the box he keeps under the counter. That would teach the old pirate to call me fat again anytime soon!

Back out on my street, the jumpy feeling returned, and I thought I caught a glimpse of that homeless guy again on the steps of a brownstone at the end of the block. Then I realized it was only a porter, cleaning the steps.

"Time to get out of town, kiddo," I thought. "You're overdue."

"Hey, babe! I got a sure thing for ya in the fifth at Belmont tomorrow!"

Eddie the Sunbather was yelling at me from his park bench on the island in the middle of the street.

Most of the time, Eddie hangs out at the OTB in the next block. Sometimes he sells a sheet at the track. On sunny days he sits on his bench, with his shirt open, improving his tan. That would be okay, I guess, if he was also a body builder, but Eddie is overweight, pushing ninety, and has long, stringy, dyed hair. Not a pretty sight. Tonight, with a brisk wind blowing off the river, Eddie wore his ancient trench coat, a scarf, and a Yankees cap.

"Some other time, Eddie," I yelled over the traffic, "I'm out on another trip tomorrow and I'm running kinda short on cash."

"Well, all right, kid," he yelled back, "but when I hit it big, you just remember I tried to let you in!"

I started back down the street, then stopped, caught a break in traffic and crossed against the light to Eddie's bench.

"Eddie. In the last few days, when you were sitting here, did you see anyone funny hanging around, anyone who didn't belong here, not a tourist, not a regular? A homeless guy, maybe, with long brown dreads and weird-looking eyes?"

He took his stogie out of his mouth and squinted up at me.

"Yeah. Yeah. Now that you mention it, babe, maybe I did. Yesterday. He was sitting on the steps of your building."

He chewed on the stogie then squinted up at me.

"He been bothering you? He better not bother you none, cause if he does, he's gonna answer to Big Eddie here. You know that, don't you?"

"Yeah, I know that." I patted him on the shoulder. "Thanks, Eddie. See you around."

Great. Just great. I had a stalker. And not even a cute one. I scooted across the street just ahead of the M5 bus and headed home.

There were no freaky types hanging around my building as I entered, just the doorman having an intense discussion in Polish with the delivery guy from the dry cleaners.

While I waited for the elevator, I checked myself out in the lobby mirror. No matter what Kim thinks, I am not fat. Not too old. Not too young. Pretty okay looking, I thought, in my black Manhattan uniform.

My hair is black, too, and my purse and my shoes. We New Yorkers look like a colony of cat burglars.

I pushed the elevator button again, like that would make it come faster. The lighted numbers showed it stopped on 6. If it doesn't come soon, I said to myself, I will take the stairs. I glanced back at the mirror, thinking that I really didn't look too bad, considering the day I'd had. I am lucky to have these big gray eyes with long enough lashes to get away with very little makeup. And I'm still a long way from Botox, thank God, because I sure can't afford it.

The elevator door opened and I stepped in as Mrs. Schwartz from 6B bounded out, pulled by her Weimaraner, Fritz, headed for the sidewalk. The elevator doors closed. A few glistening drops on the floor and a faint odor told me that Mrs. Schwartz hadn't moved fast enough for Fritz.

Tons of New Yorkers share tiny apartments with beasts of all kinds, large and small. I don't. I can't imagine it. I mean, I'm okay with dogs—I had a dog and a cat back home—but scooping poop at the beginning and end of every day, in the rain, in the snow, in January? Boarding a pet when I'm away on long trips? No, thanks. Not for me.

Like most of Manhattan, I watched *New York One News* while I ate my sandwich; then I made some calls, finished packing, and had a long, hot soak in the tub.

My bathroom, like the rest of the building, is pretty old. The plumbing clanks a lot, but I have this great tub, deep, with high sides. The hot water is included in the rent so that's one place I don't have to economize.

My phone rang while I was soaking—rang a long time—but I didn't even think about trying to answer it. I finally forced myself out of the water and brushed my teeth. After I climbed in between the sheets I was lucky to get the light turned off before I fell asleep.

When I first moved to New York, the night noise drove me nuts. I mean, Janusz is right. I am from a small 'willage,' where you can count all the red lights in your head if you think hard enough. My evening sounds were whip-o-wills and the wind blowing through the trees. I also like sleeping with the window open, which of course magnifies the noise problem.

My first week in Manhattan, I was sure I'd picked an apartment in the wrong neighborhood. In the daytime the street seemed quiet enough, but when I turned off the lights, I learned that New York quiet is not Mississippi quiet.

Horns. Voices. Garbage trucks. Car alarms. Drunk Russians. Loud tourists. More car alarms. Diesel engines. Fire trucks. Ambulances. In the middle of the night. All night. Every night.

The rest of the world thinks that the phrase "city that never sleeps" means excitement. New Yorkers know what it really means. Night noise. Of course the city never sleeps. It can't.

In time, of course, I adjusted. I tried a lot of stuff before reaching that point. The little white pills left me groggy at work. The earplugs were impossible. If I put the window down and went to sleep I woke a couple of hours later, suffocating because of the radiators.

I complained about noise pollution to the EPA. I called the Mayor's Quality of Life Hotline. I drank milk. Nothing helped.

But then, one night, for no good reason, after three weeks of insomnia, I slept. Nirvana. I simply didn't hear all that stuff anymore. I had become a New Yorker.

2

The phone woke me on Saturday morning, but when I finally answered it, no one was there.

Major bummer. Two missed calls. No number listed.

I rolled over. Probably a telemarketer.

The phone rang again, but this time, there was someone on the line. My mother.

"Mornin' darlin', time to rise and shine. Aren't you leaving on your cruise today?"

"Yes, ma'am, but not until tonight. I've had a long week, Mamma, so I planned to sleep in a while this morning. I am meeting my group at Kennedy late this afternoon."

"Oh. Well, I'm sorry I woke you up, baby. I just wanted to tell you that another one of your daddy's sisters is getting a divorce."

"Which one? Seems like one of them is always getting a divorce."

"Yes, I know. The women in the Marsh family have always had lots of trouble with men. It's just how they are. The Marsh Curse, that's what I call it. Always attracted to Mr. Wrong, never to Mr. Right. This time it's your Aunt Caroline. She's leaving that chiropractor she met in Cleveland. I can't say I'm surprised. I never thought it would last. He's a Yankee, and was married three times before he met her."

"Mamma, Aunt Caroline was married before, too, first to that professional wrestler, and then to Uncle Jack, the bible salesman. I liked him. He made me laugh."

"How could you have liked Jack, Sidney, when he turned out to already have a wife and family up in Missouri? That just shows that you're a Marsh girl, too, and have no judgment at all when it comes to finding the right man."

"You might be right, Mamma. But we can't all be the belle of the ball like you were and find someone as good as Daddy."

"No, that's true. You're right about that. They don't make many men as good as your Daddy anymore. His sisters sure have had bad luck, though. That's the gospel truth. Well, I guess I better get off the phone now, baby. It's long distance and we're just burning up money. You have a good time, now, you hear? Don't work too hard and look around on that big ship, honey. There might be a nice man on there just meant for you. I mean a *nice* man, now, honey, not one of those ole boys like your aunts are always runnin' off with and marryin'. Don't you be bringin' one of *those* home! Bye now, darlin'. Love you. Have a good time now, and be careful!"

"Okay, Mamma. Goodbye. Love you, too. Glad you called."

I ended the call, put the phone on silent, rolled over, and went back to sleep. As I drifted off, I wondered if she might be right. *Was* there a Marsh curse? And if so, did it apply to me?

⋈

The afternoon sun slanting through the mini-blinds finally persuaded me that it was time to get moving. I showered and dressed, drank iced tea, ate a sandwich and made my bed; then I rolled my bag down the hall, into the elevator, and out into the lobby.

The hallway smelled like marinara sauce. People here cook a lot on the weekend.

"You are leaving again so soon."

My favorite Pole grabbed my bag and carried it down the steps to the street.

"While you are gone, this time, your sink, I fix. Yes?"

"Yes, indeed, Janusz. That would be great. I would love for you to fix my sink."

I knew full well that he wouldn't.

The black car bound for Kennedy was at the curb, and while the driver loaded the bag I grabbed a *Post* and a *Times* from the newsstand on the corner. The street vendor cart that was always there for me in the mornings with a fresh cup of coffee, fixed just the way I like it, was gone.

New York is all about fresh. Fresh pastrami, fresh coffee, fresh bagels, fresh flowers.

Fresh driver from the car service. "So, whereya goin', doll?" he said, checking me out.

"Kennedy, please. British Airways."

"Kennedy I already know, doll," he smiled. "What I mean is, whereya goin' after that? And whenya comin' back? And when you DO come back, how about maybe a beer and a pizza sometime, you and me?"

You can't blame a guy for trying, and he was pretty cute, but I smelled married so I turned him down. Single guys' clothes never smell of meatloaf.

The car service can be sketchy because Itchy Feet won't pay the five bucks to guarantee the fancier car, so you never know. Sometimes I score and ride like Mrs. Astor, gliding down Grand Central Parkway in a sweet new Town Car with soft leather seats.

Sometimes I bounce through Queens in a beat-up glider that is 15,000 miles overdue for a brake job, mesmerized by the little cardboard air-freshener swinging from the rearview.

My rejected Italian Stallion floored it along the north edge of the park and through Carnegie Hill, apparently preferring the cross-town lights and traffic to the twilight charms of Harlem.

He was really showing off as he swung left onto the FDR, but I forgot all about him, watching the lights of the RFK Bridge reflected on the water of the East River.

I thought of other trips I'd taken—of other bridges, other rivers.

I remembered dusk along the Ganges, a faraway river that is also beautiful only in darkness. And I thought that, like the Ganges, you never know when a body might just pop up in the East.

♓

The black car got me to JFK earlier than I had planned on Saturday evening, but it was just as well, because my old chicks are always early. I rolled my bag to the meeting point inside the international terminal and pinned on my bright pink "Hi, y'all!" button.

Now that I have abandoned my Southern-belle-with-six-suitcases persona, I rarely check a bag, but for this fancy cruise, I had to bring a bit more.

"Miss Marsh, Miss Marsh, Miss Marsh!"

A blue hair helmet headed my way.

Ready or not, hon, here come the High Steppers!

I turned to smile at one of my regulars, Ruth Shadrach, her prim little self forty-five minutes early.

Ruth had faded blue eyes in a pinched face that must have once been very pretty. She wore a dusty rose twin-set, tan mom pants and sensible shoes. Her graying brown hair had been carefully styled at what was almost certainly a standing appointment and locked into place with industrial strength super-super hold hairspray.

"I have been waiting here for almost an hour, Miss Marsh. One airline man was very rude to me. He could barely even speak English! I couldn't find you. I didn't see any stewardii. I didn't see any of our group. I would have already called the travel agency if it didn't close early on Saturday. I thought I had been left!"

The others trickled in, and I greeted them, helping each one with tickets and passports and bags, bag tags and nametags. I checked the passengers off my list as they arrived, collecting the entire group before proceeding through security. An international flight requires a pretty long check-in, and it is hard to keep the early arrivals corralled until you have the whole group assembled. The siren song of the duty-free shops drives them wild.

I knew most of the group, but as usual there were a few who were not true High Steppers. Our prices for these trips are pretty good, so that often attracts extras, at least for one trip. However, for most people under forty, unless you are seriously into Lawrence Welk, one trip with this bunch is plenty, no matter how good the deal is.

I'm assigned to the High Steppers far more often than the other agents in my office, and I'm fine with that. I like them.

Some of our agents balk at leading senior groups, because of the extra care involved in such tours. I'm okay with seniors. I grew up around old ladies and gentlemen, in the older section of a small town in the South. I was surrounded by my grandparents and uncles and aunts and great-aunts and great-uncles and all their friends.

My fond feelings for my elders began then, in my childhood.

My friends who lived in the modern section of town were closer to the new school and had kids their own age right next door, but they didn't have the Misses Wells to make teacakes for them, or Mr. Billy to tell them stories. Those kids wouldn't have dared to go near that strange old woman down the block who showed me the difference between a robin's egg and a mockingbird's.

What I'm trying to say is, some people sell older people short, but I never have. I respected them when I was seven, and I respect them now. They are usually good sports and they pretty much tell it like it is. That can be refreshing, and often includes some wonderful stories as a bonus.

So I don't mind at all being assigned to seniors. It's good that I don't, because escorting your elders around the world is a job that is not always easy.

"Miss Marsh, Miss Marsh, hello, Miss Marsh ..."

3

I stood and stretched in the stuffy murk of the 747's business class cabin about fifteen minutes before the lights went up for the breakfast service.

Right on schedule.

That fifteen minute slot is just enough time to get myself together and sneak back to the tourist section before my charges start looking for me. Surely you didn't think that Itchy Feet would actually pay for me to fly in business class, did you? In your dreams!

I suspect that those who have traveled with me before have begun to catch on to the fact that I have friends among the crew on most of my regular routes, pals who don't mind letting me in the front late at night if there's room and no one makes a big deal about it. I put my shoes back on, got my stuff together, and headed back to freshen up before the aisles were blocked with breakfast carts.

As I moved down the aisle I noticed that Mr. Klein was not having quite as good a time this morning as he'd been having last night when the drinks were served. He massaged the bridge of his big beak of a nose with manicured fingers, then ran his hands through his freshly barbered gray hair, slicking it back into place. The huge diamond ring he wore flashed in the overhead light. He wore a custom-made black silk shirt, now rumpled, and gray pleated pants with an alligator belt.

His little baby-doll wife, Sylvia, was applying orange lipstick without a mirror. Strands of her platinum blonde hair had fallen from her stylish up-do. She brushed them out of her big blue eyes and stretched. That move caused Abe Klein to smile in spite of his hangover. He was admiring her abundant bust, made even more prominent by her pink angora sweater.

The Murphy family looked as if they felt pretty ragged, too. Gladys and Muriel, mother and daughter, were both huge. Their enormous bodies were wedged into the overcrowded coach seats. Pete Murphy wasn't as wide as his wife and daughter, but he was well over six feet and rangy, with a big head full of white hair and small, deep-set eyes under thick brows.

"He reminds me of an old polar bear standing on his hind legs," whispered my colleague, Jay Wilson, as we boarded.

"Hush, he'll hear you," I whispered back.

"Not a chance," Jay said, "Not over that monologue."

Gladys Murphy talked incessantly to her husband, yammering away, giving advice, giving orders. Pete's height and strong arms had served him well as he silently struggled to jam all their stuff into the overhead compartment, ignoring a litany of instructions from Gladys.

Pete's long legs looked mighty cramped after the uncomfortable night. The Murphys had already exhibited all the sure signs of first-timers, lapping up everything on the dinner trays, watching the entire movie, buying duty-free, staying up most of the night, too excited or scared to sleep.

Today they looked as gray as the London weather was predicted to be. I knew they wouldn't be ready to roll when the plane landed. Newbies never heed my "drink lots of water, sleep on the plane" mantra, part of the sermon I preach before every trip.

Flight attendants and travel agents agree with scientists who say that long flights increase dehydration, a major factor in jetlag. Drinking lots of water in flight helps to alleviate it. Seasoned travelers know to do this, and to go right to sleep, as soon as possible after dinner. I also included this advice in the printed itinerary, but I seriously doubted if the Murphys had even read it. They clearly had not slept much.

"Angelo says that we won't get to change clothes before we go on the ship, Miss Marsh, and I just can't meet all those fancy English people in these rags. I've had these clothes on since yesterday and I know how I look."

Maria Petrone, who had probably been a knockout before all the pasta, had booked this trip in celebration of her fiftieth anniversary with her Angelo, a plumbing contractor from Queens. Her dark hair, streaked with silver, fell in abundant waves below her shoulders. *Whatever she is worrying about*, I thought, *it can't be wrinkles in her clothing*. Her new teal easy-care pantsuit, studded with gold trim, looked indestructible.

"Now, Maria, Angelo is just giving you a hard time, aren't you, Angelo?" I said, smiling, patting him on his massive shoulder.

Even at his age, Angelo's muscles bulged beneath the black rayon knit of his golf shirt. His hair was thick, gray, and brushcut. A gold Rolex bordered the Navy tattoo on his forearm. He looked up at me and grinned, flashing a gold crown.

"And, Maria," I continued, "You look just as lovely as always. But don't worry; we are going to have a day room so you can freshen up before we go to the ship. Itchy Feet Travel wouldn't have it any other way."

Itchy Feet Travel would, too, if they could get away with it and stay competitive. Sometimes I nearly gag myself with mendacity, but hey, I'm a travel counselor, not a priest.

⅜

There was a slight mix-up with the luggage in baggage claim at Heathrow. The luggage was a long time coming. The bag that had gone missing was finally found. Jay Wilson, my tall, red-headed partner, directed the skycaps with the baggage handling while I helped the High Steppers through immigration and customs. Before too long we were getting the whole group and all their stuff settled on the waiting bus for the transfer to the ship.

Jay and I make a good team. Even Diana—our boss, who Jay calls "the bitch queen of the universe"—agrees with that. Jay enjoys people and can see the humor in even the most difficult situations. His warm brown eyes and wide smile make him a favorite of the High Steppers.

Ruth Shadrach grabbed me by the sleeve. She was bristling with righteous indignation. "Miss Marsh, a foreign-looking gentleman tried to steal my new red train case from the baggage cart. It's brand new. I just bought it yesterday at Macy's sale, remember? Well, he tried to steal it, but I just snatched it right back out of his hands and scolded him. He might not speak English, but he understood that, all right!"

I'm sure he did, I thought. My experience with Ruth thus far had taught me that her daily existence was filled with little dustups. The man was probably just being kind, trying to help an old lady lift her bag. Now he knows better than to try and assist an elderly American tourist.

Not getting the horrified response that she wanted from me, Ruth moved on to the others. She soon had them clucking in sympathy and shuffling toward the bus with death grips on their handbags, watching anyone vaguely exotic-looking with suspicion.

We were moving slowly that morning, which was, given our average age, to be expected. The crisp outside air was welcome after the stuffiness of the plane and the airport. As the thick mist lifted, so did their spirits.

Elderly people are much tougher than most people realize. I've found on my trips that just when I think I am really living on the edge, panting up the last few feet of the Inca Trail into

Macchu Picchu, some seniors can easily round the corner ahead of me, forcing me to abandon my assumptions about myself and them.

The skycaps and Devon, Itchy Feet's regular bus driver for the British trips, finished loading the luggage in the storage section under the bus, and I stood by the steps and helped those who needed a boost. There was the usual confusion of choosing seats and getting settled, stowing hand luggage, and of course, questions, a million questions.

"Miss Marsh, I didn't see my bag go on. That one over there is not my bag."

"I really don't like strangers handling my things."

"Will this be my seat the whole time?"

"My new luggage was very expensive, I hope it's not damaged."

"I need a front seat, I get carsick."

"When do we eat?"

"When will we get there?"

"Did you say this would be my seat for the whole time?"

I tapped on the microphone.

"Ladies and gentlemen," I began, "For those of you who are new to the High Steppers, WELCOME! Most of you have already met my colleague, Jay Wilson, and I am Sidney Lanier Marsh—Sidney, please, to all of you—your Itchy Feet Travel leader. This is our bus driver, Devon Holbrook. Devon will take good care of us today as we begin what I'm sure you will agree is the trip of a lifetime."

Jay saluted the group and they clapped.

"On behalf of Itchy Feet," I continued, "allow me to welcome each of you to Golden Heritage of the Land and Sea, a two-week adventure that we will be enjoying together aboard the magnificent Rapture of the Deep. We want to especially welcome those of you who are new to the High Steppers. We High Steppers really know how to have a good time, don't we?"

Most nodded enthusiastically. Al Bostick wolf-whistled.

Some clapped again. Angelo Petrone was asleep with his mouth open. I could see his gold tooth. A few of the rookies closer to my age looked as if they'd suddenly realized they were on the wrong bus.

The one fairly attractive man—thirty to forty years old, I guessed—just stared out the window. He looked a lot like a Latin Johnny Depp, with long straight dark hair, dark eyes and a mischievous, wicked air about him. He was attractive, swarthy, maybe South American, with a runner's build—long-legged and slender with lean muscle.

What is his name?

I plunged on.

"We will soon approach central London, where we will enjoy A Quick Peek at London, the included half-day tour described in your Trip Bibles.

"At the conclusion of the tour, we will stop for a delightful lunch at the Stout and Snout, an authentic English pub.

"After lunch, we'll make a specially arranged visit to a woolen mill where a private demonstration of the ancient art of weaving has been scheduled just for our group! And, if time permits, you might just enjoy a once-in-a-lifetime opportunity to hunt for bargains in the mill shop.

"Then finally, we'll go to our day rooms at the Duchess Hotel, where you can freshen up and maybe squeeze in a little nap before boarding the ship in Harwich.

"But before we begin our adventure, let's get acquainted. I know that some of you have traveled with one another and IFT many times before, but others are new to us, and we all want to know you better. So let's introduce ourselves. We'll begin with you, Mrs. Goldstein."

Mrs. Goldstein, beaming, reached for the microphone.

"High Steppers," I said, still holding onto the mic, "this is Ethel Goldstein, from White Plains. She has traveled with us many, many times, all over the world. Now Ethel, tell everyone all about yourself ..."

There. We were off and running. No documents missing, no bags lost, no one sick or injured or feeling neglected yet. This trip was going to be a piece of cake.

I had just wrapped myself in that comforting thought when a dirty white box truck hurled around us, horn blaring, its left front fender scraping the length of our bus. Everyone screamed and Devon fought the wheel as the bus lurched sideways and slipped off the left shoulder of the road.

4

We were lucky.

The bus sustained only minor damage—a long, ugly scrape on the right side. No one inside was hurt, just frightened and furious. Devon did a masterful job, but he, too, was angry. Angry at the "sodding lorry" and at himself for not getting the tag number. No one else had noticed it either.

In fact, two of the men, the youngish strangers in the back, didn't seem even to have noticed the accident. I still hadn't memorized their names, so I checked my list. Johnny Depp's stand-in was really Fernando Ortiz and the muscle-bound guy in the Polo jacket next to him was Jerome Morgan.

Ortiz continued reading a newspaper, with only a glance toward the window, while Morgan tapped away on a laptop as if nothing had happened. But my old honeys were all shook up.

"Okay, Jay," I murmured, "it's Showtime."

Let me tell you about Jeremiah Parker Wilson II. He prefers to be called Jay, he says because it rhymes with gay, and he is absolutely the best traveling companion that anyone could wish for, especially when escorting a tour group.

He was named Jeremiah after a stern and fortunately long-dead grandfather, a quiet and devout Quaker who I am sure must be constantly whirling in his grave over some of Jay's more colorful speech patterns and outrageous antics. Grandpa was counting on Jay to grow up, marry a nice girl, have a bunch of kids to carry on the family name, and head the family dry-cleaning business in the his small hometown in Pennsylvania. Jay's made it pretty clear that isn't happening. He moved to Manhattan just as soon as Grandpa died and he could slip the leash.

Jay has been in this wacky travel business for the last sixteen years and loves it. His wardrobe is ten times nicer than mine, because he spends every dollar he can scrape up on it. Sales at Bergdorf's, Barney's and Saks are circled on his calendar. He shops outlet malls and sample sales and haunts all the off-price stores for big-name bargains. Jay would do without groceries for a month to buy a Hermes belt. And his loft in Hell's Kitchen could win interior design awards.

I think he's nine or ten years older than I am—I'm twenty-six—but I'll never know for sure, because he'll never tell.

Because of the time he puts in at his gym, Jay is as strong as a professional wrestler, and not much escapes either him or his wit. At 6'2" and over 200 pounds, he has defused many a dicey situation with his sheer bulk. He has smiling brown eyes, wild red hair, and is currently wearing a Van Dyke beard. He loves designer clothes and outrageous costumes. Halloween and the Fifth Avenue Easter and Gay Pride parades are high points in his year. The old ladies adore him, and so do I—a fact I would eat glass rather than admit. I beg to be paired with him on my trips, and most of the time I get my wish.

"Laaadiesss," he yelled, "are your panties in a wad or WHAT?"

The tension shattered into waves of laughter. One sentence, and he had them all calmed down, happy again to be on the bus, happy to be anywhere with him. I was, too. Only Miss Shadrach still stared, white-faced, out the window.

Jay bounded down the aisle.

"Ruthie-baby, am I going to have to dance my little fanny down this aisle to get you to smile?" He loomed over her, and cradling her tiny, wrinkled face between his enormous paws, forced her to look at him.

He waggled his hips and the High Steppers roared. Ruth Shadrach, the most buttoned-up person on the bus, glowed pink with pleasure.

Jay has way more than his share of people magic. He really just loves life, and that makes him irresistible.

Two nice guys in a green compact car that had been just behind the bus when it was hit by the box truck helped Devon check the bus for damage, even opening the luggage compartment on the side of the scrape to be sure it wasn't jammed. They said they hadn't noticed the number of the box truck either, but they offered to call the police on their cell phones and act as witnesses for the insurance if we needed them.

The damage wasn't too bad, and the reckless truck driver was long gone. He had never slowed when he scraped us. Devon even claimed he'd accelerated. If there had been a name or any markings on the truck, no one had noticed it.

Everything seemed to be working properly, so Devon thanked the men, said no to the police call offer, climbed back into the driver's seat, and eased the bus back onto the roadway, waving goodbye to our new friends.

"Nice guys. Pakistani, I think," Jay said. "But we should have gotten their numbers and addresses, in case we do need them as witnesses."

"Relax," I said, reclining my seat, "We have a busload of witnesses."

And indeed we did. Most of the High Steppers had spent the entire time glued to the windows, speculating and complaining, some taking pictures, and all offering advice.

Ruth insisted loudly that one of the Good Samaritans was

"the foreign-looking gentleman who tried to steal my new red train case at the airport," but no one was listening to Ruth anymore.

⊬

We spent the rest of the day as planned—"Yes, there's Buckingham Palace. No, we will not see the Queen."—thankfully without further incident. The High Steppers kept up the pace fairly well, despite the long flight.

Besides drinking lots of water and sleeping on the plane, the only way to deal with jet-lag (I preach over and over), is to hit the ground running when you arrive. It's really true. If you don't you are messed up for days.

I also try to get my little flock to walk outside in the sun. That helps the old body-clock re-adjust. The absolute worst thing you can do is go right to bed unless it's already bedtime when you arrive at your destination. Even if you are really sleepy, hopping in the sack on the morning of your arrival makes the period of adjustment much longer.

When we finally reached Harwich, Pied Piper Jay led the High Steppers onto the ship while Devon and I sorted out bags and completed the housekeeping.

"It wasn't an accident, you know," Devon insisted, as I prepared to leave him in the ship's terminal. "That bugger meant to hit us."

"Oh, Devon, don't say that. Of course it was an accident," I said. "Who would possibly want to harm the High Steppers?"

"Just be careful, Sidney-girl, that's what I say."

I patted his arm, hugged him goodbye, and hurried through security and up the gangway. When I looked back to wave from the top of the platform, he was still standing there watching me in his brown oiled jacket, his red Yorkshire face looking troubled.

⊬

Dinner onboard that first night was terrific, even better than expected. I ordered a starter of hearts of palm, lobster bisque, a pear, walnut and romaine salad with raspberry vinaigrette, then Dover sole with a fabulous mango sauce, followed by a rich chocolate dessert so beautiful that you could hardly bear to eat it. I did, of course.

The expertise of the famous gourmet chef who plans all the meals for the cruise line was in clear evidence. No flash-frozen pre-packaged stuff here! After our overnight flight and the long day on the bus, the beautifully-served five-course meal was more than welcome. I resolved to try to attend one of the cooking classes scheduled for later in the week.

Gladys Murphy and her family ate everything on the menu. I know this because I was stuck with the Murphys at a table for four near the kitchen. During the entire meal Pete Murphy—looking uncomfortable in a striped suit and loud tie—remained hunkered over his plate, elbows on the table, saying nothing as he shoveled in his food.

Pete's wife Gladys did all the talking, mostly about Muriel.

"Muriel's real talented, Miss Marsh. You should hear her sing! She got her first singing part in the second grade at the school program and she's been singing and dancing ever since. Some people said she got the part because the teacher's husband worked for Pete, but that had nothing to do with it. Muriel won that part fair and square, didn't she, Pete?"

Pete didn't answer. He focused on his food, glancing up now and then at Muriel.

Gladys' permed magenta curls and dangly gold earrings bobbed as she talked and talked and talked, chewing all along. Between the talking and the gobbling I couldn't get a word in at all and quickly saw that it didn't matter. She didn't want conversation. I didn't see how she even got her breath. She wore a lumpy burgundy pants suit with gold sandals, a matching purse, and a ton of jewelry. The straps of the sandals were nearly buried in the extra flesh encasing her ankles.

Daughter Muriel wasn't listening. She had come to the table with a large gin in hand and ordered two more before the soup was served. Each time she ordered Gladys rolled her eyes at Pete and he shook his big head.

Muriel had longish fuzzy red hair with bangs. Her bulging pale green eyes seemed to be having a hard time focusing. Jay said those eyes looked like green grapes.

Muriel wore a purple knit blouse two sizes too small with a deep v-neck. Her tight orange skirt had wide green horizontal stripes, an unfortunate choice. Mother Nature had not been kind to Muriel, and her fashion decisions only made it worse.

In doing my duty as shepherd and host, I had turned down an invitation to dine at the captain's table. Jay said I was out of my mind. We had been introduced to Captain Stephanos Vargos for the first time on deck at the lifeboat drill.

"You've got to admit it, Sidney, that captain is absolutely gorgeous."

"I can see that, Jay. But I am not interested in the Captain. He comes on a little strong for me, and you know Zoe, that tall, blond agent with Poseidon Tours? She told me this afternoon that she made a play for him a couple of trips back and he told her he is married."

"If Zoe made a play for me, I'd tell her I was married, too. Zoe gets around, you know. I wouldn't take her word for it. But I have to tell you, Sidney, any guy that hot is going to be totally self-absorbed He's no kid. He's at least ten years older than you, and he's been around. So maybe it's better for you to leave him alone. You've attracted way too many of those smooth dudes already. And you can bet your last drachma that this big Greek is macho to the core."

Jay had a point. Captain Vargos *was* hot in his dress whites as he presided over his table, but I was pretty sure that he was also well-aware of his good looks. He is just over six feet tall and tanned, with broad shoulders and a lean waist. His hair is thick, dark and wavy and beginning to silver at the temples. There is nothing boyish about him. His smile is a man's smile— arrogant and knowing. He leaned down to whisper something in the ear of the woman on his right, and she looked up at him and laughed. Her deep blue silk dress was almost the exact color of his eyes.

"Somebody told me that it's okay to order two of everything if you want to, Miss Marsh. Is that true?" Gladys Murphy brought my attention back to the table.

"Well, yes, you can, Gladys, you certainly can ... and then there is also the Heart Helper diet and the Chef's Suggested Menu, both of which are always excellent."

"Well, I'm just gonna have two of them prime ribs and just a little tiny taste of every one of them desserts. You can keep the veggies. Don't that sound good to you?"

"You bet, Gladys. That certainly sounds wonderful. Just remember to save some room for the Midnight Buffet!"

"Don't you worry none about that, Miss Marsh! We wouldn't miss it for the world! It's called Sweet Dreams Buffet and it's all desserts. Pete and I will try everything they got. Muriel might not, though. Muriel has to watch her figure. Did I tell you already that she wants a career in show business? She's looking for those bright lights, aren't you, Muriel? Muriel wants to be a star, don't you, honey?"

Muriel ignored her. She was ordering another drink from the cocktail waiter.

As Gladys launched into a long monologue of Muriel's performance history, beginning with tap dancing recitals at age four, I made a mental note to speak privately to the maitre d' after dinner about a change in table assignments. To hell with duty. The Murphys were pleasant enough people, but a week can be an awfully long time.

ℋ

I have a favorite spot just above the Lido deck of the Rapture of the Deep that very few people seem to frequent. That is where I escaped with my wine glass after the last of the dessert plates was cleared away.

Before heading for the Lido deck stairs I had made a swing around the ship, checking to be sure that everyone was fairly well settled-in and happy.

All the High Steppers seemed to like the ship, with her bright and spacious, elegantly decorated public areas. The Rapture was a good ship, large enough with her eleven passenger decks not to feel cramped, but not so big as to overwhelm a port with too many people. She was sleek and modern with clean lines, and her crew kept her extremely well-maintained. Her hull was deep and her stabilizers worked well, allowing barely noticeable movement on deck that first night out. Some ships are built with only Caribbean cruising in mind and have a hard time handling the rigors of the North Sea or a Trans-Atlantic crossing. The Rapture was designed to take on rough seas.

Everyone had been pleased with the staterooms on the ship at check-in, even Gertrude.

"This is real nice," she said, peering into in her closet on arrival. "Not too big, but plenty of room for my things. I'm glad you told us to bring extra hangers, though, Sidney. Either they cheaped out on that or somebody stole some of them. I bet someone did steal them. Those hangers are good, but there's not nearly enough. I don't like my mattress, though. Tell them to bring me another one."

I always encourage my clients to pack some extra lightweight wire hangers. The ship's closets have a fair number of good wooden ones, but never enough for all the High Steppers' stuff. I also recommend that they pack a full-sized bar of their favorite bath soap. Nice but small bath amenities are always provided, but High Steppers prefer to stash those away in their suitcases to take home.

The staterooms on the Rapture were comfortable and spacious, with muted, tasteful colors and small but well-fitted bathrooms and closets equipped with in-room safes. There were small televisions but no in-room Internet access, as you might find on many newer ships. The beds were designed so that they could be set up as twins or a queen, by prearranged preference.

Most of the group had opted for outside cabins. A very few chose the slightly cheaper inside cabins that had no window. Amy and Charlie Wu had a balcony cabin, as did the Johnsons. Abe Klein and Brooke Shyler had each booked a suite.

Some of my group—the ones who hadn't ordered room service and gone straight to bed—were attending the welcome show immediately after dinner. Looking in on the show, I saw that the Murphys had grabbed seats on the front row center of the Broadway Showroom. Muriel seemed mesmerized by the dancers. She didn't miss a move, bobbing with the music, smiling and clapping enthusiastically after every number. It was clear that Gladys was correct; the cast members, in their sequined costumes, were apparently living Muriel's dream. Her longing was painful to watch. The Johnsons and Angelo Petrone and the Levy sisters were all enjoying the show, too, but no one was as enthusiastic as Muriel.

I didn't see any of the other High Steppers in the audience. The missing ones were probably all resting in their cabins, reading the Daily Program for tomorrow, eating pillow mints, watching the clock so they could be first in line for the Sweet Dreams Buffet.

The only group member I hadn't spotted at all since we boarded was Jerome Morgan. Dark, heavy-set and clean-shaven, Morgan had close-cut, almost buzz-cut hair and a long, hooked nose. He wore dark sunglasses most of the time and a flashy watch. The watch was the only flashy thing about him; otherwise he was very quiet in dress and manner. We had little personal information about him. At Kennedy, Morgan had told Jay that he and Fernando Ortiz worked for Abe Klein's business, without mentioning exactly what they did. He did volunteer that Abe had paid for their trip as a reward for good job performance.

Itchy Feet Travel (IFT) sells a lot of incentive travel, usually rewarding top producers in a company. It was hard to imagine either Jerome Morgan or Fernando Ortiz as super-salesmen. They did not fit the glad-handing stereotype. Both were too quiet and kept to themselves.

Morgan, who clammed up when anyone tried to have the simplest conversation with him, had disappeared into his cabin the minute we boarded. No one had seen him since. He was either seasick or really anti-social. Judging from his permanent scowl, I voted for Door Number Two. When he did appear, he just watched people with his cold little eyes. I guess if you wanted to give him the benefit of the doubt, you could call him the strong, silent type.

Ortiz was more social and had created a stir among the ladies with his lean but powerful presence and bold black-brown eyes.

I slipped out of the Broadway Showroom just as the magician was beginning his act. The spacious, tiered auditorium was filled from the top level—where the big sound and light control board was located—all the way down to the stage. His performance was a comic one, combining magic and jokes and using a lot of funny sound effects and voice synthesizers. It was really quite good, but I had seen him before on previous cruises and I thought I should finish my rounds. I wanted to be sure everyone was having a good time on the first night out.

A few High Steppers were in the casino. As soon as a ship enters international waters, the casino opens and at least one or two of our clients always plant themselves there, only emerging to eat or sleep.

I saw Al Bostick in the casino, slouched over a blackjack table, the lines in his face deepened in concentration. He was wearing the same sad old clothes he had worn on the plane. His long gray hair was slicked back and greasy and his thin lips moved slightly. I was fairly sure he was counting cards, but if the dealer noticed, he didn't say anything to Al. Behind the blackjack tables, Maria Petrone, eyes glazed over, was steadily feeding a quarter slot as if she were an orange-polyester extension of the machine.

Fernando Ortiz was slow-dancing in the Starlight Lounge with a young, gorgeous, blue-eyed blonde. Fast worker, that guy. Only a few hours on board, and he had already hooked up. Maybe he was a super-salesman after all.

I have to admit; I'm not a fan of tiny, doll-like blondes. I am tall, with all this wild black hair and stormy, gray eyes, and I am well aware that I would make a far better witch than fairy princess. Those witch parts were the ones I always got in school plays, from the third grade on.

Jay was nowhere to be found. He always cruises the ship the first night out to "see if there's anyone interesting aboard, darling," so I was quite alone, for once, and happy to be so.

There is something so truly wonderful about a big ship, at least for me. I love to travel. Anyone would, who came from my tiny little hometown. That's why I headed to New York when I had the chance.

But I always feel an extra-special thrill on a huge ocean liner when the long lines are dropped and the ship slips away from the pier. I love the parting blast of her horn and the feel of her deck under my feet as she crosses the bar and enters deep water. I might have considered joining the Navy, but my mother would have passed out at the thought. She would have insisted that the naval life was entirely too rough for a delicate Southern flower like me. You should have heard everything she said when I told her I was skipping college, and more importantly, sorority rush, to move to New York and work for a travel agency.

On the stern deck, I leaned over the rail, the wind whipping at my hair, and watched the white foam boil up behind us as the huge screws churned their way through the dark ocean. I've been on dozens of cruises in my career and have never, ever tired of it. Granted, the bingo and horse racing games and theme nights on some ships get old, but for the most part, I don't mind because I really, really love the sea.

Immersed in the moment, I didn't see or hear the approach of Johnny Depp's stand-in until he was right behind me, lips close to my ear.

"What are you doing out here all alone, Sidney?"

I could barely hear his words over the sound of the wind.

"Are you going to jump overboard and never be heard from again? It would be hours, you know, before anyone knew you had gone missing. Much too long for a rescue."

I turned to face him and noticed for the first time a thin scar marring his left eyebrow. The scar, paired with muscular shoulders, enhanced his slight aura of menace, of fascination. He was dressed in an open-collar white shirt and an expensive blazer. I caught a faint whiff of his cologne in the wind.

"Wrong, Fernando," I said, looking up at him, meeting his black eyes and wicked grin. "The High Steppers could find me. One of them ferrets me out every fifteen minutes on average."

"What a miserable way to live. I do not envy you," he sneered. "You have such a dismal life, and you don't even realize it. Those people are disgusting."

Turning abruptly, he melted into the gloom of the stern.

"Well, why did you sign on for a trip with us then," I wanted to shout after him.

But he was gone, and I wouldn't have said it anyway. IFT escorts are not rude to our customers.

The deck no longer seemed romantic, just cold, wet and lonely, spoiled by Fernando's nastiness. We were in heavy seas, and a light roll could be felt despite the ship's stabilizers. Breaking a rule, I tossed what was left of my wine over the side, watching the red drops disappear into the darkness, and climbed the outside stair to the Sports Deck. Buffeted by the wind and trying not to slip on the wet boards in my new black evening sandals, I didn't look where I was going and almost collided with a deckhand. He gripped my arms to steady me; his eyes and demeanor were oddly familiar. Had I seen him somewhere before? Perhaps on another cruise.

"Go inside with the others, lady, go inside now. It's dangerous out here."

And then he, too, marched on toward the stern without another word.

I pulled hard to open the heavy forward door against the wind and stepped quickly into the welcome noise and light of the disco.

Leaning against the bar, I ordered another glass of Malbec and waited for my eyes to adjust to the flashing strobes. I scanned the room for familiar faces. No High Steppers here, not tonight. The poor, tired dears were probably all tucked in, covered with motion sickness patches now that the seas had kicked up. My London-in-a-capsule tour had worn them out.

I was surprised Jay wasn't there. The band was good and the room was crowded. Jay is usually the King of Disco. Once, in a Mexican nightclub in Puerto Vallarta, he had jumped on the bandstand and started gatoring with such enthusiasm that the band stopped playing and the management called an ambulance. They thought the big red-headed gringo was having a seizure.

I was sorry not to see him, because I really wanted to tell him about my unpleasant little chat with Ortiz. I wasn't sure how I felt about Mr. Fernando Ortiz. He was clearly appealing to me in some ways, but sort of repellent in others, all at the same time. I wondered what Jay thought of him.

Never underestimate Jay. Under all the jazz, he is very sharp and little escapes him. Sometimes he laughs at my concerns, but he doesn't ignore them. After my vaguely ominous encounters on deck I longed for his reassurance and large, comforting presence.

I looked in the Castaway Bar, in the library, and even in the dining room, but the midnight buffet was long over. Only busboys remained, cleaning up the wreckage of the feeding frenzy. Finally I gave up and went to bed.

⽇

The luminous dial on my clock read 3:05 when I heard the steel handle of my cabin door turn for the second time.

The first time I heard it I was really still asleep, but when it turned again a few seconds later, I was wide awake and watching.

I knew that no one could enter, of course. I had turned the night bolt securely before climbing into my berth, and only the room steward and the purser had keys. I guessed some drunk just had the wrong room. But if it *was* a late-night hell-raiser, he was a mighty quiet one.

I lay awake for a long time after, listening for the sound of the door handle, for footsteps or voices in the passageway, but hearing only the faint throb of the engines and the sound of the waves. Whoever had been at my door had slipped silently away.

⽇

I was awakened again at 6:15 by Jay, pounding on the door and shouting my name.

"Okay, okay, calm down, I'm coming," I said, unlocking the door. "Come in. What is it?"

He burst into the cabin and grabbed me by both arms, nearly lifting me off the floor.

"Just get dressed right now. It's awful. I don't know what we are going to do, Sidney. Ruth Shadrach is dead."

I sank back down onto the bed.

"Dead." I stared at him. "What do you mean, *dead*?"

"I mean dead," he said, "real dead, as in not alive. So stop asking dumb questions and get dressed."

He opened my drawer and started throwing underwear and t-shirts at me.

"Here, put this on. No, not that, that's tacky, this."

I grabbed my clothes away from him.

"I can dress myself, thank you!" I yelled. "Stay out of my stuff. How is she dead? Where? When?"

"I don't know. I don't know." He ran his hands through his red hair until it was sticking up all over. "All I know is that the room steward saw the other old ladies going to the Early Riser's Breakfast this morning and thought Ruth was with them. So he knocked on the door. When there was no answer, he went into Ruth's cabin to make up the bed, and there she was. Dead. As a hammer. Someone's killed her. Dr. Sledge, the ship's doctor, is there now and the purser and they want you. So hurry up, Sidney, for God's sake, put your shoes on, and let's go!"

Strangely, we didn't meet anyone as we rocketed up the stairs to the Continental Deck where poor Ruth Shadrach, afraid to room with a stranger, had booked a single.

She looked so pitiful, lying there in the new pink nylon travel pajamas that she'd bought especially for this trip. Twice she'd told me about them and the matching robe, its sleeves now securely knotted around her throat.

"Oh, my God!" I turned away from her and buried my face in Jay's big chest.

Dr. Sledge pulled the sheet back over her.

"Miss Marsh," said the purser, "I know what a terrible thing this is for you. It is terrible for all of us. But could you please inform your group of Miss Shadrach's passing while Mr. Wilson comes with me now to the bridge to speak with the captain? Dr. Sledge will stay with Miss Shadrach, and Anthony will guard the cabin."

❋

How we got through the rest of that day, I'll never know. One of the hardest things I've ever had to do in my life was to gather the High Steppers together and tell them about Ruth Shadrach. They were stunned and saddened. Many were in tears.

"Who would do such a thing?" Mrs. Weiss said, shaking her head. "No one had any reason to harm her. No one knew her but us."

She looked around the room at the others. They were no longer the jolly band of High Steppers, but frail individuals, peering at each other with closed, suspicious, fearful faces.

"We don't know." I said. "We don't know anything yet. And at this point we don't know what the procedure will be or what the captain will do. He will let us know when a decision has been made. Each of you will probably be questioned to see if you can provide any helpful information."

"Will they bury her at sea?" blurted Mrs. Murphy, who was obviously more curious than distraught. "I've never seen a burial at sea."

"NO, Gladys, they will NOT!" Jay shouted. He had just entered the back of the room, and he looked all in.

"Now, please, everyone, go on to lunch if you can," he continued. "It's open seating, and if you can't, just go to your cabins and order room service or lie down or something and let us try to sort things out. When we have further information, we will share it with you. Right now, they are saying there will be no alterations in the day's activities, but if you choose not to participate, believe me, everyone will understand."

After they were gone, Jay and I went back to the conference room on the Promenade Deck. He had no new information from the captain.

Jay was pacing, couldn't stand still, couldn't sit, like a big cat. He ran his hands through his red hair again and again.

"They're stonewalling, Sidney. I couldn't find out anything. Everyone that I spoke with said they would get back to us later."

I sank into a conference chair and put my head down on my arms on the cool gleaming wood of the table, thinking about it all, turning the whole terrible thing over in my mind.

"Did you actually speak with the captain, Jay?" I asked

without moving my head. I thought if I didn't move it, it might stop aching.

"No. The First Officer, a guy named Avranos, said that Captain Vargos was in a meeting and could not be disturbed. But what about the High Steppers, Sid? When you told them, what did they say? How did they take it? Pretty bad, I bet. Did anyone say if they saw or heard anything?"

I looked up at him. He had stopped pacing and had perched on the big table, staring at me with a grim look in his brown eyes.

"Oh, Jay, it was awful. Poor little Hannah just cried and cried. Even old Mr. Bostick was honking away into his handkerchief. But, no, no one mentioned hearing or seeing anything. Ruth had that single cabin on the port side, remember, and the rest were all on the starboard. So if they were all in their rooms sleeping when it happened, it's not surprising that they didn't."

"So no one truly knows what happened."

"No. No one except the ..."

I just couldn't say the word.

"Murderer," Jay said, finishing the awful thought for me.

We had dealt with a lot of crises together over the years, some of them pretty bad. Nothing remotely equal to this.

Everything was complicated by the steadily worsening weather. Squalls had been predicted on leaving Harwich, and as the wind rose, the pitch and yaw of the behemoth we were riding increased proportionally. Even with her sturdy construction, the Rapture was having a hard time handling the weather.

"Great, just great," Jay said, as we began to hear glassware crash in the dining room.

"That's really what we need just now, an effing gale, with poor little High Steppers yammying everywhere and all falling down and breaking their hips!"

We assumed that the captain had immediately informed the authorities and the cruise line about Ruth, of course, but no one had as yet shared any decision as to the plan of action. Jay and I agreed to wait for their decision before laying the bad news on Itchy. We had no way to contact them, really. The storm had knocked out the cell phone system connections and the Internet in the computer room wasn't working either. We had been told that it would be some time before it could be repaired.

So here we were, sailing merrily along in the middle of a huge storm in the North Sea with the High Steppers, dead Ruth Shadrach, and whoever had killed her.

Cruise lines are equipped to deal with dead passengers. No one likes to talk about it, of course, and it's not something you want to feature in the brochure, but it happens, and when it does, they know what to do. What they are emphatically not equipped to deal with is murder.

"Jay," I said, "Did you try to come in my cabin this morning about three a.m.?"

He stared at me as if I was nuts.

"I guess that's a no," I said, "but I had to ask, because somebody did. They turned the handle on my door. If it had been you it would have been okay. But if it wasn't you, then it's definitely NOT okay."

Jay moved his stuff into my cabin that afternoon, without being asked. I told you that he is really a terrific guy, and if the High Steppers or IFT disapproved of my new roomie, I didn't care.

5

The sea was still pretty choppy the next morning, and the sky was overcast, but the worst of the storm seemed to have passed during the night. The closet doors had stopped banging open and closed about four a.m.

When the first door banged open, then shut, about 2:30, Jay sat straight up in his bed screaming, "Get out of here, you son of a bitch!"

It took a while for him to really wake up and be convinced that it was not a murderous intruder, only the big bad closet. I laughed so hard I got the hiccups.

"Not funny, Sidney, not funny! What if some madman had chopped his way into our cabin?"

"This killer is not a wild beast, Jay. This one is sneaky. He slips around like Gollum and throttles old ladies."

"That's comforting, Sidney. I love that thought."

"What do you think about a motive, Jay? There has to be a motive. I mean, who would want to kill Ruth, and why?

She didn't have any enemies. I bet about the only bad thing she ever did was not return her library books on time."

"Not to speak ill of the dead, Sidney, but Ruth was pretty

annoying. I enjoy most of the rest of the High Steppers most of the time, but I have to tell you, Ruth was not my favorite. Is being totally annoying a motive?"

"Now was that nice? And no, it's not a motive. People don't want to be nick, nick, nicked all the time, Jay, but they don't usually kill folks over it."

"Maybe there is no reason. Maybe it's just random. Wrong place at the wrong time. Maybe he was trying to rob her cabin and she caught him. I like that idea better than a sneaky murderous fiend slinking around the ship, stalking the High Steppers."

"Jay, Ruth was a retired schoolteacher, living on a fixed income. She didn't own anything a random sneak thief would want to steal. She was in her bed, in the middle of the night, in her own room, minding her own business, when she was killed. That's not the wrong place at the wrong time. That's not random. That's targeted."

"Hey, don't get all worked up, Sidney. It's four a.m. Turn off the light and go back to sleep. I'm sorry I woke you, Dick Tracy. I didn't mean to get you started. Quit worrying sweetie, go back to sleep. You need sleep. Tomorrow we'll get on the horn and make Itchy fly us all home asap. Let the cops figure it out."

Just after dawn I pulled on fleece pants and a sweatshirt, left Jay snoring on the opposite berth, and went out on deck in search of coffee.

I had decided in the long stretches of the night that Jay might be right and as soon as we reached the first port, Oslo, we would somehow convince Itchy to abort this voyage from hell and get us back to New York pronto, even if that meant refunds, something they hate to provide under any circumstances. That is, if the authorities would let us go. It made my head hurt again just thinking of it.

In the meantime, jolly old Sidney's job was to keep up everyone's spirits.

♓

I smelled Dr. Sledge's pipe smoke before I saw him. His sturdy, square body leaned against the rail, his pipe clenched firmly in the corner of his mouth. The few remaining strands of his thin reddish hair were being ruffled by the wind It wasn't raining then, but we were in heavy seas. Thick bands of dark clouds filled the sky.

He waved me over.

"Hello, Miss Marsh. This is fortunate, indeed. I was just coming to find you, and you have saved me the trouble.

"Hope you don't mind the pipe," he added, puffing, obviously not caring whether I did or not.

"Nasty habit, pipes," he muttered. His pale blue eyes scanned the darkening horizon.

"The captain informed me early this morning that, weather permitting, the authorities from Empress Cruise Lines will attempt to board the ship later today by fast boat or helicopter to clear this Shadrach thing up."

"What do you mean, 'clear this Shadrach thing up?' " I stared at him in sheer amazement.

I couldn't believe what I was hearing.

"Don't you mean, find out who killed her?" I said.

"Those are harsh words, Miss Marsh, and we mustn't jump to conclusions, must we?" He turned to face me. "I am only repeating to you what Captain Vargos told me early this morning.

"My preliminary examination indicates only that Ruth Shadrach died of strangulation. How she came to be strangled will have to be investigated. Hopefully, the matter can all be sorted out before we reach Oslo tomorrow, so the ship won't be delayed in docking."

"Dr. Sledge. Ruth Shadrach was murdered."

"Tut, tut, Miss Marsh. There you go again. I said that Ruth

Shadrach died of *strangulation*, my dear. Not that she was necessarily murdered."

"What! Of course she was murdered, you know it! How can you say anything else? You of all people! I saw her, Jay saw her, you examined her. Those knots weren't tied around her neck by accident. All it can be is murder."

He took a long draw on his pipe.

"I wouldn't be so eager to promote a charge of murder here if I were you, Miss Marsh," he said, eyes grim, pipe clenched firmly between uneven yellow teeth.

"A murder on a cruise ship would be a difficult thing for everyone concerned, don't you think? Particularly for you and your travel company. After all, if we're talking about murder here, then you and your group—her only companions—must be the prime suspects, what? Good day."

He tapped his pipe on the rail, put it in his pocket, and with a brief nod, strode off down the deck.

"Me and the High Steppers. Murderers. That jackass!"

For a moment I was blind with rage. I could barely think, much less speak.

And yet, I thought, as my brain began to recover, that is, of course, what they all will think. As Mrs. Weiss said, no one knew her but us.

Now what were we going to do? This was beyond terrible. No one had ever even died on one of my trips before, much less been murdered. But they weren't going to get away with this and blame it on the High Steppers. I needed a plan, pronto.

♓

I found most of the ladies in the tea room at ten o'clock, learning ribbon embroidery.

I'm sure that it seems as strange to you as it did to me that despite what had happened, life on board would continue fairly normally. But in fact, normalcy was precisely the goal of the ship's staff.

The Rapture is a huge ship, carrying 2,367, no, make that 2,366 passengers, most of whom had not only never known Ruth Shadrach, but also were quite unaware that anything had happened to her.

The passengers had not been informed of her death, and if Dr. Sledge's attitude this morning reflected that of the line, they wouldn't. The orders from the top must be "business as usual".

Even given the circumstances of poor Ruth's untimely demise, I shouldn't have been surprised. Cruise lines go to great lengths to hide anything unpleasant that might spoil the trip for paying customers.

The same thing sometimes happens on ships when a hurricane is in the Caribbean. Will you be relatively safe? Yes. Are your ports suddenly changed? Yes. Are you always told *exactly* why? No.

The weather conditions may be referenced and a fairly plausible reason given for the sudden shift in itinerary, just not the alarming one. No one wants passengers to panic.

Meanwhile, back at home, your family and friends, frantic with worry after watching The Storm Report hyped on television, are crashing your travel agency's phone lines.

Because of the misty, overcast day, I felt sure that only dedicated deck walkers were aware that the ship's speed had slowed considerably—that we were now taking a very long time in getting to Oslo. The notices left in the staterooms by the stewards that morning had been, I thought, deliberately vague: "Mandatory Port Talk with the Captain—Broadway Showroom—4:00 p.m."

I sat there watching my dear little ladies sew, intent on their pretty work, their tight gray perms nodding over heaps of brightly-colored ribbon. They looked so vulnerable, so good, steadily working, chattering away. Knowing that many of them, including Ruth, had pinched pennies for a long, long time to afford this cruise, I silently swore that somehow, someway, I would find the slimy creep who had done this to her and to all of us, before things got any worse.

I went to find Jay and enlist his help.

⟡

I found Jay, all right, in the hot tub. Drunk. Or at least well on his way, along with the magician and two of the dancers from the show.

"Hi, there, sweet Sidney, you little Southern magnolia, you! Come on in, the water's fiiiiiine!"

"Just what do you think you are doing?" I snapped.

"What do you mean, what am I doing, little Miss Church Choir? I am enjoying myself, that's what I am doing." He shrugged elaborately.

"What about the High Steppers, Jay? What about Itchy Feet Travel? What about poor old Ruth Shadrach?"

He took a long sip of his drink, smacked his lips, leaned back and closed his eyes.

"Have a Bloody Mary, Sidney. I recommend it. They are delicious. Dee-li-cious. I've had several already.

He opened one eye and looked at me, then closed it again and continued. "Ruth Shadrach is D—E—A—D, dead, dear girl. And I think that as soon as old Itchy finds out about it, you and I are, too. They don't like it when messy stuff happens on their tours. Looks bad for the company. Bad for business. Bad for the ship. Bad for you. Bad for me.

"So have a drink on the house while you can, shweetheart, have two. Have three. You might as well."

I stormed off down to the cabin only to find that Abdul, the room steward, was in there vacuuming. He immediately tried to leave. Stewards pride themselves on never letting you catch them cleaning. I grabbed my clipboard and pen, told Abdul to carry on, and left.

The library was—hallelujah—empty.

I sat down at the table facing the ocean and fumed about Jay.

Most of the time, like I said, he's great. But when the whisky captures him, as my Uncle Earl would say, he's impossible.

Jay or no Jay, something had to be done. We had attempted to reach my boss Diana at Itchy for instructions right after I spoke with Dr. Sledge, but had been told that all communications were still down because of the weather. Now with no Jay and no Itchy, it looked like everything was pretty much up to me.

I switched on the desk lamp and began to write, making a list of all the High Steppers, beginning with the one I had known the longest.

1. Mrs. Weiss (Hannah), 88, oldest of the group, plump and short with grizzled hair and a Miss America grin, been around the world twice, considers herself the leader. On long bus trips, she brings a deli in her purse.

2. Ethel Goldstein, 84, Mrs. Weiss' roommate, best friend and rival. Fashionably thin, Bloomingdale's wardrobe and big black-framed bifocals. HER purse contains a pharmacy.

3. Dr. and Dr. Johnson (Fred and Maxine), tall, retired economics professor from Columbia and his equally tall, history professor wife. Black, early 70s, highbrow types. Dedicated travelers; in recent years, mostly with us.

4. Mr. Bostick (Al), 79, retired theater owner from the Jersey shore. Widower. Long, oily, iron-gray hair and a lecherous grin. Will grab or pinch if you get within range. Loves to gamble, complains and swears a lot. Jay says he's a pain in the ass, but I think he's just lonesome.

5. Mrs. Fletcher (Gertrude), 79, retired NYU librarian. Tight gray perm, wears sensible knits and stout shoes, day and night. Now living with her daughter (obviously a saint) in upstate New York. I think Gertrude's the pain in the ass. Daughter's husband pays for her trips.

6. Brooke Shyler, 83, flaming red hair, socialite, upper East Side penthouse, loves travel. Rail thin and patrician, with classic features, expensive high fashion clothing, and a warm smile.

7. Angelo and Maria Petrone, 75ish, from Queens. Angelo worked his way up to owning a building contracting business while Maria raised six children, most of whom are now working in the family business. He is still muscular, but is developing a gut and has short thick gray hair, tattoos on his biceps, and a booming laugh. Maria is dark and still pretty but carrying a bit too much weight now for her small frame. She bought a rainbow of polyester pantsuits for the trip and sparkly evening clothes.

8. Charlie and Amy Wu, 60s, second-generation restaurateurs from Chinatown. The Wus are short, almost the same height, and are energetic, fit, and well-dressed. They own a lot of real estate and at least two profitable businesses in Chinatown and are rumored to be involved in many more, perhaps even some shadowy ones. Very pleasant people who are good customers of our agency, but do not mingle much with the group, preferring to book side trips on their own.

9. The Levy sisters, Marjorie and Esther. Outspoken and very liberal, politically active types from the Upper West Side. Both have a lot of gray hair left over from the '60s; Marjorie's is long and pulled back into a ponytail, Esther's is short and wiry. No makeup, no bras, Birkenstock sandals with socks. Second trip with IFT, don't expect they'll be regulars.

10. Chet Parker, slim, medium height, 30ish, antiques dealer from Chelsea. Hair highlighted blond and carefully cut. Blue eyes, fine features. New to the group. Fastidious dresser with high fashion clothing and accessories. God only knows what he's doing with the High Steppers.

11. The Murphys, father Pete, mother Gladys, fat, sad-looking daughter Muriel, first cruise, triple cabin, from Brooklyn. Pete is tall and rangy with big rounded shoulders, coarse features and a big crooked nose that once must have been broken. Gladys favors loud pantsuits with flowered print nylon blouses by day, fussy bejeweled and fringed evening wear by night. All Gladys' clothes are too tight for her and

she accents them with lots of costume jewelry. Her maroon hair is backcombed and curled. She talks all the time, leaving little for Pete to say. Muriel is beyond overweight and she, like her mother, has garish taste in clothes. She wears too much makeup and has a lot of longish fuzzy red hair, thick lips, pasty skin and bulging green eyes that sometimes do not focus well because of her fondness for alcohol.

12. Abe Klein (74) and his wife Sylvia (28), from the Lower East Side. Abe's traveled with us in the past, with the former Mrs. Klein. Abe is short, tanned, big beak of a nose and barrel-chested. He exudes an aura of power, although he says little except when exhibiting his explosive temper. He is obviously used to being obeyed. His clothes are not off the rack, but are custom-made and clearly expensive though flashy. So is his big diamond ring and watch. He met Sylvia in Vegas, where she was working as a cocktail waitress in a casino. She is small, blue-eyed and platinum blonde with a bust that does not occur in nature and a huge wardrobe featuring lots of animal prints.

13. Jerome Morgan, (40) Bronx address, background unknown, business associate of Abe Klein. Cold, silent, frowner. Dark, with very close-cut hair and conservative clothes and accessories, except for a large gold Rolex. New to the group.

14. Fernando Ortiz, (38), Manhattan address, no other information except that he, too, is a business associate of Abe's. Good-looking guy, somewhat intimidating. Just under six feet, with a slim but muscular build, longish, dark straight hair and a wicked smile that is both fascinating and sort of repellent. New to the group.

15. Ruth Shadrach, (77), deceased.

16. Jay, Devon, and Me.

There you have it. The High Steppers. I had finished my notes, but even thinking as hard as I could, I now knew exactly nothing that I hadn't already known. No motives, no suspects, no connections to Ruth other than the obvious ones, nothing strange. Well, nothing stranger than some of the people themselves and the situation in which we found ourselves.

But I did have the beginnings of an idea.

I couldn't do all the investigating myself. The ship was too big, the time too short, officialdom too uncooperative, and it looked as if Jay wasn't going to be of much use. But what about the High Steppers themselves? Old ladies in particular are the nosiest people on earth, and the most tenacious. Once they set their minds on something they do not let it go. The High Steppers, or at least some of them, could help me snoop.

There was also something in the back of my mind that kept bothering me, something that I had seen or heard that wasn't exactly right, something or someone who didn't fit, if I could just remember it.

Because I was sitting there all alone, staring out at the sea, thinking hard, junior G-man at work, it took a few minutes for me to feel that icy thrill you get when you realize that someone is watching you.

I whirled around just in time to see the library door swing shut.

6

Jumping up from the desk, I jerked the door open and looked both ways down the corridor, but whoever had been standing behind me had vanished. The only person I could see was a waiter approaching, ringing the lunch chimes with a little rubber mallet.

It had probably been a crew member, hoping to vacuum, but unnerved and weak-kneed. I sat down on the brown leather sofa, shivering, as it dawned on me for the first time just how serious this situation was.

If Ruth really had been murdered—and she had been, that was clear—I would have to be very careful in my snooping so as not to put the High Steppers or Jay and myself in any additional danger.

Stay in a group and watch your back, Sidney Lanier Marsh, watch your back. And their backs, too.

♓

The lunch chimes reminded me that I had skipped breakfast (not my usual pattern) and that I was starving. Maybe having the pants scared off you makes you hungrier. I stuffed my list in my bag and headed for the stairs.

Fred and Maxine Johnson were scanning the rows and rows of "welcome aboard" shots on the display racks outside the photo gallery, looking for their picture. They were so intent on their search that they didn't even see me as I passed, and I didn't disturb them. I shivered at the thought that the murderer might be staring back at me from one of those shots.

As I passed through the casino on the way to the dining room, I noticed that although Mr. Bostick looked as if he hadn't budged since last night, Maria Petrone wasn't there. She must have run out of quarters. Gladys Murphy sat at the slot machine close behind him where Maria had been. Muriel stood by her side, showing way too much cleavage and fogging a beer. I never saw anyone drink beer that fast unless they were in some kind of competition.

Sylvia Klein, wearing a short, turquoise terry cover-up and leopard-print flip-flops, was perched on the next stool, at the dollar slot, with a matching beach bag on the floor beside the stool. It had the letters S and K monogrammed on it in gold.

Bostick tried to snag me as I passed by. "Hey, toots, don't ya have time for an old man?"

"Not right now, Al," I smiled, keeping my distance. "Lunch is ready. Didn't you hear the chimes? Aren't you hungry?"

"Nah, I'll grab a pizza later."

He clutched my arm and pulled me toward him. For an old guy, he was really quick, and really strong.

"When you get time, doll, I wanna have a little gab with you about Ruthie."

His bleary old eyes filled with tears. He wiped them quickly with a dirty old handkerchief and blew his nose.

He had my full attention now. He was so busy honking into the handkerchief that I managed to slip out of his grip and put a barstool between us. He reached for me, but patted Muriel on the rear instead. She was thrilled. Her face turned bright red.

"Ruthie?" I said. "Do you mean Ruth Shadrach?"

"Yeah, Ruthie."

He cleared his throat.

"She left a bag in my room Sunday night, see? Said for me to give it to you sometime. Said it wasn't hers, that it got delivered to her by mistake, and that one of her bags was missing, her red traincase. This one is a red traincase, too, but she said it wasn't hers. I don't know. They looked the same to me, but her key don't fit this one, so I guess she was right. She tried to call your room to tell you about it, but you didn't answer. I guess you was getting to know one of them sailors."

He leaned across the barstool and stole a look down my shirt. "I could bring it by your cabin later tonight sometime," he said, "and we can pry it open and take a peek at it in private if you like, just the two of us. What time are you gonna be there?"

I took another step backward.

"I don't really know, Al, but if you really want to bring it by, anytime is fine. If I'm not there, just give it to Jay Wilson. He and I are sharing a cabin now, you may have heard, and I'm sure he'd like to talk with you about Ruth, too."

He backed off then and settled back on the stool at the blackjack table.

I had to ask. "Al, what was Ruth Shadrach doing in your room Sunday night? She told the others that she was going to bed early."

"That she did," he winked, smiling to himself, "that she did. Ruthie and me had a little something going on the side, see. She wasn't no babe like you or nothing, but she was all right. You know what I mean? Don't ever count out them quiet ones. Sometimes she rode the bus all the way out to my crib in Jersey for a weekend. Ruthie the Riveter I called her. Ruthie was a good old girl."

He grinned and reached for me one more time, but I moved faster than he did. "See ya later, cutie pie!" he yelled.

Bells started ringing at the dollar slot machine when I was

almost out of the casino, so I paused and looked back. Sylvia had gotten lucky. She had a pay-off. Al ignored the bells and the rain of coins spilling into the metal tray at Sylvia's machine. He was frowning, concentrating on the cards he'd been dealt.

Muriel looked annoyed at Sylvia's good fortune, and Gladys was loudly complaining to anyone who would listen that the machines were all rigged. She climbed off her stool in a huff and headed toward the dining room, Muriel lumbering after her.

I didn't stick around to defend the casino. I was out of there.

♓

When I got to the dining room, the door was open and the inevitable line outside was gone; the early-birds were already seated.

My bunch was scattered among four large tables and two smaller ones on the port side. Abe Klein weren't present. I had seen Abe earlier, stretched out on the terry-covered lounges among the potted palms that surrounded the Catalina Pool. The Rapture has a retractable roof that can be closed in cold weather, transforming the heated pool and deck area around it into a solarium. A buffet lunch in an adjacent dining room is always available, served in casual cafeteria style for those guests who prefer a less formal meal. The dress code is relaxed—pretty much anything goes.

Lunch in the main dining room on board the Rapture is open seating, meaning that you can theoretically sit where you choose. In reality, the dining room staff tries to pair you up with others, filling each available seat at a table before ushering anyone on to the next one.

They say that this practice encourages camaraderie among the passengers, but it really just makes it easier for the staff.

Because some passengers dislike this routine and the assigned seating at dinner as well, some cruise lines are now offering true open seating. The ships of those lines present a choice of restaurants and meal times. Besides the main dining room and buffet, meals are also served in smaller, themed restaurants that require reservations and come with a surcharge. We urge individual clients who are deciding on a cruise to always consider which style of dining they prefer before choosing a ship. Some passengers are enthusiastic in their praise of the newer meal arrangements. Others prefer the more traditional routine.

Luckily, when I arrived at the dining room there was no maitre d' or assistant maitre d' at the door to seat me. They were all busy seating others.

I paused just inside the door for a quick scan of the room, not wanting to have to eat with damn frolicking Jay and company. I didn't see him and didn't want to even guess where he might be. I was still plenty mad at him, and though I knew we would eventually make up, I was not ready for that olive branch just yet.

I walked quickly past the High Steppers enclave, smiling and waving, and settled at a small table near the window.

I looked out at the whitecaps on the waves without really seeing them. The ship was bouncing around pretty good now, despite the stabilizers. Every now and then you could hear something else crash in the kitchen. I didn't care. I'm a good sailor, never get seasick, and Empress has lots of dishes. My mind was busy grappling with the disturbing image of Bostick and Ruth as a duo.

"May I?"

I looked up at a spanking white uniform, immaculate, crisply pressed and replete with gold braid. It was Captain Vargos.

He seated himself across from me without waiting for an answer. In my experience, some cruise ship captains equate their personal magnetism with that of film stars, and this one seemed to be no exception.

Rahim, the busboy, filled our water glasses and handed us lunch menus. The head waiter approached our table with two eager-looking passengers, but after a glance from Vargos, he seated them elsewhere. Their faces fell. Passengers love to dine with the captain.

"There now, Captain Vargos," I said, "you've disappointed your public. And isn't it rather unusual for you to be in the dining room at lunch?"

I closed the menu and willed the waiter to appear.

"It is indeed unusual, Miss Marsh," he said, leaning forward, "but then, this is an unusual voyage, and you are an unusual lady. May I call you Sidney? I have sent you one dinner invitation already that you have ignored, but now that we have this crisis on our hands it is imperative that we meet. We must work very closely together. It is essential, *n'est-ce pas*? So I am here today for the express purpose of having lunch with you. I left orders to be informed when you arrived."

Rahim offered bread and a wink, and the sommelier opened a bottle of white wine.

Antonio, the waiter, appeared for our order.

"I'll have the chef's recommendations for today, Antonio," Captain Vargos ordered. "And for you, Sidney?"

"I'll just have the luncheon salad." I said with regret.

With no breakfast, after the night I'd had, I'd been looking forward to the whole nine yards at lunch, but I didn't want to spend any more time with Vargos than necessary. Jay and I had clearly been shut out of the loop of information regarding the investigation of Ruth's death. I resented that and knew I wasn't going to be told anything new or significant by this Greek god.

"I don't quite understand why you need to speak with me at all, Captain Vargos," I began, looking up into those deep blue eyes. Despite my resolve, wading into those depths, I almost lost my train of thought. "I was told that once the cruise officials landed onboard this afternoon, they would assume all responsibility for the investigation."

"That would certainly be true if the authorities had been able to board today," he replied. "Unfortunately, the wind has again gained such strength that a fast boat docking or a helicopter landing is out of the question. Either one would be unsafe. I have been told that we must simply delay the inquiry until we can reach port. Therefore it becomes once again my responsibility, and yours. No?"

He took a long sip of wine before continuing.

"At four o'clock I will announce to the passengers the unfortunate news that one of our guests has died. We will observe a moment of silence. They will assume that her death was due to advanced age and that the cruise will continue on as stated in the itinerary after this regrettable delay, necessitated by inclement weather.

"We will, of course, encourage them in this assumption." He fixed me with a piercing blue stare. "Beyond that, I will tell them nothing. I must insist that you and Jay Wilson do the same. I will also announce that all shipboard activities, including the Captain's Cocktail Party and Masquerade Ball planned for this evening, will take place as scheduled."

"But Captain," I protested, "A woman had been murdered on this ship."

He looked around to see if I had been overheard, but no one was seated at the next table, and the noise level was fairly high. "We don't know that, Sidney, now do we? We know that she is dead, of course. But we don't know why or how she met her death. And we won't know until we dock in Norway and an official investigation can be conducted."

He watched me in silence as Antonio placed a plate of prosciutto and melon before him.

"Until then," he continued, "this ship and everyone on her—including you, Sidney—are under my command. I am asking you and your colleague not to discuss the circumstances of Ruth Shadrach's death or share any wild speculations regarding it with anyone. I do not want panic. As captain of this ship, I could issue these as orders, but I prefer that you honor my request."

"But Captain—"

"I'm sorry, Sidney, but I must insist that every attempt be made by my crew and the cruise and hotel staff to carry on as if nothing unusual has happened. I strongly suggest that you do the same." He picked up the bottle from the silver cooler at his elbow and said, "May I?"

After filling my glass and his own, he lightly touched his glass to mine, all the while watching me carefully with his deep blue eyes.

I could see why Zoe and every other woman on this ship found this man attractive. I regretted that he was already taken and I was sorry we had not met another time, in another place. He *did* look and act like a movie star, and lunching alone with him in that beautiful setting under other circumstances would have been pretty special.

But he clearly would be no help in solving Ruth's murder. He had his job as captain to consider. I had my job as travel leader and my mission—to find out who had killed Ruth and why. I wasn't sure how best to respond to Captain Vargos' "request," so I concentrated on finishing my lunch.

The lovely Salad Niçoise and the chilled Chardonnay were not very satisfying. At that moment I would willingly have traded all the gorgeous food and wine and flowers on the Rapture of the Deep for an Amstel Light, just one of Kim's pastrami sandwiches, and a stool at his ratty counter.

7

"I just don't think it shows the proper respect, that's all I'm saying."

Gertrude Fletcher sat front-row center in the Crystal Lounge, primly patting her tight gray curls into place, waiting for the vegetable-carving demonstration and class to begin.

"When you get to be my age, Gert," said Hannah Weiss, handing out little paring knives, instruction sheets, and raw vegetables, "you'll find out that you gotta keep moving. Things happen. People get sick. People die. That's just how it is. Life goes on. It's sorta like George Burns said, 'When the guy in the black coat knocks on your door, you gotta go!'"

"Well, I think Ruth would want us to dress up tonight and have a few little drinks." Brooke Shyler looked down at the emeralds on her perfectly-manicured fingers. "Why, Ruth herself was really looking forward to the masquerade ball," she continued. "She even brought a costume. Think of it as a memorial."

"Yeah, a memorial," Ethel Goldstein nodded. "A memorial. That's nice. We'll think of it as a memorial."

"I still think they should have buried her at sea instead

of keeping her in the icebox with the radishes," said Gladys Murphy. "I never seen a burial at sea."

Time for moi ... Sherlock Marsh. I began carefully, mindful of Vargos' warning. "Girls ..." They love to be called girls.

"Did any of you notice anything odd about Ruth Sunday night during dinner? Anything strange?"

They nodded in unison, like old bobble-headed dolls, letting me know that this topic had already been well-discussed.

"She wouldn't eat," Ethel said.

"All that gorgeous food and she wouldn't eat," Hannah added. "Steamship round of beef, roast spring lamb, white asparagus, barely tasted it. She just picked, picked, picked. When I asked her why she didn't eat, she just looked out the window and said something about the bus and her little red suitcase."

"That's right, she wouldn't eat," Maria Petrone added. "And she didn't even stay for the Crepes Suzette. She just got up and left, right after our waiter, Vlamin, fired it up."

"I can't wait for the Baked Alaska tonight," said Hannah. "I just love those flaming desserts. So good, so pretty."

"What is Baked Alaska?" asked Muriel Murphy.

"What, you never had Baked Alaska?" Ethel peered at her over her big black bifocals.

"She never had Baked Alaska." Hannah looked at others, shaking her head, and then at Muriel and explained, "Baked Alaska is this delicious cake, filled with ice cream and then covered all over with that sweet, fluffy stuff—I can't think of the name of it right now—and then baked. Then the waiters flame it up, turn out all the lights and march around the dining room singing, "Hot, Hot, Hot" with the Baked Alaskas on their heads. It's beautiful. You should see it. And it tastes so good."

Her sweet little wrinkled face glowed with nostalgia.

"That was the Baked Alaskas that we saw this morning in the big freezers when we went on the galley tour," Hannah continued. "They looked so delicious, all lined up on the racks and ready for tonight."

"The fluffy stuff, Hannah, is meringue," Gertrude snapped. "And that's not on the menu tonight. The Baked Alaskas are on Caribbean Night. That's tomorrow night. If you would read your Daily Program, you would know that we have French cuisine tonight, because of the *Bal Masque*."

She finished with an acid smile. "Did you see Ruth while you were in the freezer?"

"Now, Gertrude, you know they wouldn't keep Ruth with the Baked Alaskas. You're just trying to make everyone sad again and spoil the whole thing." Ethel made a vicious cut into her turnip and turned her back on Gertrude.

Gertrude had the last shot. "I just don't think it shows the proper respect, that's all," she said, for the fifth time. "And I'm not dressing up tonight like some hootchie-cootchie dancer, either!"

"Just *imagine*, Sidney, Gertrude Fletcher as a hootchie-coochie dancer!" Jay said in my ear.

He stepped over the back of the chair and plopped down beside me. "Still mad?"

"Hell, yes, I'm still mad, party boy." I whispered, "We've got this big mess on our hands, and the High Steppers to take care of, and we still haven't talked to Itchy, and, oh, by the way, sugar britches, a killer roaming around the ship, and *you* get hammered and hide in the hot tub with the magician. I'd like to make you both disappear!"

"But you can't," he murmured, "and you wouldn't if you could, because you love me. And I've got news. While I was in the room taking a little aspirin, Captain Vargos called and asked me to come to the bridge again. I don't know why he needed to see me in person unless he was trying to make an impression. All he wanted was to tell me again to shut up about Ruth. He said that he is ordering everyone—particularly us— to carry on as if nothing is wrong. So, my sweet, at least until we get to Norway, the drill is business as usual on the high seas. He said he'd already put the word on you. That means you'd better put a smile on that sad little face and get ready to party tonight, my angel, because there's nothing else to do unless you and Fletcher want to go sit down below with Ruth."

I really wanted to stay mad at Jay, but I just couldn't. I do love him, and between us we've covered a lot of ground together over the years, some of it pretty rocky. I also needed an ally.

And, after all, it's not fair to get angry with the tiger because he has stripes.

We sneaked out of the veggie demo and grabbed mugs of coffee from the Buccaneer Bar before heading to my special hideout overlooking the Lido deck.

The wind was strong, all right—the captain hadn't been exaggerating—and you couldn't see far into the mist. There were no stars. Thick clouds scudded across the sky. We ducked into my favorite little shelter above and behind the Lido Bar, now as deserted as the pool it served in better weather.

I outlined my plan for Jay, who thought it was a very, very bad idea.

"Look, Sidney, you are not a detective, or a trained investigator, or any of that stuff. You are a travel agent, not a cop, and you could get yourself in a whole lot of trouble messing around in all this. What if you DO figure it out? What if you find the killer? What are you going to do then? Arrest him? Whip out the nunchucks?"

What indeed? Somehow, my plan hadn't gotten quite that far.

"I don't know, Jay. But I've got to do something. I can't just sit around and sleep and eat and hope for the best. Besides everything else, we've got to get this thing solved so they'll let us go home. Do you really want to spend the next couple of months locked up in some historic, freezing old hotel in Oslo while the High Steppers are questioned by Interpol or somebody? And what about our careers?"

I finally had his attention. He was silent for a minute. Then he turned and looked hard at me, suddenly serious.

"Okay, I'll help you, and you may, *may* be right. But you have to promise me, Sidney Lanier Marsh, promise me that you won't do anything that might get you iced like Ruth. Don't forget, little Miss Clouseau, that Ruth was a big chicken. She probably had ten locks on her apartment door at home, but her cabin door was not forced, not even locked. So the only way this perp could have gotten into her cabin was if she opened the door for him. That means he was someone she knew, someone she trusted. Someone *we* know and trust. This isn't a game, sweetie. The same thing could happen to you."

8

After Jay left, I tried to put his warning out of my mind. I knew I couldn't think long about the risks I was taking or I would chicken out. I also knew that even though Jay had promised to help me, and even if he really meant it, he has trouble staying on task for long, particularly when he finds the task distasteful.

I went to finish questioning Al Bostick. He had never brought the mystery bag by the cabin, and I'd never finished our conversation about it, either.

Our plan for the day was simple. While I tackled Bostick, Jay would talk to Ortiz and Morgan. That wasn't exactly earthshaking, but it was a good start. After making his handsome offer to "do this little detective job," Jay declared his intention to work on his costume for the party. He loves to dress up.

The one time that I wanted to find him, of course, Mr. Bostick wasn't in the casino, and the blackjack dealer said that he had been gone for quite a while.

I didn't think Al Bostick would be working on any costume. I had never seen him wear anything but a faded black shirt and sagging pleated pants. I couldn't imagine what kind of costume he would choose in any case. A bookie? A racetrack tout? He wouldn't need a costume for either of those personas.

The slot machines were getting some heavy use tonight. I had a hard time making myself heard over the clatter of the payouts and the ringing of the bells, not to mention the crooning of the singer in the Moonbeam Room next door.

The dealer's thick Welsh accent didn't make my task any easier. The casino, like the beauty salon and the shops on The Rapture, is run as an outside concession, a British one. All the dealers and the pit boss are British.

A cruise rep once told me that some of the casino vendors on ships set the slot machines to pay out big at the beginning of a cruise to get everybody playing and in a party mood. Then later in the week, he claimed, they tighten them back up and make a killing.

I don't know if that's truth or cruise legend, but it certainly has been rumored for years. It could be true, I guess. Casinos have to close the entire time while a ship is in port and they reopen when it sails back into international waters. Plenty of time for a little tinkering.

I looked in the shopping arcade—no Bostick there—and then I had a long conversation with Amy and Charlie Wu, who were pricing designer watches.

"I saw him in the casino. Did you look there?" said Amy.

"He's always in the casino. I can't imagine what he'll do when we get into port," Charlie said. "Maybe then he'll eat and sleep.

"But enough about Al. We are interested in the German Christmas Market Tour you have advertised for this winter. Is it still available? Can you tell us something about it?"

While I was talking with the Wus, the shop clerk set up a kiosk of long silk scarves, mostly knock-offs of designer scarves, but really beautiful in their own right.

After the Wus left to find costumes for the party, I lingered over the gorgeous silks, trying to rationalize a purchase. I ended up buying a lovely, pale pink pashmina, also some nail polish remover and a paperback book. I gave up on Al and went down to the cabin.

I was in the shower when I heard Jay's key in the door.

"Put a towel on and come out right now, I've got a surprise for you," he bellowed over the noise of the water.

I took my time drying off, ignoring the hammering on the bathroom door.

After I stepped out into the totally dark cabin, I almost dropped my towel in a sudden blaze of light as he yelled, "Surprise! Surprise! What do you think? Don't you love it?"

He could have been an extra in *Moulin Rouge*. I have seen Jay in a lot of strange get-ups over the years, but this one topped them all.

He wore a red spandex bodysuit to which he had somehow attached strand after strand of clear Christmas chaser lights. He must have begged or bribed his way into the ship's show props to get them.

Tiny, white lights raced around his legs and down his arms. On his head was a crown of sparklers which I was sure he planned to ignite at the proper moment. He had sprayed his hair gold. I hoped it didn't ignite along with the sparklers.

The only flaw in this otherwise splendid creation was limited mobility, because to achieve maximum impact he had to be plugged into a wall socket.

Even for Jay, that costume was over the top.

I sat down on the bunk in my towel and howled until my stomach hurt and tears ran down my face.

Jay, delighted and encouraged by my reaction, began to dance.

"Stop it. Stop. Stop it. You've got to stop. I can't stand it," I gasped as he flexed back and forth, striking bodybuilder poses with chaser lights rippling up and down his body.

"They're going to love me, aren't they?" he smirked.

"I'm not going in until just before dinner. I want them to get the full effect when I arrive. Please have me announced."

He unplugged himself from the wall, covered the whole thing with a long black overcoat, and left.

⊁

Somehow, in spite of all the desserts I'd been enjoying, I struggled into my standard black cat outfit that I bring for all of these masquerade things.

Mostly, it is a black dance leotard and tights, with a tail, a mask, and a headband with ears. It is easy to pack and I don't care if Jay's seen it about a million times. It works for me.

I brushed my hair, put on the cat ears, and longed to spritz on some free French perfume that my buddy Helga—the boutique manager—had just given me in the shop. She saves samples and the old testers for me sometimes when the new ones come in.

I put the bottle away in my suitcase. Unfortunately, I can only enjoy wearing a fragrance, especially heavy scents, when Jay is not around. He can't tolerate perfume. He's not just being a toot about it—he would love to wear it himself—but he is really deathly allergic. If it touches his skin, he breaks out in a blistering rash, can't breathe. Poor guy even has to use unscented soap.

I knew he would really wow them tonight in that crazy costume. I laughed again, picturing how he would look. Unbelievable. There is only one Jay.

I turned off the lights, locked the door, and headed for the Starlight Lounge.

People were already lining up for photographs with Captain Vargos when I got to his cocktail party. I ducked past that line, feeling his eyes on the tail of my cat suit.

"Thish ish shoooo exschiting!"

Muriel Murphy's round green eyeballs were trying to focus between gigantic false eyelashes. She was dressed as a nightclub performer and stuffed into a low-cut sequined costume.

Obviously she had been into the champagne for quite a while. I learned on the first night out that besides food, Muriel also has quite a problem with alcohol.

My dad has seven sisters, and one of them—my Aunt Minnie, a very buttoned-up Methodist—refers to drinking alcohol as "taking a drink." In her pinched-up opinion, "taking a drink" is the first step before "taking dope." Aunt Minnie would thoroughly disapprove of Muriel. My old high school friends would just say Muriel was "bad to drink" and some of them would be able to match her shot for shot, but they would never consider partying with poor Muriel.

It was quite an evening. Everyone had gone all out on the costumes. Some were brought from home, others rented in the gift shop or created on board. But none were in Jay's league. Not even close. There were hula girls and sailors, comic book characters, nuns and priests. Elvis was in the building, along with Prince Charles, Sarah Palin, Obama and Michelle, you name it.

Waiters passed silver trays filled with beautiful canapés, shrimp tempura, cucumber sandwiches, and eggs topped with caviar; others kept the champagne flowing. A small combo played on the bandstand ... big High Stepper favorites like "Tie a Yellow Ribbon," "Tiny Bubbles," and "Bill Bailey."

I danced with most of the men in our group: Charlie Wu, Angelo, Dr. Johnson, and Pete Murphy. Chet Parker swooped by with Marjorie Levy.

To my surprise, Fernando Ortiz and Jerome Morgan were there, all decked out in full costume and seemingly caught up in the festive mood. Fernando even swept off his black hat and bowed, flashing a mocking smile at Hannah and Ethel. The little ladies, who missed the "mocking" part, looked pleased.

Maybe he isn't so superior after all, I thought. He seems to actually be enjoying the party.

But when Muriel Murphy sat down at their table, both men immediately left, heading for the bar. I watched Fernando, as Zorro, talking in low tones at the far end of the bar with Morgan, as Darth Vader. Or at least Darth was the right size and shape for Morgan. With the mask and costume, it was hard to tell. Later I saw Fernando dancing with Sylvia, who in her costume had a lush, uncanny resemblance to Marilyn Monroe.

In fact, everyone but Jay and Al Bostick seemed to be there. I was right about Al—the party was not his sort of thing—but Jay's arrival should be imminent.

I got a fresh drink and posted myself near the door as promised, waiting for Jay and watching my gang have fun. At 7:45 I heard Jay hissing "Lights, lights!" at the door, so I dimmed the switch for his grand entrance.

He slipped inside the room in the darkness, dropped the raincoat, and plugged himself in. The magician stood on a chair behind him and lit the sparklers.

He was magnificent.

As predicted, they loved him. In time with the music, he did his little dance, made all his moves. They hooted and whistled and cheered, not just our group, but everyone. I've never seen him happier. He didn't even mind when the waiters doused his sparklers and shooed him out of the room before he could set off the fire alarms.

The dinner chimes sounded, and I was turning to leave when Captain Vargos took my elbow and propelled me out the door, saying, "Tonight, the elusive Sidney dines with me."

9

"Do you see what I see, Angelo? Sidney is eating dinner with the Captain."

"Yeah, and I bet before the night's over, he gets lucky. He's slick, that one."

"I wish he'd get lucky with me, don't you, Hannah?

"I don't know, Ethel, I've forgotten."

♓

Shards of the High Steppers' conversation drifted up to the Captain's table.

Blushing, I stole a glance at Vargos, whose blue eyes glittered with amusement. He raised his glass in a toast: "Here's to the High Steppers, my lovely Sidney, and to a magical evening."

I would have loved a magical evening with this man. There was just one big problem. His wife. I had been attracted to him from the moment I met him, but when Zoe told me he was taken, the bloom was off the rose. Married guys fooling around just don't do it for me—no matter how attractive they are, and this one certainly was. I think they are all weasels.

"A better toast would be to the faithful Mrs. Vargos and all the little Vargoses who I'm told are waiting for you back in Athens, Captain."

There was a moment of silence. I was surprised to see him look genuinely perplexed. "There is no Mrs. Vargos, Sidney, although I admit I have encouraged that assumption on occasion when I felt it necessary. It's easier than saying, 'I'm sorry, but I do not find you attractive,' don't you think? I am not married. Many captains are, but marriage is not easy for a ship captain. It is difficult to make a marriage and family work well with such long separations. Command of a ship like this is very demanding, very difficult, and actually quite lonely. I am on duty, working away from my home base for months, in faraway ports and at sea."

"Well if it is so hard and lonely, why do you do it?"

He gestured toward the huge windows that filled the stern end of the dining room. A faint moon had emerged from the clouds and was gleaming on our wake, illuminating the churning sea.

"That's why, my dear," he said, smiling down at me. "The sea, as they say, is my mistress. I do this job because I must. It's all I ever wanted to do, from the time I was a small boy at Piraeus. But I consider it to be a fortunate voyage indeed when I meet and find myself attracted to a beautiful woman."

He reached over and covered my hand with his. His touch was so electrifying that I felt as if his hand had burned a hole in mine. I heard an explosion of giggles from the High Steppers table and, blushing again, pulled my hand back from his.

He laughed. "You are delightful. And I was pleased to learn from my staff this evening that you are following my orders and have stopped questioning them. I'm glad you realized that you must obey me. Perhaps you'd like to come to the bridge after dinner for some cognac and view the stars with me through the telescope in my private quarters? I am becoming quite an astronomer."

That "orders" and "obey" remark brought me back to my senses.

"Thanks, Captain Vargos, for the invitation. But I have other things on my mind. An unsolved murder, for instance, that no one but me seems to be taking seriously."

I put down my napkin and pushed back my chair. "Good night, Captain, and thank you for the hospitality. As far as your orders go, I'll do the best I can."

I almost collided with a waiter as I fled the dining room, heading for the open deck and some fresh air. I was grateful to find the deck deserted so I could vent in private.

If my grandmother and Aunt Minnie the Methodist could have heard the words I used when I reached the deserted rail of the Promenade Deck, they would have wanted to wash my mouth out with soap, twice.

What made me really angry was the sure and certain knowledge that deep down inside I knew that I was deeply attracted to him, in spite of his arrogant, macho orders and assumptions. I wanted to believe him and not Zoe about the existence of a wife. I wanted to trust him. I didn't want him to turn out to be a lying rat.

"My, my, my, what ugly words! You should have been a sailor. I don't see what you're so upset about. Why were you swearing? What happened? It looked to me as if you were having a fine time up there with old lover boy Vargos."

In my rush to the rail, I had not seen Chet Parker, lounging in the shadows on a deck chair, smoking a cigarette. His perfectly cut white dinner jacket and boyish blond hair gleamed in the reflection of the ship's lights as he climbed, laughing, out of the chair and moved toward me and the rail.

"I really don't think it's any of your business, Chet," I steamed, blushing all over again in the knowledge that my profanity had been overheard.

Parker was still laughing and now he laughed harder than ever, choking on the cigarette smoke. "Oh, God, you are so funny. Oh, God, I wish you could have heard all those old women talking about you and that gorgeous captain. Won't they be disappointed that you turned him down?"

I couldn't answer. Not and keep my job.

He looked at my face and burst out laughing again.

"Well, Sidney," he said, wiping his eyes, and tossing his cigarette butt over the rail into the ocean, "good night, good night. I hope you have a good night. Now let me go see who I can find to show me some stars!"

I could still hear him laughing even after the door shut behind him.

Right then, I just wanted to quit and go home, and by home, I meant all the way home, to Mississippi.

Life is much simpler in a small town in the South. You know everyone. They know you. They mind your business, all right, and that can be annoying, but most of the time it's because they really care about you. And it's home. You are safe. No mystery murderers or lying rats there. Well, *some* lying rats, maybe. But at least you know who they are. I leaned on the rail, watching the pale moon on the sea, my anger fizzling into sadness. I was suddenly quite homesick.

I was just about to resolve to quit the travel business forever and run home to Mamma when I felt Jay's big arms wrap around my shoulders.

"Hey, kid, time to head for the cabin. Give old Uncle Jay a big hug and forget about all this other mess. We've got a big day tomorrow, and you could use the sleep."

Have I told you how much I love Jay? As angry as he makes me, he is still the best friend I ever had, and he is always, well, *usually*, there when I need him.

⋈

When we returned to the cabin, we found fresh towels in the bathroom, beds turned down, room lights lowered, mints on the pillow, but no Daily Program. Abdul, the room steward, usually puts the DP for the following day on our beds along with our pajamas, artfully draped.

The Daily Program is a useful little sheet listing all the ship's activities, theme night information, the day's weather, stuff like that. Jay and I also use it to remind the High Steppers of any meetings scheduled with our group. The next day's sheet was supposed to run a notice for the High Steppers to assemble in the Starlight Lounge at 9:00 a.m.

"Oh, hell, Jay, I forgot to check on Al. I never found him to ask what he wanted to tell me about Ruth."

"Give it a rest, Sid. Al can wait. I don't give a rat's ass about Al. Let the cops take care of it all tomorrow in Norway. Let's talk about tonight, instead. Wasn't my costume terrific?"

"Yes, it was, Jay. You were marvelous. I think it was the best costume you ever made. Now stop posing and turn the light off. I'm ready for this day to be over."

The Daily Program shot under the door.

I grabbed it and climbed back into bed. I hadn't gotten past "6:15—Morning Power Walk with Amy" before falling asleep.

♓

I had already showered, dressed, and grabbed a quick coffee before we docked in the morning; I wanted to watch the ship maneuver into the harbor at Oslo.

The arrival into a new port is one of those great things about cruises, and one that I love most.

I stood at the rail, the hot coffee mug warming my hands in the crisp air, watching as the pier came closer and closer, admiring the old stone buildings in the morning mist.

Like all of the Scandinavian harbors in the summer, Oslo's is a busy place, with commercial vessels, ferries, fishing boats, pleasure craft, and cruise ships all jockeying for position.

Jay joined me at the rail just as the long ropes were being tied to the big stanchions that lined the dock. We watched as the gangway was maneuvered into place.

The cruise line suits and the Norwegian immigration officials had come aboard very early on the pilot boat, and, according to the cruise director's PA announcement during breakfast, the ship was already cleared for disembarkation.

"How did they manage that, Jay, with Ruth and everything?" I said. "I know Empress swings a big stick here, but I thought we would be hours clearing, if we were cleared at all. I am amazed that Norwegian cops aren't swarming all over this ship.

"Well, I hate to have to be the one to tell you this, Sidney, because I know you're going to yell. The purser called our cabin while I was shaving. You had already left. Sid, they are listing Ruth's death as a suicide."

I couldn't believe what I was hearing. Like, the words didn't compute.

"Jay, we *know* that's not true. We were *there*. We *saw* her."

"The room steward got there first ahead of us, remember? He was first on the scene so his story is golden. They've already cleaned up her cabin, and now he swears it was suicide. And Dr. Sledge is backing him up, so I guess what we saw or know or say or think just doesn't matter. I told the Empress Line brass what we saw, and they said we must have been mistaken, that our mistake was understandable because of the shock."

"What about the police, Jay? The police didn't want to talk to us?"

"I asked if we would be speaking with the police and the answer was emphatically no. 'Absolutely unnecessary,' the purser said, 'the case is closed.' We were also offered a free upgrade to a suite with a balcony because of our 'distress,' Sidney ... an offer that, you will be happy to know, I declined. I'm thinking of asking if it's still good, though. I don't have much moral fiber."

Well, that does it, Jay. We've got to get through to Itchy, just as soon as we go ashore, before the bus gets here for the shore excursion. Something has to be done, and this thing is way too big for us now. We have to have help."

⧓

Because of the time difference, calling meant waking up New York. Calling from the pay phone on the pier, I used the agency calling card and reached our manager Diana at home after ten rings. She was not pleased.

"We are fully aware of the Shadrach situation, Sidney, not because either you or Jay bothered to inform us, but because of a courtesy call I received yesterday afternoon from Captain Vargos of Empress Cruise Line." The sleep in Diana's voice had changed to ice. He wanted to offer his condolences and reassure us of his personal distress regarding Miss Shadrach's suicide. He was shocked, *shocked* to learn that our very own agents had not contacted us immediately with the news."

"But Diana, they told us the phone service was down, email, too, and you are not listening. Please, Diana, please listen. We know she didn't kill herself. She was murdered, Diana. She didn't ... we tried ..."

"We will speak about this when you return to New York, Sidney. In the meantime, just try to do your job. If anyone else kills themselves, I would appreciate a phone call immediately. *Immediately*. Do I make myself perfectly clear?" With a sharp click, the phone went dead.

Yeah, Diana. You sure do. Crystal.

A lot of other things were becoming clear, too.

⧓

We assembled the High Steppers in the Starlight Lounge and gave them each a color-coded sticker for their shore excursions. Some were going to the Viking Museum, others to the Kon-Tiki, and some were just going ashore to walk around, check out the Royal Palace, or shop.

"Sidney will be escorting the red group to the Kon-Tiki and the Vigeland Sculpture Park, and I will go with the blue group, you lucky people, to the Viking ships and the Hadeland

Glassworks. If you get lost, just watch for my hat!"

Jay jammed one of those plastic Viking helmets with the horns on top of his wild red hair. He really looked a lot like a Viking. A mad one, of course.

"Now girls, those of you who are shopping on your own will need to remember to be back on board no later than 5:30," he continued. "Remember now, my angels, the ship sails at 6:00, and it's a long way to Copenhagen. If you miss the sailing, I hope you are good swimmers, 'cause you'll have to get to the next port on your own. Okay, Blue Group, you're Vikings now, and we're off to ravish and pillage. Follow me!"

Jay's blue group filed out, giggling, loving his craziness, most wearing fanny packs and gleaming white tennis shoes. Angelo Petrone stepped out of line to pull me aside. "I heard you paging Al Bostick, Sidney, and I wanted to tell ya that I seen him about midnight last night with one of them Brazilian dancers from the cabaret. Man oh man! They was ahead of me in the hall headed to Bostick's cabin and believe you me, they was feeling no pain. I ain't seen Al this morning, but if you're waiting on him, I think you had better fugetaboutit. He ain't going on no bus trip, with no High Steppers, you know what I mean?"

I drew a line through Al's name on my clipboard.

"Okay, Red Group, are we ready for the Kon-Tiki?"

10

The shore excursion bus rounded the corner and rolled to a stop near the Grand Café.

I tapped on the microphone. "Well, High Steppers, this was a terrific day, wasn't it? Please join me in a round of applause thanking Helga, our wonderful local guide, for all those fantastic stories about the history and legends of Norway. I learned a lot, and I know you did, too! Now, please, a big round of applause for Helga and for Olaf, our driver."

Scattered applause reflected both the weariness of the group and their dissatisfaction with the step-on guide and the local tour people. Big tips for Helga and Olaf would not be forthcoming, I thought, nor would they be deserved.

Olaf's sullenness was exceeded only by Helga's inept performance of her duties. Not only had she managed to make Thor Heyerdahl's epic adventure seem boring, she also lost members of the group all along the way as people bailed out of the over-priced tour to return to the ship on their own.

Tour directors and the ship's shore excursion teams on big ships often find themselves at the mercy of the local tour agents. It is impractical for the line to operate their own tours with so many ports and passengers, all with varied interests. So they vet and hire local tour companies to arrange and conduct them. Most of the tours arranged by the local agents and offered as shore excursions by the ship are good, but occasionally they are not. Checking out the online reviews of previous passengers on the cruise line website before you book is always a good idea. It helps a lot in making a more informed choice as to which tours you would enjoy and which you might not. The price of the excursion, times and duration and level of difficulty are also provided, along with notations about the inclusion of meals and shopping stops.

It's fine for passengers to book onshore tours or arrange local guides or taxi tours independently of the cruise line if they wish. But if you do so, you should remember that you are on your own if something happens that causes you to be late in returning to the ship. If you are delayed with a tour booked with the cruise line, they will hold the ship's sailing until the shore excursion bus returns. If you are late and touring on your own, the ship will sail without you.

Private or custom tours can be booked by the ship's concierge desk, arranged yourself via the Internet or telephone with a local vendor in advance of your cruise, or onshore with a local agent upon arrival into a port. If you hire a taxi tour, be sure to agree on the price before setting off. In a small or limited port, tours and vendors may fill up, so advance booking is best, and you should always make sure that the agency or outfitter is reputable and comes with a reliable recommendation.

"Sidney, is this a shopping stop?" Sylvia Klein wanted to know.

"Yes, indeed, Sylvia, it is. In Jorgensen's, just down the street, they sell the most incredible Norwegian sweaters and ski caps. It is one of the recommended shops that Michael, our cruise director, described in his shopping talk. If you mention your ship and cabin number in Jorgensen's, you will definitely get a discount. You might even win a prize!"

I checked my watch.

"We will have forty-five minutes here before returning to the pier, High Steppers, so just have a look around or maybe enjoy a coffee and meet us back here promptly at five o'clock. Please remember to take your port maps with you, and if you forgot to bring yours, I have some extras here in my bag. Our bus, number 216, will be parked right here, and I will be just over there, at the Grand Café, waiting for you. You may also return to the ship on your own if you wish, but please let me know if you are doing that, and remember that the ship sails at six. We must all be back on board no later than five-thirty. Now, are there any questions?"

Hands went up.

"What time does the ship sail?" said Sylvia Klein.

"What time do we have to be back on board?" said Marjorie Levy.

"What was that bus number again?" said Maria Petrone.

"Where is the john?" said Pete Murphy.

♓

I was sipping espresso at a corner table in the Grand Café imagining myself as one of Ibsen's Bohemians when the Viking helmet appeared on the horizon.

Jay's group dispersed and within minutes he plopped down at my table and ordered a Hansa beer.

"I would have made a good Viking," he said, leaning back in his chair, stretching those long legs.

"Oh, really? What makes you say that?"

"Well, see how great I look in this hat? Just like a Viking. The only problem is that those old Vikings spent all their time riding around in their dragon boats raping and pillaging. I don't think I would do all *that*, but maybe I could have just chopped off a few heads with one of those cool axes or something."

His beer arrived. He paid the waiter and savored his first sip.

"Ah, that's good," he said, leaning back again. "Speaking of chopping off heads, Sidney—did you get Diana on the phone? In all the confusion this morning I couldn't ask."

"Yeah. I got her. But not before the captain did. She totally believes him and the suicide story and everything, and from the way she was talking, we'll have plenty of explaining to do when we get back ... if she'll even listen, which I doubt. I got my head chopped off, all right. I'd say we are pretty much toast."

"What did I tell you, Sidney? What did I tell you? That woman is horrible. And we might as well cave in about Ruth because no one wants to believe anything else anyway, not even the High Steppers. Especially not the High Steppers. I don't think you've noticed, Sidney, but the High Steppers aren't exactly grief-stricken about Ruth. The old girls are used to their pals cashing in their chips. Happens all the time, like Hannah said. It makes them sad, but as long as it's not them, no one wants to ruin their vacation, now, do they?"

"No, Jay, but we owe something to Ruth, you and I, no matter how anyone else feels. She was our responsibility. And besides, what about the killer? Aren't you worried? We can't cave in. Somebody really bad is roaming around loose on that big ship."

"I know that, Sidney. I am well aware of that, my little conscience. Just be sure that you are."

And with that, he drained his beer, jammed on his helmet, and strode off toward his bus, gathering his flock as he went, charming them all and leaving me to do all the worrying by myself, as usual.

♓

Don't tell the High Steppers, but Oslo is not my favorite city.

Granted, seeing real, actual Viking ships is beyond cool and the museum that houses them is unique and interesting even to people who are not into history. And the Kon Tiki is totally amazing—when you think about Thor Heyerdahl heading out across the vast Pacific Ocean bound for Polynesia riding a bunch of lashed-together balsa logs. I am fascinated by his books, *Kon-Tiki* and the even more interesting sequel, *Aku-Aku*. The city of Oslo itself is visually pleasing and well laid out. Other than that, in my humble opinion, Oslo is a snooze.

The main thing Oslo has going for it, I think, is that it's not Helsinki, where after a gander at the big shipyards and a whirl around the Sibelius monument you can have a high old time sipping on cloudberry liqueur and munching on a little reindeer pâté. Maybe I'm wrong. There's a good chance that my impressions of both cities have been unfairly prejudiced by the company I keep.

I instinctively prefer the magnificent scenery of those countries—the mountains and the fjords—to their cities. Oslo and Helsinki are both kept clean and neat and have some very impressive public buildings. I shouldn't make a judgment, I guess, after three admittedly brief visits. I know I must be missing something, because both have many fans. Perhaps I just need a better tour guide.

After all, one of the reasons I love travel is that I find something interesting wherever I go. I just feel more kinship with some places than with others.

So I had no regrets as I stood by the aft rail watching the lights of the most famous city in Norway fade into the mist. It wasn't quite dark, though the early dinner seating was well under way, just that eerie twilight that passes for evening in Scandinavia in the summer.

Maybe I always come in the wrong season. I should return alone for a long visit in deep winter. I could watch the magic of the Northern Lights, cook myself in a hot tub, allow someone to beat me with birch branches, and then jump naked into a snow bank.

Right. I guess I'm just not the fjord type. I prefer summertime, hot, steamy Southern nights, Jack in the Black, smoky barbecued ribs washed down with sweet lemon iced tea, and red-clay hills covered in kudzu.

Dreaming of Dixie, I was caught by surprise when two strong arms slipped around me and pinned me against the rail, and someone started nuzzling my neck.

"Okay, Jay, okay. Give it up. I know you love me, but don't overdo it. A High Stepper might be watching and get the wrong idea."

"Ah, but it is not Mr. Wilson who holds you close, not this time," Captain Vargos said in his deep voice. "I missed you at dinner."

I turned to face him, swallowed once more in the depths of his blue eyes. He pulled me close and I knew he was just about to kiss me when something began buzzing at his waist. Releasing me, Vargos snatched his cell phone from his belt and snarled into it, "Vargos."

As I watched him listening intently to whatever the caller was saying, my doubts were fading, melting away in the moonlight. I no longer believed he was lying about the wife. Zoe can be a cat, and her information must have been wrong. And, if he wanted to keep his day job, he *did* have to answer to Empress. Instead of escaping while he was distracted by the phone call, I waited, in the curve of his arm, for him to finish his conversation.

It wasn't much of a conversation. He just stood there listening, holding the phone to his ear, jaw clenched, looking grim.

Finally, whoever was on the other end finished speaking.

"I'll be right there," Captain Vargos said. "She's with me now. I'll bring her. Send someone to find Wilson."

He looked down at me, his eyes troubled. "We have an emergency, Sidney," he said quietly. "There's no time for explanations. Just come along quickly, if you will. Follow me. This way, please."

Releasing me, he jerked open the heavy door marked "Authorized Personnel Only" and bolted down the port stairway. I followed. I had no choice.

♓

Muriel Murphy wouldn't get her first Baked Alaska that night after all.

Al Bostick lay naked on top of all those exotic desserts in the freezer, frozen solid, a plastic trash bag knotted around his throat.

Vargos took off his coat and wrapped it around me. I shook uncontrollably from the cold, the shock, and the horror that had been Al Bostick.

"Come out of here. You've seen enough," he said. He turned to a busboy. "Please bring her some coffee."

Vargos took me up one flight of stairs, sat me down in the executive chef's office, and gave me his handkerchief to blow my nose. It seemed so strange to me—sitting there looking through the glass door—to be watching the evening meal in motion, as if on a normal evening.

Waiters and busboys hustled heavy trays, and chefs, cooks and kitchen help all worked together like one efficient machine. Meanwhile, on the level below us, two burly Asian deckhands stood guard in front of the door of the frozen food locker. I stared in frustration at the captain, tears rolling down my cheeks, wiping my nose with his handkerchief.

"There is no reason for you to look at me like that, Sidney. I didn't kill him."

"Maybe not, Captain Vargos, but if you hadn't tried to hide Miss Shadrach's murder, if you had ordered a full investigation immediately, hadn't gone along with the cover-up, this may not have happened. Al Bostick might still be alive."

He pulled me to my feet then, strong hands gripping my shoulders, and I looked up into those dark blue eyes.

His voice was deep and gentle. "Sidney, I am not an evil man, and I am not unfeeling. I only did what I had to, what I was told to do, that is all. There is no cover-up. No conspiracy. The cruise line sincerely regrets Miss Shadrach's unfortunate death and has just been trying very hard to keep things pleasant for the sake of the other thousands of passengers until this voyage is completed. You know how important that is. Please be reasonable. Today's unfortunate tragedy will have to be investigated thoroughly, too, until an explanation is reached and the culprit is found. Please try to understand."

"All I know, Captain, all I understand, is that my High Steppers are getting killed, and every official connected with this ship, including you, is acting as if it's not happening, as if it doesn't matter."

He removed his hands from my shoulders, walked around the desk, and spoke briefly into the telephone.

"Someone will be here in a moment to escort you to your stateroom, Miss Marsh. For your own safety, please don't attempt to leave it again this evening. I will have a tray with your evening meal delivered to your cabin, and when I wish to speak with you again, I will send for you."

And with that he walked out of the door, slamming it behind him.

The door opened again and a husky Russian in a cook's helper uniform motioned for me to follow. When I didn't move on my own, he grasped my upper arm in a firm grip and, without a word, marched me past the pastry racks, out through the double doors and down the passageway, into the staff elevator and up to my cabin.

He waited for me to open my door with my key, then motioned for me to enter. Despite my protests, he closed it firmly, and I heard the master lock above the knob click into place. I immediately tried to open the door, but it was firmly bolted.

11

I was infuriated and insulted. Here I was, locked in my cabin and treated like a child. I tried the rest of the evening to escape, first by beating on the door until the big guy opened it, then pleading and finally shouting at him. Nothing worked. My guard just folded his arms like a big genie, shook his head, and closed and locked the door again.

My room phone wasn't working; it obviously had been turned off. My cell phone said "No Service."

I broke my best hairbrush when I threw it at the door. After that, and a good cry, I felt better.

About 11:00 p.m., to my great relief, a knock on the door brought a steward with a dinner tray, and hot on his heels, Jay.

You would think that in such a crisis I would have no appetite, but the opposite was true. I was starving. I tore into the dinner tray, blessing the chef.

"Really, Sidney, it's as if you spent the last week on a diet of bread and water. Where are your manners?"

I didn't answer for a minute. I was too busy chewing.

"Funny, Jay, really funny. To hell with manners, Jay, and to hell with you, too," I said when I could. "You can't criticize me. You had your meal. You weren't starved. You weren't a prisoner."

"Oh, come on, Drama Queen. Give Vargos a break. He may have had your best interests at heart, trying to keep you safe until a few things could be sorted out."

"My. Best. Interests?"

"Calm down, Sidney, calm down and listen. Just hold on a minute. Listen to me. Everything's okay. It's all okay. It turns out that Bostick's death is not even connected to Ruth or the High Steppers or us or anything after all. They've already caught the guy who did it—some Chilean deckhand."

"What do you mean, Jay?"

"Well, see, it seems like this guy, this deckhand, had a thing going with some dancer from the cabaret, and when he found out that she had shacked up with Bostick, he lost it. That was the end of old Al.

"All they have to do now," he continued, with this happy little smile on his face, "is figure out the police jurisdiction—which is kind of complicated, of course—and we're on our way.

I stared at him without saying a word, but he refused to meet my eyes.

He continued babbling. "Oh, and you'll be happy to know that I already called Diana from the bridge. She's okay with everything. So just chill out, sweetie, everything's fine. Everything's cool. And look! I brought you a chocolate martini!"

"How do they know for sure that the deckhand is the murderer, Jay, or that this death has no connection to Ruth or the High Steppers?"

"They've got it in black and white, Sidney. Black and white. The guy wrote a confession, see, in a note, right before he jumped overboard."

"Jumped overboard. Is that what you said, Jay? Jumped overboard? He wrote this handy dandy confession and then jumped overboard? He was overcome with remorse, I suppose.

His poor little old heart was just broken all to pieces?"

"Right. So now we don't have anything to worry about, do we?"

I climbed into my bed, switched off my light, turned my face to the wall, and pretended to sleep. Not because I didn't have anything to say or anything to worry about.

Because there was no point in continuing a conversation with someone who deliberately refused to use his brain.

♓

I was scarfing down poached egg and toast in the dining room when we sailed into Copenhagen.

Normally, I try my best to be at the rail for the sail-in when we enter a port. I love sail-ins and I truly love Copenhagen, but I'd had a tough time falling asleep, overslept and barely had time for breakfast.

Copenhagen is terrific and I was really rushing because I didn't want cause any delay for my group or myself in going ashore. Shore time in a city and country you love is precious indeed. Choosing the buffet on the Lido deck would have allowed me to see the sail-in, but I didn't want to risk an encounter with a certain ship captain. He was never in the dining room at breakfast, certainly not when nearing a port. After the horrible events and bitter words of the previous evening, I needed space and time to think.

The High Steppers had been shocked, of course, with the news about Al Bostick but not overly saddened or even too surprised. He had not been at all popular. Many of them were repulsed by his mannerisms and his dress. He had insulted most of the women, loudly and regularly referring to them as "old bats."

"That's tough about Al," Angelo said, when he heard the news. "But that rascal was playing way out of his league. A man his age, coming between some hot-blooded guy and his girl … Well, I ain't saying he had it coming or nothing, but he was asking for it, messing around like that. I had no problems with Al, kinda liked the guy. But my wife, man, I can tell ya, he sure wasn't her cup of tea,"

Angelo's assessment was the nicest I heard. No one proposed a memorial service.

I thought the day onshore, off the ship, would be good for everyone. We all needed a breather.

In this port, I was scheduled to escort the all-day City and Castles Tour through the shining metropolis of Copenhagen and on to magical Northern Denmark and two of its magnificent castles. I had been looking forward to it. I had done the same tour once before and knew that both the castles and the scenery are lovely.

Before leaving the cabin, I put some serious money, a credit card, and my passport in the little pouch I wear around my neck and under my shirt while on excursions. My ship's card, a few euros for drinks and snacks, and a little string bag for purchases went in my left pocket. I stashed my compact camera and cellphone in my right.

I always try, with varying degrees of success, to get my clients to store their valuables wisely. In areas where pickpockets work, the lack of a purse keeps you from being a target. Plus, sightseeing is a lot more fun and less tiring if you don't weigh yourself down with an extra thirty pounds.

Jay was gone when I woke—not too unusual, because he often ran on the jogging track early in the morning—but this morning he'd probably gotten an early start to avoid talking to me.

That suited me just fine, because I really didn't want a lot of conversation with him either until his moral compass had swung back to normal.

Before I finally slept, I had thoroughly dissected that incredible fable that Jay had spun for me in the light of my deep and intimate knowledge of his psyche. I concluded that— while our clients might want to fully accept, even welcome the convenient explanation of Al Bostick's untimely demise—he couldn't possibly expect me to buy it.

Jay is not a simpleton. Far from it. So there was no way that he could possibly believe that (a) Bostick's death was not connected to everything else; or (b) that the deckhand/alleged murderer—if he even existed—could be anything other than another innocent victim of whatever awful thing was wreaking havoc on the Rapture.

My group had somehow become deeply entwined in this terrible and dangerous mess, whether anyone wanted to admit it or not, and no one seemed to be inclined to want to face up to it or do anything about it but me. I had asked Jay to go with me to Bostick's cabin to look around for any clues, but he told me the cabin had been immediately sealed by the ship's purser and was being guarded against unauthorized entry until the investigation was completed. I could tell that he was glad of that fact, which meant he wouldn't have to deal with it. He was totally shrugging off Bostick's death.

Jay is a decent man, the best friend I ever had, and he is no dummy, but sometimes he strays from high moral ground in favor of expediency.

Someone had tossed him this ridiculous story about the deckhand, and he had grabbed it with both hands because that was the easier option.

♓

"Sidney, Sidney, there you are! Aren't you going with us on the tour to Hamlet's Castle? I need my sticker, and they have already called some groups to assemble on the Continental Deck gangway." Gertrude Fletcher pounced on me like a duck on a June bug, glaring down at my breakfast through her bifocals.

"Oh, my goodness, yes, Mrs. Fletcher. I'm so sorry," I said, hurrying to finish. "I'm afraid I overslept. I'll be right there."

I rose, grabbed my bag and sunglasses, and followed her out of the dining room.

"Well, you'd *better* hurry, or we'll be left," she sniffed. "Jay Wilson's tour has already gone. I guess *he* managed to get up on time, no matter *what* the two of you *did* last night!"

I bit my tongue and followed in Gertrude's wake to my shore excursion group waiting on C Deck, thinking that the mysterious Chilean deckhand had really gotten it wrong.

He had snuffed the wrong High Stepper.

12

The High Steppers waited impatiently in the sun while Phillip Wu and the Murphys took at least five hundred pictures of the statue of The Little Mermaid. The graceful statue is certainly beautiful and beloved by the Danes, but nobody needs that many pictures of her. Gertrude finally barked at them to stop.

"Enough, already. Get back on the bus. You're wasting our time!"

For once, I think everyone was secretly cheering for Gertrude.

Every now and then someone steals the lovely little mermaid from her rock but somehow the Danes always find her, fix her and put her back. She has become a national symbol and is a monument to the enchanting tales of one of their native sons, Hans Christian Andersen.

We climbed back on the bus and Kirsten, our very knowledgeable local guide, continued her narrative. "Copenhagen was once a fortified city with high ramparts, surrounded by a deep moat. As you can see, it is now a city of canals. Her citizens actively use the canals, sometimes even living on them in houseboats."

The bus crossed a bridge and we looked down on a derelict boat where a scantily-clad woman with long blond hair tended potted plants. A thin, bearded man, naked except for some bright purple shorts and some impressive tattoos, was smoking something that probably came from the plants.

I heard my old biddies fussing behind me, clucking about the Danish hippies, and I reflected that it might not be such a bad thing to be sitting on that beat-up boat in the bright morning sun, wearing an old bikini, listening to the blues, sipping a cold one. Instead, I rolled over the cobblestone streets in the bus with the High Steppers as Kirsten continued her narrative.

"We will soon pass the magnificent Christenborg Palace, now the seat of the Danish Parliament. In olden times, Denmark was an absolute monarchy.

"Before long we will be leaving the city and traveling to the north of Denmark, where we will be visiting some of the most famous castles of the Danish kings and nobles, including the highlight of the tour, the very beautiful Kronborg Castle at Elsinore.

"Legend has it that Kronborg was the castle of Shakespeare's famous Danish prince, Hamlet. Whether or not the legend is true, I'm certain that you will enjoy such a beautiful castle, situated along the narrow stretch of water dividing Denmark and Sweden.

"Across this narrow strait, the lord of the castle once stretched a giant chain to stop passing ships and demand that they pay a toll.

"Now if you'll look to your left, just beyond that wall ..."

I was no longer listening. Kirsten knows her stuff, and I usually enjoy what she has to say, but with the sudden deaths of two of my clients, I had a lot on my mind.

So much that I pulled the little black plastic knob, reclining my seat, and shut my eyes, worrying, worrying, tuning out the tour as we rumbled through the gates of the ancient city.

⊬

The bus left the tarmac and entered the long driveway leading to our first castle.

Looking back at the High Steppers, I caught the Murphy ladies watching me and whispering. I knew that they and probably Gertrude Fletcher—seated alone across from them— had been talking about me.

It happens every trip. Gossip about the tour leader is either an occupational hazard or one of the great unadvertised pleasures of a group tour, depending on your perspective.

When we reached the first castle, Kirsten counted us off and then led the way across the drawbridge into the courtyard, waving her red umbrella for us to follow, brightly explaining the finer points of medieval Danish architecture.

In her wake, the High Steppers picked their way carefully across the uneven stones, slowly moving single-file past the ticket-taker through the massive south doors of the castle keep. Jerome Morgan impatiently pushed his way around the shufflers to go through the gate ahead of them.

Chet Parker joined me on a bench in the courtyard and lit a cigarette. "You don't mind, do you?"

I shook my head. "No. I don't do the smoking sermon. Not my style. Your lungs are your own business. I used to smoke. But don't you want to see the dungeon, Chet?"

"Too boring. I like my dungeons with lots of torture machines, racks, iron maidens, stuff like that. This one just has mice. I've been here before."

"Really?"

"Yep. Several times." He unbuttoned his cuffs and folded them back carefully, perfectly, above his wrists, exposing tanned arms and a Cartier watch ... real or faux, I couldn't tell. "Empress didn't tell you about me?"

"No. Tell me what about you?"

"Glass Slipper."

"Oh." I guess I should have known, but I don't handle the financial end of the group trips. The sales agents and accounting do that. By the time I get the passenger list the final payments have been made.

Empress Lines' Glass Slipper Host Program is one of a number of similar deals that some cruise lines quietly maintain to ensure that lonely ladies have a good time on their vacations. Each line has some cheesy name for it. Around the office, we just call them all Gigolo Programs.

The way it works, an attractive, articulate man is offered a substantial discount on the price of his cruise. In return, he is expected to dance a lot and charm the ladies, particularly the lonely, elderly, or unattractive ones, ensuring that they leave the ship at the end of the voyage in a rosy, romantic glow, eager to book another cruise.

The dancing hosts are screened, somewhat, and supposedly given a background check. Mild flirtation is allowed and even encouraged. Serious involvement, which might lead to repercussions for the line, is not.

Sometimes, though, a rich widow returns from her vacation with the ultimate souvenir, a boy toy.

Blond, handsome, and fastidious, Chet Parker was a perfect Glass Slipper Host. I should have known.

"They don't exactly fit in with the High Steppers, do they?" Parker said. "Neither one of them has spent over two minutes with anyone in the group since we left New York."

Following his gaze, I spotted Mr. Silent—Jerome Morgan—standing high on the ramparts, looking out to sea with binoculars, his yellow shirt rippling across his big shoulders in the wind. Morgan seemed intent on something in the distance. Fernando Ortiz, in a dark blue windbreaker, stood beside him, shading his eyes with his hand.

"No, they don't," I said, "but that's not unusual. There are always a few who don't fit. The tour price attracts them."

"It would attract me. Cheap is the only way I can go. I couldn't vacation like this at all if I had to pay full price. I love European travel, but I really don't have the money," Parker said. "Without my discount I wouldn't get any farther than Fire Island."

He stood to crush out his cigarette, and then sat back on the bench beside me.

"But I've gotta tell you, Sidney," he said, "this trip is giving me the creeps. First that old lady offs herself, then Bostick screws the dancer and gets himself killed. I don't know. It's getting weird."

He brushed a strand of hair back from his forehead and took his designer sunglasses from his pocket.

I didn't say anything, just leaned back against the cold wall of the castle, admiring its beauty and smelling that unmistakable, musty ancient stone smell, mingled with a faint whiff of tobacco and Chet's cologne.

"What do you think really happened to Al, Sidney? Was it really all about the dancer?"

I wondered if I could trust him. After all, he did sort of work for Empress and supposedly had been checked out.

"I don't know, Chet," I said finally. "I just don't know. But you would think that in a crime of passion, the deckhand would have killed Bostick in his cabin when he found him with the girl. So what was Al doing in the freezer?"

"Yeah, that's right. What does the girl say?"

"Nobody seems to know. And nobody seems to know where she is, either. They say she left the ship when we docked and no one's seen her since. You would expect Empress and the cops to be on her like white on rice, but she supposedly just strolled off the ship and vanished. Don't you think that's a little odd?"

"I think it's a little convenient," Parker replied. "They don't want trouble, you know that. No bad publicity. You know how this stuff works, Sidney. Someone may have even paid her off, sent her back to Brazil. Who knows? We'll probably never know. There's really no point in trying to find out, either."

"No, I guess not. She would probably be really hard to track down, too, even if I had a way to find out her name and home address. Especially if she didn't want to be found."

"True. There's another thing about this that really bugs me, Sidney. If the deckhand didn't kill him, then how on earth could Al Bostick have ended up naked and strangled in an off-limits crew area, in the freezer?"

"No one seems to know, and unless someone confesses or comes forward with more information, we may never find out. Right now, if anyone knows anything, they're not sharing."

"Al may have been lured in there by the killer, Sidney. Or maybe he went with the dancer for some kinky reason and was followed by the killer."

"Eeeuw."

"Yeah."

"Whoever killed him also had to be really strong, and crafty, there's no doubt of that."

"We may never know how it was managed, Chet. No one has reported seeing anything. The time of death was placed by Dr. Sledge as 'sometime during the wee hours of the morning.' That's between mid watch and first watch, when most of the crew and passengers on the ship are sleeping. I guess now they can call that time of night on this ship 'the dead man's watch.' "

"Thank you for that spooky little spin on nautical terms, Sidney. I love thinking of that."

"I'm just saying …"

"Speaking of spooky, want to hear something funny? Some of the old ladies think that the dancer was cursed or something because she worked in the Broadway Showroom. There are rumors swirling that it is haunted."

"Haunted? How ridiculous is that? Where did they get that idea?"

"From some tale they were told on the ship's tour. You know how those things go, Sidney. Add a good ghost story to a tour and you can always jazz it up. Maria Petrone gave the Haunted

Showroom story a boost, too. She swore that she heard weird voices late at night coming from the Showroom as she headed back to her room from the casino. I wish it was haunted. I loved the big shows on my first few cruises but I'm bored with them now. Those shows get pretty tired when you see the same one, night after night, cruise after cruise. That's the only drawback I've found to the Glass Slipper. After a while, no surprises."

He paused. "Tonight's special treat will be great, though," he said. "Would you like to go to Tivoli Gardens with me? I don't think I can stand another evening of dancing with the Levy sisters."

"I'd love to," I said, "but when we get back from this tour there won't be time for Tivoli. We're sailing at five o'clock."

"Oh, no, we're not," he replied. "Didn't you hear the captain's announcement this morning? We're going to stay in Copenhagen at least until midnight. The ship can't sail until the Danes finish the paperwork on Bostick and the deckhand, or, as the captain put it, 'until certain formalities have been completed.' "

"I didn't hear it. I overslept."

I wondered why I hadn't been given notice of the itinerary change. If the Captain expected me to be a part of his team and follow his orders, the least he could do was keep me informed.

"Well, because of the delay, we have to blow off Helsinki on Friday to stay on schedule for St. Petersburg," he continued. "To make it up to the passengers, they are being treated to a night at Tivoli."

He stood up, dusted off the back of his pants, and lit a cigarette. "Come with me to Tivoli, Sidney, to the best amusement park in all of Europe. Forget the serious stuff and all these dull people for one night. We'll have fun."

I thought about Jay and the captain and the whole mess. A night at Tivoli away from it all sounded pretty good.

In fact, it sounded great.

"Sold! I'll meet you at the bottom of the gangway at eight."

13

At the next castle, Kronborg, I stood on the high north wall at the top of the great stone tower overlooking the sea, watching the sun glitter on the strait of Oresund. Sweden was clearly visible on the far shore.

A Russian freighter passed fully loaded with her hull deep in the water, bound for St. Petersburg, I supposed, followed by a Silja Lines ferry. A lone fisherman sat in a small wooden boat, rocking in the wake of the great ships.

Something flashed in the sun. Was the fisherman trying to signal his presence to the ships' captains? I would be signaling if those giant ships were bearing down on me. I would be waving my arms and hollering big time.

Below me, the Murphy family stood on the path at the water's edge, photographing one another using a big, old-fashioned camera, with first the sea, then the castle, as a backdrop. Their camera flashed again and again.

Didn't they realize that the castle was too big and they were too close for it to show up? People take the most random pictures on trips and then wonder why their friends nod off when forced to view them.

I moved to my right, from the shadow into the sun, and found Fernando leaning on the parapet. Through his binoculars he was watching the ships and the Murphys, too. Morgan was nowhere in sight.

"Well, hello, Sidney," he said without turning. "You move very quietly, like one of the ghosts that haunt this castle. And may I say that you look lovely today, much prettier than a spirit."

"If I am a ghost, Fernando, then perhaps you are, too. But not, I think, the prince of Denmark."

He laughed softly and lowered his binoculars, turning to face me. It was the first time in the entire trip that I had seen him really relaxed. His dark eyes were warm with amusement. He looked pretty good himself, in his white shirt and dark blue jacket, silhouetted against the bright blue sky.

"No, I am not the prince of Denmark, Sidney. Far from it. You'll have to look farther to find your Hamlet."

"And I was wrong." he said, suddenly very close to me, "though you move as quietly as a mouse, you are no ghost either, are you?"

Startled, I took a step backward, away from him, and clumsily stumbled over a rock, almost falling onto the parapet.

He caught me easily, laughing out loud now, breaking my fall. I looked up at him, wondering what it would be like to kiss him, and he knew it. I could see it in his eyes. My face burned redder than Brooke Shyler's hair.

"Come with me to Tivoli tonight, Sidney, after you tuck those dreadful people into their beds. You'll learn that I'm not a ghost, that I am very much alive. I think you will enjoy the evening."

I looked down and saw the Murphys staring at us, mouths open. I shook his hand from my left arm, tried to summon some dignity, and stared at my watch as if it were made of rubies.

"Thanks, but I can't, I'm busy," I stammered. Standing next

to him like that made me inexplicably nervous. "Oh, my goodness!," I blurted, "Look at the time! The group will be at the bus in twenty minutes. We must be going."

I turned to start back down the stone steps, but his left hand shot out to take my arm again and reel me in.

"Have dinner with me tonight at Tivoli, Sidney, won't you? I can promise you a memorable evening."

"I can't," I said, looking up at him, "I promised Chet that I would go with him."

"Well, when you change your mind," he said, releasing me, "and I hope you will, I'll have a table for two reserved at The Peacock for nine o'clock. Nine o'clock. Don't forget. I'll be there, waiting."

Without a word, I started down the winding stairs, tripping again, almost missing a step in my haste.

His teasing voice echoed behind me. "Be careful, lovely Grace, it's very dangerous. There might not be anyone there to catch you next time. Remember, nine o'clock. I'll be expecting you."

I rushed down the path to the bus, almost knocking down Muriel Murphy in my haste, stewing to myself over the conceit of the men in my life—Fernando, Chet, Captain Vargos, even Jay.

Men! I steamed, Either I have no guys in my life or too many. And each of them is convinced that he is the greatest .I can't deal with this. It's way too complicated. I'm going to quit this job and go to work at Macy's just as soon as I get back to New York. In the maternity department, where I won't have to deal much with men. Or maybe I could go back to school and learn to run a mammogram machine.

An old nun in dusty black vestments sat on a bench outside the courtyard wall, her gnarled hands twirling wooden spindles as she wove coarse thread into delicate lace.

She lifted her head as I blasted by her, nodding to me with a slight smile, making the sign of the cross to give me her blessing, as if she could read my thoughts and found herself in total agreement.

I need all the blessings I can get, I thought. Maybe I won't go back at all. Maybe I'll just find a good convent around here somewhere, take my vows, and spend the rest of my life with the kind sisters, peacefully making lace.

I was among the last ones on the bus, not a good thing for a tour host. Gertrude and the Murphys would probably write me up. I thought I caught Muriel glaring at me, though Muriel was generally so strange anyway that it was hard to tell.

In my haste, I didn't even stop at the gift shop or the bathroom, just climbed the bus steps and plopped down next to Kirsten, closing my eyes.

She began her bright and cheery monologue. The stragglers filed in, Fernando included, and the bus backed out of the parking lot and headed back to Copenhagen.

♓

Hannah and Ethel had spent far too much time at the Kronborg gift shop selecting troll dolls for their grandchildren, so we were almost forty minutes late arriving at the pier.

By that time, I deeply regretted skipping the restroom break. Back at the ship, I was last in the long, slow line on the gangway through security. When I was finally aboard I rushed down the stairs and corridor of B Deck.

I unlocked the cabin, flung my bag on the bed and, unbuttoning my pants, jerked open the bathroom door.

Jay stood at the sink, shaving, a towel wrapped around his waist. "Well hello, Nancy Drew. Thank you for knocking. How's it going? Caught the murderer yet?"

"I'll be back when you're finished, smartass. Don't use all the towels."

I slammed the door and blasted back down the hall and up the stairs to the ladies' room outside of the Crystal Dining Room.

When I re-emerged, Maria Petrone stood just outside the dining room door, studying the evening menu placard on the gold easel.

"How does it look to you, Maria?" I said. "Delicious?"

"Man, yeah, it does. It says Danish Middag. What is a middag? I never heard of no middag, did you? But whatever it is, it looks great. I don't know what I'll pick for my main course." She leaned closer to the placard, squinting at the calligraphy. "I might have the roast pork with red cabbage and some of the poached salmon, too. Gladys Murphy says that it's okay to have both. Then 'apple dumpling with warm cream and a hint of schnapps.' I love apple dumpling. Mario will take the steak. He always takes the steak, no matter what night it is. What are you having?"

I studied the menu.

"Hard to say, Maria. With so many selections it's difficult to choose, isn't it? But I'll be eating light tonight or not at all. There is great food at Tivoli. Aren't you going?"

"Nah. I been to Coney Island plenty of times."

"Oh, but Maria, it's not like that, really, nothing like that. Tivoli is much nicer. It is special."

"I hear what you say, Sidney, but I don't want to go. Nuts to that. I told my Angelo, I ain't missing my high-dollar middag and show for no amusement park. You young people go and have a good time. Tell me all about it when you get back. But I ain't chowing down on no hot dog and pop tonight. No, ma'am. I can do that back in Queens."

"Miss Marsh is quite right, Maria. Tivoli is delightful."

Brooke Shyler joined us, impeccably dressed in black silk pants and a white shirt that I guessed was from Agnes B.

She and Maxine Johnson held nearly empty champagne flutes. They had just come from the Starlight Lounge, where the Mariner's Club party for returning passengers was in full swing.

"You must go, Maria," she insisted, with Maxine nodding

in agreement. "Everyone loves Tivoli. They always have, ever since it was built back in 1841 by permission of the king. Hans Christian Anderson wrote about it in "The Nightingale." It's very romantic. You and Angelo should go and ride the swan boats or the carousel. You could have a schnapps and watch the fireworks. It's lovely. Maxine, tell her."

"It's really not like an ordinary amusement park, Maria," Maxine said. "Fred and I wouldn't miss it, and neither should you. Especially for a pork roast."

I hoped Brooke and Maxine would convince Maria. If many of the others embraced the Petrones' reasoning, only a small group of High Steppers would be going on the evening excursion, and I hated for them to miss the unexpected treat.

A lot of them don't go out much at night even when at home on familiar ground. They would certainly be apprehensive about leaving the ship after dark in a foreign port.

I went back to the cabin to shower, hoping that I had given Jay enough time to get out of my way, but he was still there, waiting for me.

"You'd better step it up, Sid, if we are going to be on the first bus. I thought we might stay at Tivoli for a couple of hours and then get back in time to dress for the Fairytale Ball. I found us some costumes. I'm going to be a troll and you can be a pixie. The pixie suit will be really cute on you."

"Sorry, Jay. I'm afraid that I'm the troll tonight. I'm not going to Tivoli with the High Steppers. You are. I've been accompanying most of the High Steppers around Kronberg all day while you went to the art gallery with Brooke and a tiny group in a private car. Tonight is my night off. I'm not working. I'm going to Tivoli with Chet Parker."

"You are *what*? Going to Tivoli with Chet instead of me? I don't believe it."

"Believe it, Jay, believe it. And I won't be back in time for the Fairytale Ball either. Now if you'll excuse me, it's my turn in the shower."

Grabbing my robe, I went in the bathroom and closed and locked the door.

He yelled for a while, but I really couldn't make out what he was saying over the noise of the water. I wasn't listening anyway. Finally I heard him go, slamming the cabin door. On his way out he childishly turned off the bathroom light, leaving me to shower in the dark.

The switches and plugs are on the outside of the bathroom door on the Rapture, and on a lot of ships—so that you can't electrocute yourself, I guess. In your bathroom at home in the U.S., with wet feet and floor, you might plug into 110 volts and just do a little dance, but on this ship, grounding 220 could take you out.

Reluctant to leave the warm water, I stood under the showerhead in the dark until the shampoo was all rinsed away, then turned off the water, wrapped my hair in a towel, pulled on my robe, and groped the wall outside the door for the light switch.

A big hairy hand snaked out, grabbed my wrist and jerked me out of the bathroom and into the room. It scared me so much that I couldn't even scream.

"Hah! Got you. Now dry your hair and come on the bus with me. I'll tell Chet you changed your mind."

Furious, I wrenched my arm away from him and shouted, "I am NOT going with you tonight, Jay Wilson. Not on the bus. Not to Tivoli. Not to the costume party. Not ANYWHERE. I need a night off. I DESERVE a night off. I am going to Tivoli with Chet Parker and I am going to have FUN. Without the High Steppers. Without YOU! Get that through your head. I am not going with you."

He finally got it.

"Okay, Sidney, okay," he said in that little crybaby voice he gets when he's miffed. "Have it your way. I understand. Of course you prefer Chet's company to mine. I completely understand. And I really didn't want you around anyway. You would look like crap in a pixie suit. Your ass is too big."

And this time he really did leave, all huffy and sniveling.

Maybe I shouldn't have been so hard on him, but it had been a long day, and I had had just about enough of Mr. Jeremiah Parker Wilson II for a while, particularly until he decided to start doing his share of the work.

14

Eight forty-five p.m. and Chet was nowhere.

I waited as long as I could stand it, knowing that at any moment, Jay and the High Steppers would be filing off the ship, headed for the bright red tour bus. It was waiting, caution lights flashing, at the end of the pier.

Furious with Chet and with myself for provoking a fight with Jay for apparently no good reason, I jumped into the first cab in the taxi line and sped off alone for Tivoli.

I paid the driver at the east entrance of the gardens, gave my pass to the smiling ticket taker, and rushed down the first path I saw, not wanting to be lingering in the entrance area when the shore excursion bus arrived.

There was not much of a crowd, at least not in the east end of the park. Indeed, no one was on that dark path but me, and I began to get a spooky feeling that someone was watching from the overhanging shrubbery or following me, stopping when I stopped, walking when I walked.

"You are being totally ridiculous," I told myself firmly. "You are not being followed. It's a big park, and no one but Chet and Jay even knows that you are here."

I sat down on a bench near an empty bandstand to consider my options, none of which seemed very attractive.

As I saw it, I could either hide in the bushes until after Jay and the High Steppers arrived and then grab a cab back to the ship and go to bed, or have a grand old time at Tivoli all by myself.

Or I could take Fernando Ortiz up on his dinner invitation.

I followed the signposts to the entrance of The Peacock.

The maitre d' was a short stocky Dane with thinning silver hair, a luxuriant moustache, and twinkling blue eyes. "Yes, Miss, may I assist you? Did you have a reservation?"

"Um, maybe. Well, you see, I might be meeting someone here. I mean, someone might be expecting me, but I don't know. I don't see him. I'm not really sure. Maybe not."

"I see," he said. "Are you, perhaps, Sidney Marsh? If so, we have been expecting you."

I nodded.

"This way, then, please, follow me."

Fernando sat alone, sipping a martini. He rose as we approached and the maitre d' handed me a menu and seated me across from Fernando, facing the window with a view of the lake.

What am I doing here? I thought. Avoiding Jay? Chasing Fernando? Why am I so nervous? What am I, a teenager? No. I am a fool.

Fernando smiled as if reading my thoughts again, damn him.

"Ah, Sidney. How lovely you look, and right on time, too. Now what will you have to drink?"

Whiskey, I thought, *and lots of it. This man makes me so nervous!* But I said, "A glass of malbec would be nice, thank you."

"Malbec it is, then. Would you ask Gustav to bring us a bottle of the Mendoza malbec, please, Karl, and perhaps some of the pâté and flatbread for a starter?"

Karl bowed and moved away, signaling to a waiter.

"Tell me, Sidney, where did you develop a taste for Argentine wine? My home is in Columbia, but I also enjoy the wines of Argentina. Have you been to Buenos Aires? Perhaps you know the tango? We must go dancing. I expect we would be very good together."

Cheese City, I thought. But irresistible, of course, because he is so very good looking. This just might turn out okay after all.

⊬

The Peacock dinner with Fernando Ortiz was one of those rare and amazing evenings that I would have memorialized in a scrapbook—if I kept a scrapbook.

I'm sure that you don't want to hear all the sappy details of our sparkling repartee and meaningful glances, or how we drank too much wine and slow-danced under the stars on the terrace, so just let me say that Ortiz is definitely hot, and I had a great time. It was maybe one of my top ten dinner dates ever.

That's why it was such a shock when he abruptly looked at his watch, called for the check, gave me a quick peck on the cheek, and left me sitting there alone with my tango fantasies at the beautiful, candlelit table.

Crap, I thought. The Marsh curse strikes again!

As the meal progressed, I had envisioned us strolling slowly together, arm in arm, beneath the twinkling white lights of the gardens; perhaps riding the carousel or the dragon boats, or winning a big teddy bear on the midway.

Now the only big teddy bear in my room tonight would be Jay.

Ah, well, I thought, mustering up all the pride I could as I said goodbye to the waiter, maybe it's for the best. Relationships with clients are tempting, but not usually a good idea.

I tried to wrap that prim little thought around myself. At least he hadn't stuck me with the check.

Instead of a check, I received a note.

"Who gave this to you?" I asked the waiter.

He shrugged. "He did not give his name. He said he was a friend of yours. He gave it to me at the height of the dinner service, when we were the busiest. I don't remember what he looked like, really, except that he was a very large man, and dark. An American, I think. He gave me a twenty dollar tip."

"Would you know him if you saw him again? Is he still here in the restaurant?"

He looked around the room, which was largely empty now. We had lingered far too long. He shook his head and picked up his tray, "No, Miss, he is not here. We are closing soon. I don't know if I would recognize him again or not. As I said, we were very busy when he gave me the note. I did not get a good look. Excuse me now, Miss, I am needed in the kitchen."

I opened the folded paper. The note said:

> I am your friend. I have been following you and your group since New York and it is now time for us to meet and talk. I mean you no harm. Do not be afraid. You have nothing to fear from me. Please mingle with the crowd near the carousel just before midnight. I will find you there and tell you all you need to know.

Should I meet him? Should I be afraid, despite his assurances? Was I crazy to consider such a meet? Maybe. But the carousel was usually a mob scene. I would be safe in a crowd, I thought. And maybe, finally, I was going to get the break I needed.

I couldn't resist. I had to know what he knew. My mother's voice whispered in my mind: *Curiosity killed the cat.*

The fireworks were beginning as I left the Peacock. It was getting close to midnight. I would have to hurry to make it to the carousel before the rides closed for the evening. The wind was blowing fairly hard, it was getting colder and thick clouds were moving in from the sea, obscuring the stars.

In my somewhat fuzzy state, I was not exactly sure of the

way out. I could hear tinkly music, so I knew that I was near the carousel.

I started down the dim path to the left and was headed for the carousel when a sudden illumination of the fireworks overhead gave me a glimpse of Pete and Gladys Murphy on the path ahead. They were deep in hushed, intense conversation with Dr. Sledge, of all people. They were watching two other figures farther down the path, a man and a woman locked in a passionate embrace, standing in the deep shadow of the fun house.

I stopped, too, and quickly stepped off the path into the bushes so neither group would catch me spying.

"I tell you something's got to be done about her and fast," Gladys said. "People are starting to suspect things. People are talking."

"Yeah," Pete said, "this just ain't working out at all like you said it would. It ain't working at all."

"You must both be patient," Dr. Sledge said. "These things take time, what? Give it some time, I say."

"Yeah, well, you've been saying that all along and things are only getting worse," Gladys hissed. "Those old bats are nosy as hell, and Sidney is getting closer to the truth all the time. She's got to be stopped!"

Gladys was practically shouting now, shaking her finger in Dr. Sledge's face.

He tapped his pipe out on the heel of his shoe. "Calm down, Mrs. Murphy." His voice was cold, his expression hard as he removed her hand from his arm. "I will not have you shouting at me. You must listen. You must follow my orders. You know we have a scheme to follow. Any deviation ..."

I had been inching closer through the trees, straining to hear. At that moment I stepped on a stick, which broke with a loud crack. I tried to melt back into the thicket, thankful for the clouds that suddenly obscured the moon.

"Hush!" Pete said. "Both of you. Someone's coming. We'll

talk later, on the ship. But you haven't heard the last of us, Dr. Sledge. Gladys is right. She's got to be stopped, and soon."

I stepped back onto the path and collided with Muriel Murphy, who, feeling no pain, was woozily weaving her way toward her parents. I clutched her arm to steady her, to keep her from falling. She was sweating, breathing hard, and every breath was a cloud of gin.

"He almos' knocked, bastard almos' knocked me down," she blubbered, tears streaming down her face, mascara running into the crevices of her cheeks, "he said 'get out of my way, fat bitch' "

"Who did that, Muriel?"

"Jerome Morgan, thass who. Morgan, Morgan, Morgan, hogging the path, bumping into me, calling me 'fat bitch.' He can't call me names. Called me a drunk. Called me a fat bitch. He better not call me names, Schidney, he better not!"

She was really worked up now, poor thing. Mascara dripped off her chin and her face was red and blotchy. Had she tried to come on to Morgan?

"Look, Muriel, forget about Morgan. I'm sure he didn't mean to hurt your feelings and I'll speak to him about it. Your parents are just ahead of us, see there? Let's join them. Don't let this spoil your evening."

I steered her forward toward Pete and Gladys.

"Look at them two, would ya," Pete laughed, as we approached. But he wasn't talking about me and Muriel, he was looking the other way. "Why don't they just get a room?"

Just as a blue and gold chrysanthemum lit the sky, I saw the faces of the couple as they finally parted and walked rapidly away in opposite directions. It was Sylvia Klein and Fernando Jackass Ortiz.

I was close enough to the Murphys then to release Muriel's arm and head her, still wailing, down the path toward Pete. He put his arm around her, patted her back, and looked at me over her head, mouthing a thank-you. I nodded, gave a quick wave and headed back up the path in the opposite direction, away from the Murphys, away from Fernando and Sylvia.

"Wowzers. Look at that," said a disembodied voice that came from a bench by the edge of the path. "Bet old Abe Klein has been asleep for hours. She must have drugged his cocktails. Tell me, what do you think attracts all these guys to Sylvia? Is it her big, baby blues or those great big knockers? And why are you hiding in the bushes, spying on them? I've been looking for you everywhere. You were supposed to meet me at the park entrance at 8:00."

Of course, I hadn't seen Chet Parker in the gloom. All I could see even now was the glow of his cigarette.

I looked back toward the fun house, but Sylvia, that big rat Fernando, Dr. Sledge, and the Murphys had all disappeared.

I turned to face Chet. Could he be the writer of the note? But no, he was clearly referring to our earlier 8 p.m. meeting time, not midnight at the carousel.

"We were *not* supposed to meet at the public entrance. We were supposed to meet on the pier, as you well know, Chet. I was there at 8:00 and you were not. So where were you?"

"Would you believe trapped in the Starlight Lounge with the Levy sisters? No? Well then, what about ..."

"Look, Chet, don't give me any excuses. Just go back to the ship and call it a night. The park is closing soon. No, don't explain. I don't care. And I've got to go now. I'm meeting someone near the carousel and I want to get there before the rides stop, if they haven't already. No, don't explain, Chet. I don't care what you have to say, I really don't give a rat's ass. But if you ever mess with me again, you are toast, my friend. Hear me? Toast. Your little glass slippers will never dance again, at least not on Empress Lines."

This pointless conversation would probably have continued for much longer if a long, shrill scream hadn't come from the direction of the carousel.

Parker and I looked at each other and, without another

word, took off running toward the sound.

⯈

A crowd had gathered around the carousel. Everyone stared in shock and horror at the sight of the body—a large, dark-skinned man, seated on a carousel horse, tied by his neck to the pole, flopping back and forth, back and forth, as the carousel turned round and round, its gaily gilded and painted wooden animals moving up and down with the music. The macabre figure seemed to be swaying in time with the tinkling, music-box melody.

The wire holding the grisly equestrian in place had cut into his neck, and dark red blood had bathed the front of his shirt and pants. It was coagulating in a black-red puddle beneath the hoofs of the horse. His eyes—large, gray-green, and now sightless—seemed to stare back at the crowd, the lights of the carousel bizarrely reflected in them.

The onlookers, even the screamer, fell silent, waiting and watching in horrified fascination for the bloody horse and its terrible rider to come around again.

It seemed as if hours passed before the police arrived to shut off the machine and secure the area. In reality it was probably no more than a few minutes.

Chet and I moved in stunned silence away from the grotesque carousel. The dead man was clearly not one of the High Steppers, *thank God, not another one*, though his clothes—some kind of uniform—indicated he might have been a member of the ship's crew. With all the blood, it was hard to tell.

"Let's go, Sidney," Chet said. "We'd better get the hell out of here. They are going to cordon off this area. If we stick around much longer it could be hours before we are allowed to leave, and we might miss our sailing. Stop staring and let's go. That poor guy is probably not from the ship. He must be a local. I've never seen him before in my life."

But I had.

He had stumbled over me in the New York subway.

I was almost positive that it was the man I had named "Homeless Guy." What was he doing at Tivoli? Who killed him, and why? Was he the author of the note, the man who said he had been watching me, following me? Was he the man I was asked to meet at the carousel? Or was that someone else … maybe even his killer. Had someone silenced him before he could share his information or reveal his identity?

15

We sailed at midnight. Fast-moving, thick clouds were building in the west. Lightning snaked from the cloudbank into the sea. It would storm soon, I thought, certainly before morning.

I stood alone by the rail in the darkness and watched the Rapture clear the docks, then the harbor. Watched until the pilot boat picked up the harbor pilot from our ship. Watched until, with a final wave and a parting blast of his horn, the pilot boat turned back toward Copenhagen and the ship mounted the deep swells of the North Sea.

Then, as the waves grew larger, crashing against the bow, and the lights from shore gradually dimmed, I watched, bathed in mist, until at last there was nothing at all left but the ship and the blackness of the sea.

I heard ladies' heels approaching from the stern. In my state of mind, the last thing I wanted was conversation with a High Stepper, so I stretched out on a deck chair in the shadows and closed my eyes, hoping that whoever it was would overlook me or think I was asleep.

The footsteps came closer and the deck chair next to mine

creaked slightly with the weight of a new occupant. I could smell Chanel.

"Hello, Brooke," I said, without opening my eyes. "Did you have a nice evening?"

"Actually, I did," she said. "I went to dinner in Copenhagen with old friends. They sent a car for me. But I came back to the ship fairly early and was sitting on my balcony when I saw you return in the taxi with Chet. You looked rather forlorn, so I thought you might want company. I called your room, but there was no answer. Then I thought that I might just find you here and *voilà!* Here you are. What's wrong, my dear? Has something happened, or has it all just gotten to be a bit much for you?"

I looked into the beautiful, wise eyes of my good friend, and I lost it.

All the troubles of the past two weeks came pouring out. Jay, Ruth Shadrach, Al Bostick, Diana, Chet Parker, the carousel, the homeless man, Ortiz, my biological clock, everything.

She didn't speak until I had finally run down and dabbed my eyes with her monogrammed linen and lace handkerchief.

"You know, Sidney," she said, "one of the very few advantages of old age, in my view, is that you learn to put a lot of things that once seemed vitally important into perspective. Younger people, yourself included, seem to believe that it is their mission to solve all the world's difficulties; that the fate of all mankind rests on their shoulders, that everything that happens is their personal responsibility. But the longer you live, my dear, the more you come to realize that you must do what you can, and then leave the rest to fate, or as you would say, to the Almighty."

She paused to give my arm at little pat.

"There is obviously a great deal going on here," she went on, "that neither you nor I understand. It may indeed be dangerous for you and for us all, but we must see it through without alarming the rest of the group unduly. Creating panic among the High Steppers would serve no purpose, and it would be terribly cruel. It would spoil everything for them and perhaps put them in even greater danger. You, of course, have an enormous responsibility."

I sniffed, and she handed me the handkerchief again before continuing. "You must proceed with extreme caution— particularly if you can't make the tour company see your concern and authorize an early return. There may be a perfectly normal explanation for everything that has happened, though I doubt it. This thing with the homeless man is most disturbing."

She was silent for a few minutes, then continued, "Yes, dear Sidney, you must be very careful. There is grave danger here. But I think you were quite right not to involve yourself in the police investigation. After all, you couldn't identify that man. You never knew his name. And it is possible, after all, that you may have been mistaken. The light was poor, you were some distance from the carousel, and you had had an upsetting evening and several glasses of wine."

"Brooke," I said, "I'm pretty sure it was the homeless man."

"Well, it seems very odd to me, dear, that a homeless man could follow you all the way from New York and somehow meet his end on a merry-go-round in Copenhagen. I don't see how that would be possible. You must have been mistaken. That note may have been from someone else entirely, someone who was afraid to reveal himself in all the commotion at the carousel. The author of the note may even have tired of waiting and left before you arrived. You said yourself that you were delayed by the Murphys and Chet Parker."

She shrugged. "As for your other concerns, well, Jay will come around, Sidney; he is given to fits of pique, you know that, but he is basically a sound man. And Mr. Ortiz ... well, dear girl, there are many fish in the sea. I wouldn't lose a lot of sleep over the loss of that one. Another will swim along, eventually, you'll see."

I thought over what she said, and for a long time neither of us said anything, just watched the sea and the dark sky and the distant lights of passing ships in silence.

Finally I asked, "Brooke, why do you come on these trips? You are a wealthy woman. You can go anywhere, do anything, stay in all the best hotels, go to all the glamour spots. Why are you a High Stepper?"

"My dear, I love being a High Stepper. I have done and still do all of those other things. But I think the High Steppers are a kick. I like them. They are good people, genuine people; they are real. I also enjoy my friends in New York, of course, but I get tired of charity balls and gallery openings and clubs. So many of my dear friends, with their young, young faces on old, old bodies, are so very sad, so very predictable. They care little for the stuff of life. Most of them are far more interested in their appearance and their health and those tiny dogs that they stuff into their purses. Very dull. The High Steppers are funny and very loyal, genuine friends. With them I see more of the world as it is. It's hard to get a true feel for a foreign country, you know, from the penthouse suite of a five star hotel."

She looked clearly into my eyes and smiled, as though trying to coax the same from me. "Now come along dear, and let's go to our rooms. It's late and we need our beauty sleep! We don't want bags under our eyes, do we?"

I left Brooke at the door of her suite and, energized by her sensible advice, marched down to my cabin for the confrontation with Jay that I had been dreading all night, prepared to give the apology that I knew I owed him.

But when I unlocked the door, he wasn't there. Neither were his things.

He had moved out.

16

The yellowish green numbers on my travel alarm clock read 3:06 a.m.

I rolled over on my back, feeling the motion of the ship well underway as it plowed through the Baltic. It was storming again, and when I parted the curtains and looked out, big bolts of lightning illuminated the heavy sea.

Someone hurried past my door, then another and another. I heard high-pitched laughing. Low, sharp commands followed; then I heard even more rapid footsteps. I reached for the light switch and pressed it, but nothing happened. The electricity was off.

I was alone in the cabin. Jay had not returned.

Groping my way across the room, I pulled on my fleece and my gym shorts and slid my feet into flip-flops. Then I quietly unlocked and partially opened the door and peeked out.

The passageway was dark and empty, illuminated only by the emergency lights. No other doors were open.

I spotted Abdul's white jacket in the dimness, headed toward the stairs, and hurried to catch up with him just before he turned the corner.

"Abdul, what's with the lights? Why is the power out? What is going on?"

"Not to worry, Miss Marsh. Not to worry. Small electrical problem, that's all. Will be back on soon. Everything okay now. Everything fine. Now back to sleep you go, okay? Not to wake old ladies, yes? Everything fine."

But it was not fine, not fine at all.

The passageway was silent. Whatever had awakened me was gone, and as I reached my door, the corridor lights came back on. The lights in my cabin were working now, too.

Frustrated, I climbed back into bed, my brain in turmoil, searching for the sense of all of this. The more I thought about it all, the more muddled it became.

I tried to read for a while, but the faces of Jay, Ortiz and the High Steppers danced across the pages. Finally I turned off the light and just stared at the ceiling until morning.

♓

The flower arranging class was in full swing when I entered the Starlight Lounge on Thursday morning. Seated at three long tables by the windows, a group of High Steppers watched intently as the ship's florist explained how to cut a rose under water to make it last longer in a floral arrangement.

I slipped into an empty chair between Hannah Weiss and Amy Wu.

"Good morning, Miss Marsh," Hannah stage-whispered. "We missed you at breakfast. You should eat a good breakfast. A young girl like you can stand to put on a few pounds. I had Swedish waffles this morning with cream and strawberries, and Ethel had prunes, of course, but then after that she had ..."

The florist, a very talented but high-strung Asian man from California, stopped speaking, put his hands on his slender hips, and stared at Hannah.

"Oops," Hannah said, red-faced, "sorry. I'll be quiet now. I'll be good, I promise. Keep going. I won't interrupt again."

What a jerk, I thought, picking on poor little Hannah. How can he be so mean to a sweet old lady?

The hotshot designer opened another bundle of roses and resumed his demonstration of French hand-tied bouquets. I was no longer interested in anything that guy had to say. I focused instead on my group, studying their faces, trying to piece together the puzzle that this trip had turned into, hoping to get my sadly diminished group back home safely.

Chill out, Sidney, I thought. Brooke is right. There's really nothing you can do. You can't freak out over all this, or you'll go nuts. Relax. If you're going to find anything out, you're going to have to stay calm.

The Daily Program listed many activities, as is always the case on days at sea. That means more work for the cruise and kitchen staff but less work for me. On port days, it is just the opposite.

Then the dog and pony show is up to me and Jay.

I planned to chat purposefully all day, all over the ship, to anyone and everyone, gathering whatever scraps of information I could piece together to solve these murders.

Brooke had kindly offered to do the same. I knew I could trust her to be discreet. She had gone to the perfume seminar to talk with the High Steppers there, and after that, she was going to hear what the bridge players had to say.

The florist finished with a flourish, holding a drawing for the arrangements that he had created during his demonstration.

"Oh, my goodness, I won! I don't believe it! I never win anything!" Ethel Goldstein was thrilled with her Gerber daisies. "I'm taking these back to my cabin and heading straight for the casino! This is my lucky day!"

Maxine Johnson also won. The ladies clustered around her, admiring the lovely bouquet of pink roses, hand-tied with a silk ribbon.

Maxine admired it, too, and then presented it to Hannah

with a smile. Esther Levy scurried to her cabin with her vase of bright yellow tulips.

The florist and his assistant began packing up as the catering staff set out coffee, tea, lemonade, and big trays covered with paper lace doilies and heaped with fancy cookies.

There was a thirty minute break between activities. The next class to be held in the room would be a napkin folding demonstration put on by the dining room staff.

After helping myself to coffee and a generous serving of cookies, I joined the girls at a large round table in the corner. They were gossiping about Sylvia and Abe Klein, who had apparently had a huge public spat in the disco after the midnight buffet.

"Abe was really drunk. He jerked Sylvia off the dance floor where she was slow dancing with Pete Murphy, and then he yelled at her and called her a slut," reported Marjorie Levy.

"Yeah," said Hannah, stirring her coffee, "and then Murphy told Abe that he didn't have any right to talk to Sylvia that way, even if she is his wife. Abe tried to swing at Murphy, but Murphy just stepped out of the way. Abe lost his balance and fell right on his keister, and everybody laughed. Then Sylvia started crying and ran out of the room."

"She wasn't upset about Abe being mad at her, see," said Gertrude, barely able to conceal her delight. "Sylvia was upset because Abe said real loud, 'I paid for those tits that you are shaking at everybody, and I can say anything I want.' "

Annoyed with Hannah and Gertrude for butting in on her story, Marjorie again took up the narrative. "Sylvia locked Abe out of their cabin and wouldn't let him in for anything. Abe beat on the door until the neighbors complained, and the little room steward ran and got the hotel manager and Jay Wilson. They took Abe away with them, and we don't know what happened after that because nobody's seen any of them at all this morning."

"Well," I said, "where was Mrs. Murphy during all of this?"

"Nobody knows," Hannah said, rolling her eyes. "She wasn't in the disco, that's for sure, because old Pete was dirty dancing then with Sylvia. He was squeezing her ass with both hands!"

"Hannah!" Ethel protested.

"Well, speak of the devil," Esther said, "here comes Gladys, poor thing. Hush, now, all of you. She'll hear you."

"Good morning, Gladys," trilled Gertrude. "Did you sleep well? Where's Pete?"

"Pete's sleeping in," Gladys answered. "He's all tired out after his big night at Tivoli Gardens."

"I thought he might be tired from all that dancing," Gertrude needled, "Did you and Pete really even go to Tivoli? You weren't on the bus. How did you get there?"

Gladys' beefy face turned even redder and she bristled.

I rushed in to make peace.

"Of course they were at Tivoli, Gertrude, I saw them there myself with Dr. Sledge. They must have taken a cab. That's how I got there."

To Gladys, I said, "Changing the subject, I meant to ask you about Dr. Sledge. I didn't realize that you and he were friends."

Gladys, happy to be off Edith's hook, pointedly turned to face me, keeping her back to the others. "Well, you see, Miss Marsh," she stammered, "Dr. Sledge's brother is, uh, my mother-in-law's doctor."

"Really?" I said. "What an amazing coincidence! Did you know our Dr. Sledge before the trip?"

"No, no," she replied, "we just got to talking one day when we went to get some medicine for our daughter Muriel. Dr. Sledge said that he has a brother who is a doctor, too, in Tallahassee, Florida. I said that my mother-in-law lives in Tallahassee, Florida, with my other daughter, Harriet Finkelstein, and her husband Bill. One thing led to another, and what do you know, we found out that Dr. Sledge's brother is my mother-in-law's doctor. Small world, isn't it?"

"It certainly is," Gertrude said, "if Dr. Sledge's brother really *is* your mother-in-law's doctor. It sounds pretty far-fetched to me."

"Yeah," said Hannah, "that's real confusing."

"Well, he certainly *is* my mother's doctor, Gertrude," Gladys shot back, "and I know that for a fact, because I called Mom from Copenhagen to double-check. She said he sure was, so there!"

Just then the assistant maitre d' announced that the napkin-folding class would begin in five minutes.

He asked for a volunteer to help pass out the napkins and printed instructions. I rushed to assist to avoid refereeing a fight between Gertrude and Gladys. When I had given everyone their materials, I waved goodbye to the girls and slipped out on deck for some fresh air.

I hated to agree with Gertrude on anything, but the story sounded pretty far-fetched to me, too. There was also the matter of the puzzling argument I had overheard on the path in the park. I had forgotten all about it because of the events that followed. So what was going on with Dr. Sledge and Gladys? What was Dr. Sledge up to?

♓

Angelo Petrone had just finished skeet-shooting off the aft deck when I found him.

"Nice shot, Angelo. I didn't know you were a marksman."

"Not as good as I once was, Sidney, but I try to keep my hand in."

"Angelo, could I ask you something? Have you got a minute?"

"Sure thing, Sidney. Here, let's have a seat, out of the wind. What's on your mind?"

"Angelo, the other night, when you saw Al Bostick with the dancer, where were they? You said in the hallway. Were they near the kitchens?"

"Nah." He shook his head. "They wasn't nowhere near them kitchens. I passed them on Continental Deck, Sidney, and then they went into his cabin. And that's the last I seen of him. I don't know how he got to the kitchens. It seems funny, don't it? The way it turned out."

"Yeah, Angelo, it does. It sure does."

♓

Dinner that night was formal and I had a terrible time getting dressed because I just didn't allow myself enough time. I got shampoo in my eyes, turning them blazing red, I goofed up my eye makeup and had to redo it, and I couldn't find the round brush that made my hair behave. After finally rolling my hair in hot curlers, I grabbed my dress from the closet and discovered that the hem was out. Jerking the curlers out of my hair, I rummaged through a drawer, found some tape, stuck the hem in place, pulled the dress on over my head, and blasted off for the dining room, hoping that the doors weren't already closed.

The lights in the big room were low, with candles and flowers centering tables overlaid with crisp white linens. The huge crystal chandelier was dimmed. A harpist was playing, and a strolling violinist. Wine was being poured, waiters were circling, taking orders, and the dinner service was about to begin.

I slid into my seat just as Captain Vargos rose to give his welcome toast.

He looked handsomer than ever in the dark coat of his formal dress uniform. The gold epaulets on his broad shoulders gleamed in the candlelight. Seated next to him was a beautiful young blond in a silvery blue dress, her perfect hair curling down her bare back. Her lovely face smiled up at him as he completed his toast.

Resuming his seat, Captain Vargos stared coldly, directly, at me and then quickly turned his head, smiling, as if hiding a laugh. He had been staring, not at my face, but at the top of my head.

Reaching up, I discovered the big plastic hot roller that, in my haste, I had failed to remove from my hair. *Great look, Sidney*, I thought, *now he thinks you're really cool.* I snatched it out, hoping no one else had noticed. My face blazed with heat as I tucked the stinking thing into my purse.

17

I couldn't rest that night, not at all. I was getting very little sleep on this cruise. Too much was wrong; too many bad things were happening.

I had made myself look like a fool at that damn dinner, my love life was non-existent, and my boss and my best friend were both mad at me. Two of my clients were dead, along with a random guy I might have recognized, and I was no closer to finding out *why*, much less *who*.

I felt as if this whole trip was inexorably headed toward some terrible end, just as our ship steadily plunged at full speed through the dark water.

The ship's destination, however, was fairly certain; mine was not. I was handling everything badly, acting like an idiot, running around like a chicken with its head cut off, and I didn't have a clue how to fix anything.

If Jay had been there, I would have woken him up and talked it out until his street smarts produced some answers, a real plan of action. He would have ultimately said something totally outrageous and made me laugh. But he wasn't there, and that was my fault, too.

I looked at the clock. Three a.m. I thought some more. I looked again. Three fifteen. I had been tossing and turning like this, staring at the ceiling, forever. Plus, I realized, I was hungry. I hadn't eaten much dinner. The midnight buffet was long over and it was too early for breakfast, but, hey, it's a cruise ship. There's always food somewhere, right? I could have called room service—they have it 24/7—but I was ready to get out of that room for a while. Maybe escaping the room would also help me get away from my thoughts.

Now, I know it was pretty goofy of me to ramble around the silent ship alone at that hour, but I was sure that I could be quick and careful, and after all, it was three o'clock in the morning. The murderer was probably asleep, like everyone else but me. Even murderers have to sleep sometime, don't they? According to Jay and everyone else, there hadn't been any mad murders anyway, only a sad suicide, a crime of passion, and a totally unrelated incident ashore involving the grisly death of a stranger. A stranger who had wanted to tell me something. I knew that much was true.

But still, I was pretty sure I could get away with a quick snack run. I was starving, and totally sick of that cabin, tired of looking at Jay's empty bed.

I stripped off my nightgown and pulled on gym shorts and a T-shirt, the first things I grabbed out of the drawer. I didn't even consider makeup. Who would I see at this hour?

As predicted, I met no one in the hallway, not even Abdul. Steering clear of the elevators, I zoomed up two flights and then slipped out on deck for the fastest transit to the back of the ship. The deck was deserted, too. I didn't linger. The wind was icy, and I was soon shivering in my skimpy little outfit.

There was always coffee and some kind of snack in the casino bar, so I headed there.

To reach the casino from the port deck, I had to go all the way around the Broadway Showroom outside in the cold wind and enter on the other side, or else take a shortcut through the darkened theater, which you really weren't supposed to do. But there was no one around to see, so I skirted the brass "Showroom Closed for Rehearsal" sign and pushed open the heavy door. Signs like that rarely stop me, anyway, unless the High Steppers are watching.

I stepped inside, and in almost total darkness felt my way down the aisle, trying not to collide with anything as I headed for the opposite door.

I had just reached the middle of the dance floor, just below the stage, when I heard the laughing behind me.

I froze, stock still, listening and shivering all over. I couldn't tell whose voice it was—whether man or woman or maybe the ghost—or even pinpoint the source of the sound. I was almost in the center of the big room, and the eerie cackling seemed to be coming from all around me. The laughter echoed and grew louder and louder, booming in the dimness. Then I realized that a spirit was out of consideration unless the spook was at the big master sound board, playing with the magician's voice synthesizers and special effects. I could just make out a shadowy figure—whether man or woman, it was too dark to tell—seated behind the big board. But in the dark? At three o'clock in the morning?

I inched quietly forward across the dance floor, hoping to creep slowly to the exit and escape unnoticed.

Suddenly I was blinded, surrounded by a pool of white light. The weirdo had turned a spotlight on me. I stood transfixed, in the center of the pool of light, the only light in the room.

Music boomed out, Sinatra singing "New York, New York."

That dreadful laughter began again, and then a voice, still unidentifiable, distorted by the sound system's special effects, whispered, echoing, through a microphone, "Dance for me, little dolly, dance. Dance as if your life depends on it."

And so I danced. There in the darkened showroom, in the middle of the night, in the center of the spotlight, I danced, desperately trying to think of an escape, until the clapping and giggling and music ended, and the light went out.

And then I ran, and ran and ran, ran like a scalded dog, out of the Broadway Showroom, past the photo gallery, through the arcade, down the stairs, down, down, down, never looking back to see if the banshee was following, until I finally reached my door and slammed and locked it behind me. I slid down the door, sobbing, to the floor, that horrid laughter still ringing in my ears.

During that headlong flight, I had met no one, seen no one, passed no one, heard not a living soul. It was as if the ship was not the Rapture of the Deep after all, but instead, The Flying Dutchman.

♓

When I woke, just after seven, I wasn't sure if the night's events had been real of not. Perhaps, I thought, it had all been a horrible nightmare, a product of my overwrought imagination and the stress of the last few days.

But there were my shorts and shirt in a heap on the floor by the bed.

It had been real, all right. It had happened. I just didn't know how I was going to deal with it.

I found some aspirin in the bathroom, then lay back on the bed, waiting for the little dwarves in the iron boots to stop jumping up and down in my head.

For a long time I stared at the ceiling, trying to decide what to do. In the end I decided to do nothing.

As dangerous as it might be, and as hard as it might be, I resolved not to tell anyone what had happened until I had a better idea of the big picture. Telling would only cause a big hullabaloo with little result. There would just be a lot of talk, but no one would do anything. I knew all too well what the official line would be.

Jay would be alarmed at first, but then the image of my command performance would overwhelm him, and for years hence he would tease me about it. What a great story to tell over cocktails! He wouldn't be able to resist.

Could the puppet master have been Jay, playing a trick on me to exact some twisted kind of revenge?

No, that scene had been too strange even for Jay, and too cruel. Jay takes jokes pretty far sometimes, but he is not cruel and he has never been mean to me. Despite our differences, Jay was one of the few people on board I knew I could trust.

And, I thought, if I remained silent, perhaps whoever had carried out the prank would let something slip; then I would know who the enemy was.

I had not been harmed, not really, and no one knew what had happened except me and the madman. This thing had to end somehow, and the more I thought about my humiliation and fear, the angrier I became.

My fear had turned me into a performing monkey, terrorized me into dancing for the amusement of an insomniac freak. While I spent my morning cringing over the spectacle I had made of myself, that damn ghoul was probably laughing his head off just thinking about it, or maybe something sicker.

But what about the threat? Dance, if you want to live? Had I just stumbled onto some kooky drunk messing around with the sound board or had I been followed into the theatre? Was I being stalked? Was my tormenter actually the murderer?

Whoa, Sidney, I thought. *Don't go down that path. Nothing but hysteria there.* No, I had to be strong, and brave, and above all, smart. Careful. And no more solo midnight rambles! Maybe I really did need to tell Jay what had happened, even if it meant enduring a lifetime of teasing. I resolved to give that a lot of thought.

But first, I had to find Jay and make up. No way was I spending another night alone.

18

Looking for Jay, I searched the Rapture's public areas, literally from stem to stern and from the Sun Deck to B Deck.

No Jay.

I asked around among the High Steppers, but no one had seen him since the bus returned from Tivoli just before the ship sailed.

"Are you sure he came back with the bus?" I asked Fred Johnson.

"Oh, yes," Fred nodded, "though he was acting pretty strange, I thought, even for him. He was rather subdued, sort of distracted. Maxine and I both remarked on it."

"Did you notice where he went after you came aboard?"

"No. We were almost the last to board. We rode up in the elevator with him, but we got off on Promenade Deck. Jay said good night and continued on up in the elevator. I don't know where he went after that. Is something amiss?"

"Oh, no. No. Nothing's wrong. I haven't seen him this morning, that's all."

"He's probably sleeping. He had quite a bit to drink, Miss Marsh."

"Oh."

Well then. That explained a lot.

"I am meeting Maxine for lunch in a few minutes," Fred continued, "Will you join us?"

"No thanks, Dr. Johnson. I'd love to, but I'd better see if I can find Jay right now. Perhaps tomorrow."

♓

I found Edgar, the ship's concert pianist, in the Starlight Lounge, practicing for his evening performance.

He was playing Chopin's Military Polonaise, his favorite, and I sat in the back of the darkened room until he finished, not wanting to interrupt, enjoying his music.

Edgar trained at Juilliard and for a while he was on the concert stage. He never achieved stardom, however, only moderate success. He had been almost ready to give up and find another way to earn his living, when a chance meeting with an old friend in Miami resulted in a contract with a cruise line.

Now, twenty years later, his piano has taken him around the world. He is tall, balding, and British, with a great handlebar mustache. He is also a very funny man, and he does a sort of comedy concert show on some nights and serious classical recitals on alternate afternoons. He practices everyday for four hours, mostly, he says, to keep his fingers limber.

"Bravo, bravo, maestro, bravo!" I said, clapping as he finished.

Edgar turned and peered into the dimness of the cavernous room. "Ah, there you are, my dear Sidney. My audience of one. How nice. Thank you. Come closer, please, I am ready for a break. Tell me, are you here for a reason? Is it my superb playing, my mastery of the keys? Or is it that you just couldn't wait until dinner to see me again?"

For the last couple of nights I had been dining at Edgar's table, having bailed earlier in the week on Murphy and Company.

"Both. Your music is magnificent, of course, but I did want to ask you something."

"Fire away, then, dear girl. I am putty in your hands. Do you want to ask how thrilling it would be to sleep with an elderly British concert pianist? No? Well. What then?"

"Edgar, it's Jay. I don't know where he is, I can't find him anywhere in the public areas, and no one has seen him at all today. He got pretty smashed last night, I'm told, so he may just be holed up somewhere, holding his head. Or he may be hiding, pouting because of a little disagreement that we had, which was, I'll admit, my fault. He moved out of my cabin in a snit, and I don't know where he went. I wouldn't worry, but as you well know, some funny things are happening on this ship. Have you seen him?"

"Indeed I have, my darling, you should have come to old Edgar first thing and not wasted time running about. I wasn't supposed to tell you this, but I shall. I shared the hair of the dog with Jay not two hours ago on his balcony."

"His balcony! What do you mean, Edgar? B Deck doesn't have balconies."

"No, dearest, but the Neptune Suite does, and that's where our boy is ensconced. In fine style, I must say."

"The Neptune Suite! He's in the Neptune Suite? How in the world did he manage that?" I thought for a moment. "Oh, my God, he didn't break in, did he?"

Edgar shook his head and laughed, "No, no, no, no. He is there quite legally. By invitation. How he managed it, I can't say. You'll have to ask him."

He turned back to the keyboard as I thanked him and left, calling out to me over his shoulder, "Think nothing of it, love, but mind you, I shall demand a full report at dinner tonight. You will undoubtedly want to share a bottle of port."

⊬

I rang the doorbell of the Neptune Suite, calling out "Room

Service" in my best Spanish accent. No answer. I rang the bell again.

"Room Service for Meester Weelson."

I heard steps approaching the door, stopping as he peered out though the peephole. Not that it did him any good, because my finger was over it.

I rang the bell again and curiosity got him. I knew it would.

He jerked the door open and stuck his head out. When he saw me, he tried to slam the door, but I was too quick for him. I had slipped inside.

"Beat it. Scram. Go away, Sidney, please leave. I have nothing to say to you."

"Well, I have something to say to you, Jay Wilson, if you'll let me into the pity party for just one minute. I came to say that I was wrong to treat you the way I did, and I'm sorry. So there. I apologize. Now will you forgive me?"

"I don't know," he said. "Maybe. It depends. But first you've got to tell me who you really went to Tivoli with last night, Sid. I know it wasn't Chet, because I saw him leave the ship when we did, in a cab by himself. So who were you with? Don't lie. I can tell when you lie."

So I told him all about my ridiculous dinner dates, down to the last detail, ending with the horror at the carousel. I didn't mention that I thought I had recognized the murdered man, or about my nocturnal tormenter. I was still trying to decide whether to tell him about that or not. By the time I had finished, he wasn't mad at me anymore, just preachy.

"Sidney Lanier Marsh, Chet doesn't matter—he's just a fluffball—but I hope someday you learn to avoid sketchy guys like Fernando and Vargos. Now here you are, playing around with both those bad boys. Tell me, though, I can keep a secret, which one is better?"

It took all of my will to control my temper after that cheap shot, but I managed it, probably because deep down I knew I had it coming. "When I find out, Jay, you'll be the first to know. Okay, my friend, we're even. Actually, you win. You always win, don't you? Truce?"

He smiled and nodded slowly. "I guess so, Sidney. I never have been able to stay in a fight with you for long, have I? Come, relax and I'll get you a drink. Welcome to the Neptune Suite!"

I sat on a pale blue silk loveseat beside a marble table supported by gold dolphins and Jay poured two glasses of Dom from a bottle chilling in a silver cooler. He was wearing a silk robe embroidered with the words "Neptune Suite" and a little trident on the pocket.

He might have appeared very impressive, except that his huge hairy legs sticking out from the bottom of the robe spoiled the effect.

He handed me a glass, clinked it with his, and I knew I'd really won, though he wouldn't make it easy. I'd still have to grovel a little to be totally back on his good list.

"How do you like my suite, by the way? Nice, isn't it? Although the gold seahorse faucets in the Jacuzzi are a bit much."

I looked around the room, taking it all in, thinking it all over.

"Would you like to move in?" he said. "There's plenty of room.

"Jay," I demanded, "What are you doing in this suite? I want the truth. How did you get here?"

He didn't say anything, wouldn't even look at me.

Then I knew.

"You caved, didn't you? You told them that it was all fine, that you had changed your mind and would back up whatever version they wanted to spin about Ruth and Al and everything. In exchange, you got the Neptune Suite."

I headed for the door. He still hadn't said anything, wouldn't meet my eyes.

"No, Jay, I'm not moving in," I said as I started to back away. "I couldn't sleep one wink in this place, knowing that I had totally copped out for the sake of gold faucets and a Jacuzzi."

19

Vinny, one of the assistant pursers, shook his head firmly at my request.

"No can do, Sidney. No way. I can't give you a key to Mr. Bostick's cabin or a copy of the passenger/crew manifest without authorization."

"But, Vinny," I lied, "Captain Vargos said he wants me to have both those items so I can help him figure out how to keep the High Steppers safe. After all, I am the tour leader. He wants me to have those things. He said so."

"Weak, Sidney, weak. Think I'm buying that? Not even if Santa Claus says so. Empress would have my job if they found out. They just released Bostick's cabin today and it stays locked until it can be cleaned out and his stuff packed up. I can't let anyone in there."

"Well, they won't find out you did unless you tell them, Vinny, because I sure won't."

"Sorry, Sidney, I can't do that. Not even for you. I couldn't even do that for the President."

I turned to leave, then realized that Vinny was still standing there with an expectant look on his face.

The light bulb went off.

"Vinny, what if President Abraham Lincoln said to give it to me?"

"No, ma'am. Not for President Lincoln. Not even for President Andrew Jackson. But President Grant, now, old Grant might be a different story. He's powerful, Grant is. He swings a lot of weight. Old Grant's an influential man."

I grimaced, considering my dwindling bank account.

Vinny was driving a hard bargain, but I really wanted that key and the manifest.

"Okay, Vinny. An envelope will be left with Satish for you at the bar in the Moonbeam Room. By the end of your shift, say about six-thirty. Okay?"

"Okay, Sidney, and them items you was interested in will be under your cabin door after first seating. Pleasure doing business with you, but keep it zipped, understand?"

My new plan of action was to stop drifting along, hoping that everything would be all right, and make some careful but concrete moves toward finding the killer. I needed real information and the facts I knew were pretty thin.

Sometime during the night I had realized that if at all possible I must search Mr. Bostick's cabin for Ruth's bag and any other clues on the off chance that Empress hadn't already had it sanitized. The key would make that possible.

We had missed our chance to check out Ruth's cabin after she was found. We were so shocked and stunned by her death that it didn't occur to us until a day or two later to attempt a search. By then, it had already been cleaned and refitted.

The purser had sealed Mr. Bostick's cabin when his death was discovered and until the official seals were removed, no one could enter it. The hour after dinner, during the show, would be our first opportunity for a quick look.

I bought the copy of the manifest to check out exactly who was on this ship. Somewhere in the hundreds of names there might be a clue, some connection to the High Steppers. It was a long shot, for sure, with all those names, but it was all I could think to do, and I might get lucky. I not only wanted to try and identify the supposedly murderous Chilean deckhand and the dancer, but any other "persons of interest" as well. One of the bartenders told that me that the deckhand was a guy named Raoul, from Santiago, and that the dancer's name was Esmeralda.

I had not brought my laptop on the cruise, but there are computers for passenger use in an annex off the ship's library, and if I found any interesting names and addresses, I could do a search that might yield a hit. Or maybe an Internet café in Stockholm would be more private, and therefore safer. I would have to think about that one, but first, I needed the manifest.

The computer rooms on ships are always filled with seniors. They love writing letters on the Internet, mostly complaining about stuff to their congressmen, I think. Or maybe telling the President how to run the country. They like to share their thoughts out loud with anyone available to listen, too, so the computer room is never really private.

Yes, it was time for some digging, and as soon as possible.

I didn't know who all the players were in this deadly game that was unfolding, or how they all fit together. But some of picture was becoming clearer.

In the wee hours of the night, I had finally realized the identity of the mysterious deckhand who on that first night out of Harwich had bumped into me on the rainy deck and warned me of danger. I knew him by sight, I just didn't know his name.

I had last seen him at Tivoli, taking one final ride on a carousel.

♓

Brooke was sipping from a tall frosted glass of Pellegrino with a thin slice of lemon when I finally found her at a quiet corner table in the Crystal Dining Room. It was fairly late, almost 1:30, and most of the herd had already finished lunch and gone to bingo.

"Hi," I said, sliding into my chair. "Hope you haven't been waiting long."

"Oh, no," she replied, "I just got here myself. I never lunch early, you know. I've ordered the Brown Derby Cobb Salad, and here is Alberto to take your order."

Alberto approached the table and handed me a menu. I chose iced tea with lemon and mint, and the European Toast—a delicious sandwich of cheese, tomatoes and olive on a crunchy toasted bread—served with a side salad of arugula, bibb lettuce, pears, and walnuts.

Moheet, the busboy, brought my tea.

Brooke laughed. "Do Southern women have iced tea in their veins?" she said. "Well, Sidney, where's Jay? Did you find him?"

"Forget Jay, Brooke. Jay has completely lost his mind. He's gone as crazy as a shot rat, and there's really no hope for him this time until we can get him back to New York and into therapy.

"We can't count on him for any help whatsoever," I continued, buttering a roll, "He's out of it. Trust me on that. But what about you, Brooke? Did you find out anything useful?"

"Yes," she said, smiling. "Yes, I did. First I went to the perfume seminar. That was amusing, but I didn't learn anything new. "

She ticked off her results on her long, slender, fingers. "Then I played bridge for a while with Marjorie Levy and Chet and Fred Johnson. Still nothing. But then I went to the beauty salon for a manicure, and Sylvia Klein was there having her roots done. She didn't notice my arrival. She was too intent on telling Monique, the hairdresser, and anyone else who cared to listen, her plans for leaving Abe and the ship in Stockholm."

"What?" I said, leaning forward, "Leaving the ship? No kidding? Did she say why?"

"Oh, yes," Brooke nodded, "At length, but I couldn't hear all of it because Gladys Murphy, who was having a shampoo and set, started talking just then in a loud voice about the shopping in Stockholm, so I didn't get all of Sylvia's plans. Sylvia had obviously been talking for some time before I came in, too, mostly about how Abe had mistreated her. But I heard enough, I think."

"Well, out with it, what did she say?"

Alberto arrived at that moment with our lunch, and Brooke's blue eyes sparkled with delight at the enforced delay in her narrative. She knew how eager I was for her answer.

When Alberto had finally finished fiddling around with the table and departed for the kitchen, Brooke continued, "Sylvia said, 'I'm thinking about leaving old Abe when we get to Stockholm, so I want the works, Monique, while he's still paying for it.'

"Then Monique said, 'Leaving him, how will you leave this bad man? Where will you go? What will you do?'

"Sylvia replied, 'I've got ways, and I've got friends, and I've just about got it worked out, too. Abe and his pals can kiss my ass. Last night was the coop de grease'—I think she meant *coup de grâce*. 'I'm sick to death of the whole thing and Abe, too, but before I leave this ship, you better believe I'm headed straight to the boutique to see how much more damage I can do to his charge account.'

" 'What if he tries to stop you,' Monique said, 'what if he won't let you go?'

"Sylvia laughed and said that he better not try to stop her, that she knew too much. 'He better keep me happy and he knows it, I've got insurance' she said. There was more, but I couldn't hear the rest because of Gladys and the hairdryer."

Brooke laughed, "Perhaps you could ask Sylvia about her plans tonight at dinner, in your official capacity, Sidney. After all, you need to know if a member of your group is leaving early, don't you?"

"Yes, certainly," I said, "but what about Abe? Do you think from what you heard that he is leaving too?"

"I don't know. That dreadful Murphy woman's voice simply drowned out everything else that Sylvia said, almost as if she meant to; but of course, Gladys was just being her usual charming self. Anyway, by the time Gladys finally stopped talking, my manicure was finished and Sylvia was under the dryer, so I left."

Alberto appeared with coffee and the dessert menus. He also brought a thick, white envelope, embossed with the ship's insignia.

I stared at it, recognizing the handwriting.

"Well, aren't you going to open it?" Brooke said.

I broke the seal and read the short note inside, scrawled in slashes of bold, black ink.

> Dear Miss Marsh,
>
> Your presence is requested immediately on the bridge.
>
> —*Stephanos Vargos*
> Master, m/s Rapture of the Deep.

"It seems I'm being summoned," I said, finishing my coffee and pushing back my chair.

I took a deep breath.

"This should be interesting."

20

I climbed the steps to Bridge Deck and knocked on the door marked "Authorized Personnel Only."

The first officer opened the door, looked out, and motioned for me to enter. "Good afternoon, Miss Marsh. Please come in. Captain Vargos is expecting you."

If you've never been on the bridge of a modern cruise ship, you may have some romantic notions about the ship's wheel and compasses and astrolabes and such. If so, you've seen too many late movies.

I guess they can still work all that stuff, but the reality is that computers and sonar and GPS and other mysterious electronics now rule the waves.

Before 9/11, ships used to all offer bridge tours on days at sea, and the passengers really enjoyed them, but in our new age of heightened security, the bridge is mostly off limits now to passengers. Many lines have also stopped galley tours and skeet shooting.

Everything about the Rapture's bridge looked efficient, high-tech and complicated. The sight of all those precision instruments and sonar screens and stuff immediately reminded me that the task of piloting this monster safely across a deep and dangerous ocean was a difficult and serious business indeed.

These modern behemoths are so slick and so big that you tend to forget that underneath you is a whole lotta water. When the wind begins to rise and the whitecaps appear—as they had around dawn—you start to think about that. Or at least some of us do. For others, it takes a full gale before their attention is drawn away from the meals and the shows.

The main room of the Rapture's bridge reminded me of the cockpit of an airplane, only much, much larger. The front wall was made almost entirely of thick, tinted glass, fronting a room filled with electronic instruments and radar, sonar and computer screens. Other rooms, adjacent to the main one, included the captain's office and private quarters.

First Officer Avranos escorted me to the captain's office and knocked on the door.

"Enter," the captain's deep voice answered.

"Ah, Sidney," he said, rising from behind a handsome mahogany desk, "it is good to see you again, and it is good of you to come so promptly. Please have a seat. May I offer you some refreshment? No?"

He nodded to the officer. "Then that will be all, Avranos. Please close the door on your way out and see that we are not interrupted."

Steady, Sidney, I told myself, think before you speak this time.

He sat once again in his fine leather chair behind his massive desk, watching me with those dark blue eyes. He wore a white shirt and pants and a dark pullover sweater with epaulets gleaming on the shoulders.

I sat, too, squirming a bit under his gaze as I took in my surroundings.

The office was handsome, with highly polished mahogany furniture and paneling, gleaming brass fixtures, and a midnight blue carpet. There were few personal items. His master's license, framed, and some nautical engravings were hung on the walls along with stylized charts of the constellations in black ink on thick white paper. An expensive brass telescope, mounted on a tripod, stood in the corner. No photographs of people, no memorabilia.

Everything was very neat, painfully precise.

He leaned back, elbows on the arms of the chair, fingers tented, staring at me in silence. His dark hair was beginning to gray at the temples and, though he was clean-shaven, a shadow of beard darkened the firm line of his jaw.

His stare was intent, unnerving.

"You wanted to see me, Captain Vargos," I said finally, "and here I am. In your note, you indicated that it was urgent, so I came immediately."

He rose and came around to the front of the desk, where he stood before me and leaned against the polished wood. He folded his arms and again did nothing but stare.

We got off to a bad start, I thought, wishing that things had worked out differently between us.

"Yes, indeed, it is extremely urgent," he said. "I don't know quite how to approach you about this, Sidney. I'm not sure how to proceed. You are so defensive, so stubborn, so elusive. I asked you here today to warn you for the last time to stop meddling in matters that do not concern you. If you do not heed these warnings, there may be grave consequences. I hope that this time you will accept my advice in the spirit in which it is offered. My only concern is for your safety and that of the other passengers."

"Yes, Captain, I appreciate that, and I'm sorry that."

"Please, Sidney, let me finish."

"But, Captain ..."

He raised his hand, cutting me off.

"I was informed this morning, Sidney, that you are again asking questions, potentially dangerous questions, of the hotel staff and others about the identities of the missing dancer and the deceased crewman. I am not suggesting at this point—nor do I have reason to believe—that either of them met with foul play, but if they did, then your questions could certainly put you in jeopardy. I do not know who the woman is, or where she is, and I do not believe that anyone on my staff does either. As for the crewman, his background is being investigated."

"But, Captain ..." I said again.

He shook his head.

"The circumstances surrounding this man and woman are not your affair, Sidney, nor are they the business of your group. As I said, these matters are being thoroughly investigated; you have my word on that. You are not a trained investigator, or an officer of the law, and you certainly have no authority to ask such questions."

He leaned forward, watching me intently. "I must insist that you stop your so-called investigation immediately. I have cautioned you before, and you have foolishly ignored my warnings. I am telling you now, I am *ordering* you, to cease this activity at once. If you do not, as master of this vessel, for your own safety, I will have you confined to quarters."

"What? What did you say? Confined to quarters?" I glared up at him defiantly. "I don't think so, Captain Vargos. I don't work for you. I am not an employee of this ship, or Empress Line, and all I have done is to pose a few simple questions in hopes of unraveling a dreadful mystery that has resulted in the murder of two innocent people, people charged to my care—murders that you and this line will barely acknowledge, let alone try to solve."

He reached down and grabbed me by my arms, pulling me out of the chair. He was furious, and I thought that he was going to shake me.

"Don't you understand what I am trying to say, you silly girl? Don't you know what you are doing? You must listen to me. I am not, *not*, working against you or your group or anyone else. I am on your side. I am your captain. Your safety is my responsibility, my prime concern. I have been protecting you all along, and believe me, protecting you is not easy, with all of your attempts at detective work."

His tight grip on my arms loosened, and the hard glare in his eyes softened. "I care about what happens to you, Sidney Marsh. I care very much, no matter what you think." His eyes darkened, studying mine. "But believe me, I certainly can confine you to quarters, and if you don't stop this immediately, I will."

I pulled free of his grasp and took a giant step backward, toward the door. "Okay, Captain Vargos, okay. I've got it. I hear you. Thank you for your concern. Aye, aye sir. I certainly appreciate your position, and from now on, I will be sure to obey your orders."

I jerked open the door, stepped through it, and slammed it behind me, ignoring the curious glances of the ship's officers.

Like hell I will, I said to myself as I bolted down the stairs.

♓

When I opened the door to my cabin, there was Jay, sprawled out on his old bed, propped up on his pillow and mine, reading the passenger/crew manifest that I had bought from Vinny.

"How in the world did you get this?" he said. "This is the real deal, isn't it?"

"Yes it is," I said, snatching it out of his hands, "and never mind how I got it. What are you doing here?"

I looked at the bags piled in the corner.

"Is that your stuff? I thought you moved out. I thought you were living in the Neptune Suite."

He smiled. "I guess I do have a conscience after all, Sidney, because it was bothering me. We've been pals for a long time, lady, and you mean more to me than the Neptune Suite. And maybe I discovered that somewhere I do have a little bit of integrity after all. But, hey, I'm back. Aren't you glad?"

Jay is impossible, of course, but yes, I was glad.

♓

In the shower, I thought everything out and decided that now that Jay and I were a team again, it was time for us to really step up the action before Vargos clamped down.

Just why he would clamp down at this particular time was a mystery. Was he somehow involved in the crime? Nah. I didn't think so, I couldn't see it. But you never know. Was he just a company man, marching to the direct orders of Empress to put a lid on it? That seemed more likely. Maybe he really cared about my safety. That would be nice. I savored the thought.

Who knew?

Most of the High Steppers go to the early show before dinner, so I decided that would be the perfect time to check out Bostick's cabin.

I turned off the water, wrapped my hair in a towel and myself in a robe, and stepped out into the cabin to lay out my plan for Jay.

He was gone again. There was a note on my bed.

> You are hogging the bathroom again, piggie. I can't wait on you any longer. Try to look amazing tonight. Don't wear that tired old blue thing you always wear.
> See you at dinner.
>
> —J.P.W., II (The Magnificent!)

Tonight was another formal night, so I wiggled into a new black sequined number that I had snatched up, no kidding, at a Midnight Madness clearance sale. I twisted my hair up and secured it with a diamond, well, *rhinestone* pin.

There. Jay would approve of this outfit—yes, he would. Maybe it wasn't totally amazing, but it was close. I have to admit he was right about that blue dress. It's seen better days.

I added long silver and CZ earrings and was digging in my drawer for my evening bag when the phone rang.

I picked it up. A mechanical sounding voice whispered, "Back off, Sidney Marsh, or you are next."

"Who is this?" I demanded, but my answer was a quiet click. The call had ended.

I hung up and sat down on the bed, weak-kneed, my stomach churning.

Great, just great, I thought. *Now even the perp is in on Warn Sidney Day.* I felt a now-too-familiar frisson of fear, but stamped it firmly down with anger. I was scared, but also just plain mad. I was determined to maintain that anger. It would be my armor.

I considered telling Jay, but if I did, he might insist that I heed the warning. I wasn't doing that. I wasn't giving in. Not now, not after all that had happened. After all, if the caller really meant to harm me, he would just do it, not call up and tell me about it in advance. Robot-Voice wasn't going to hurt me. I was just being terrorized again. That thought infuriated me. I slammed the door behind me and rushed down the passageway to dinner.

21

The entrées that evening included a choice of lobster or prime rib.

Feeling like a Murphy, I ordered both. Does fear and anger make your hungry? For me, that night, it did. I also killed two glasses of wine before the soup course. Edgar, Jay and I were seated at Table Seven, a small table for four on the far side of the dining room. No one else was seated with us. The High Steppers were seated some distance away, in the middle of the room, near the Captain's table.

Edgar, ever the gentleman, didn't comment on my gluttony, but Jay never minces words.

"Oink, oink, Sidney! Are you ordering two desserts, too?" You better ease up on the groceries, sweetie. That little sparkly dress looks great on you, but it barely covers your ass as it is."

"You're just jealous of my dress, Jay, because you can't wear it," I shot back.

"Now, now, children," Edgar said, "Stop quarrelling and gaze upon Mrs. Petrone. Ah, there's a sight to behold! A vision in scarlet!"

Angelo and Maria Petrone were just being seated across the

room at Table Six. She was, indeed, beyond amazing, in a very low-cut red and gold satin dress with a lot of gold fringe and sparkles and a slit up the front of the skirt. This was a dress for a pop-tart, not a woman of her age.

All the High Steppers were dressed in their finest. Hannah, Ethel and Gertrude had fresh hairdos from the beauty salon, and were wearing tea-length dresses in dusty rose, ice blue, and mauve.

Chet Parker, the Johnsons, and Brooke were seated at the Captain's table. Both of the men were in black-tie; Maxine wore a green silk knit dress that had to be a St. John, and Brooke was classic, of course, in a long white Dior.

"Captain Vargos is watching you, my darling," Edgar said, "have you noticed?"

Are you kidding me? I thought. I noticed. Believe me, I noticed.

"Check out the Murphy family," Jay said. "The fashion police need to make an arrest at Table Four."

Pete Murphy was squeezed into an ill-fitting rental tux from the gift shop. His hot pink cummerbund was coordinated with Gladys' garish lime green and pink sequin gown. Daughter Muriel's skin and fuzzy red hair were not enhanced by her tight, very low-cut, green-bean colored dress.

Muriel glanced in our direction. Her round green eyes glowed, accented by gigantic false lashes. Her thick scarlet lips parted in a dreadful smile. But she wasn't focused on us. She was watching Table Eighteen by the window, where Fernando Ortiz sat, deep in conversation, with a short, Middle-Eastern man.

"Hoo, boy, he better look out," Jay snorted. "I'm glad she doesn't have the hots for me!"

"I am told that she aspires to be an actress and a singer," Edgar said. "I interrupted her terrible singing yesterday when I went into the Broadway Showroom for my rehearsal. Completely off-key. A horrible experience! She said she was practicing for the talent show, and I could tell that she truly believes that she will win. Very sad, really."

Edgar looked at his watch, placed his napkin on the table, and pushed back his chair. "I must be off now, my dears. I am scheduled to play Beethoven tonight in the Boom Boom Room. Such a travesty!"

After Edgar left, I laid out my plan for Jay, who agreed, I think, just to keep the peace and get me off his back. All he really cared about at this point was getting this gig over with and returning to New York pronto. I didn't tell him about my robo-call warning and I still hadn't shared my own horrible experience in the Broadway Showroom. I was keeping all that to myself for the time-being. I thought Jay might back out on the investigation of Al's room, and this was our first and only crack at it. Jay can be a big chicken.

I felt the Captain watching me again, but I wouldn't meet his eyes.

He won't catch me alone for any more little chats or to give me any more orders until I've solved our mystery, I vowed. After that, we'll have to see.

The meal ended with Cherries Jubilee, sort of a shipboard staple. Like Baked Alaska, it is served aflame and is prepared tableside by the headwaiters. They must believe these culinary demonstrations enhance their chances for big tips at the end of the cruise.

It doesn't, at least as far as the High Steppers are concerned. They figure everything is part of the deal. They won't pay one dime for extras.

Still, the flaming ceremony is pretty, and the dessert, a cruise-ship staple, is yummy. Jay and I both lapped it up and lingered over coffee. He spared me any more cracks about my appetite for food or drink, having put away more than his share of both.

By now, the dining room was almost empty. The captain had left his table. The High Steppers always rush out right after dessert so they can fight for front-row seats for the cabaret.

After dinner we stood at the doors of the Broadway Showroom until we were pretty sure that most of the High Steppers were seated and enjoying the show.

Then we headed for Bostick's cabin.

22

"Someone's coming. I hear someone coming. Quick, quick, quick! Into the closet. Quick! Turn off your light."

Jay and I dove into the closet in Bostick's cabin, burrowing behind the man's nasty old clothes just as the footsteps stopped outside the door. We had just begun our search and now here we were, Laurel and Hardy, stuffed into the tiny closet. Barely breathing, we heard the cabin door open.

I expected it to be the steward, but the overhead light remained off. Whoever had joined us also preferred darkness.

Not a good sign.

Under the door I could see a thin beam of light moving along the floor, probably looking under the bed. I held my breath and prayed.

Soft footsteps moved closer. A cabinet door opened. A pause, then the sound of a door closing. A dresser drawer glided opened next.

Great. Just great. Someone else was searching the cabin. The closet would be next and then we were busted. I tried to press deeper into the smelly darkness but there was little room, especially with Jay trying to do the same thing.

The closet door slid partially open, the tiny light beamed in, and a gloved hand began to slide the hangers along the rod on Jay's side. I felt him shudder.

Just at that moment, we heard a distant clatter from far down the long passageway. The hand froze for a moment, then withdrew. The closet door slid shut, and we heard the soft footsteps moving quickly away.

I could smell Bostick's shoes and my own sweat.

The pencil beam clicked off, and I heard the cabin door quietly open and close.

"I think I just peed in my pants," Jay whispered.

"Thank you for sharing," I whispered back.

We heard distant voices approaching in the passageway, becoming clearer as they approached. As soon as they passed, we would be able to slip out, too. I heard Jay exhale, but we did not move a muscle or make any other sound. The voices and the metallic clattering sound were directly outside the cabin now—deep voices, Russian. We waited for them to continue past the cabin, but instead they stopped, opened the cabin door, switched on the lights, and entered.

Heavy footsteps. One of them said something that earned hearty laughs from the others. The bathroom door opened. A toilet flushed. Then I heard wheels, and thuds, and drawers opening and realized that the cabin's contents were being loaded on a cart. I knew then that it had to be crew, with orders to clean out the cabin.

Our only hope of escaping discovery was if the cart was small and filled before they got to the closet. I knew the linens would take up a fair amount of room, but Bostick hadn't had much stuff.

The bed creaked under the weight of one of the men, and I heard paper rustling, pages turning, then chuckling, followed by comments in Russian and more laughter. A pager beeped, the bed creaked again and the cart thudded against the doorway. Then they were gone, locking the door behind them.

We stumbled out of the closet and into the room. I realized I was trembling.

"Holy moley, that was close! Your bright ideas almost did us in this time, Sidney. We've got to get out of here before either those Russians or our other friend comes back. It's like a freeway in here. They must have posted a notice somewhere that this cabin had been released."

I glanced around the room, hoping against hope to find something, anything, quickly that would make our risk worthwhile. Everything belonging to Bostick except the stuff in the closet had been removed, and we had already determined that the closet contained nothing but a few nasty old clothes.

Jay stuck his arm under the bed and came out with a bondage magazine.

"Looks like those guys missed this one when they looted old Bostick's stash. Thank God for chains and leather. If they hadn't found this juicy stuff they might have had time to look in the closet before they were called away. Let's get out of here. If Ruth's red bag was ever in this room, it's gone now. Someone must have beaten all of us to it. Come on. Let's get the hell out, Sidney. *Now*, before the phantom returns for another look."

⋊

Back in our cabin, Jay locked the door and then we hashed everything out, beginning with my first sighting of the homeless guy in New York. I finally told Jay all about recognizing the guy on the carousel after receiving the note at the restaurant and the details of my horrible night in the Broadway Showroom. He was shocked and sobered. After that, and our little evening adventure in Al's closet, I had Jay's full attention. He was finally taking me seriously.

"Okay, Sidney, I admit it. You are right. The fun and games are over. Our visitor in the dark tonight had a knife. I saw it on the table when the closet door opened, reflected in the beam of the flashlight. I do not, *not* like knives. I wasn't too worried when I thought The Strangler was lurking around because I'm pretty big and it would take someone even bigger to strangle me. But knives are another thing. Knives are really bad. I don't do knives. I am not ending up as sushi."

"A knife, Jay? Really, a knife?"

"A real knife. Long. Sharp."

"Okay." I took a deep breath. "Okay. Well." I took another long breath. "Let's try to stay on task, Jay. You were asking about the homeless guy."

"Okay, okay. Shelve Jack the Ripper. Back to the homeless guy. When you saw him in New York, Sid, were you afraid of him?"

"Well, yeah, sort of, especially when Eddie said he saw him on my steps. But he can't be the killer, Jay, because Homeless Guy is dead. Besides, if he'd wanted to kill me, he wouldn't have warned me with a note."

"Homeless Guy never really did anything to you, did he? Never said anything?"

"No. Not in New York. He followed me, and yelled at me once to stop, but I couldn't hear what he said. He never said anything I could understand until we were on the ship, and I didn't realize even then that it was him."

"What? Homeless Guy was on the ship?"

"He was on the ship, and he warned me about the deck being dangerous. I thought he meant *slippery* because the deck was wet and the sea was rough, but maybe it was more than that."

"How did you know it was the same man and why didn't you say anything about it?"

"Because I didn't realize it was him at the time. He was dressed differently, like a crewman. You know how hard it can be sometimes to recognize someone out of context. It was only later that I knew it. Something about the way he walked … and his eyes, Jay, they were a weird color, kind of muddy gray-green. I remembered his eyes."

"And then you didn't see him again until …"

"Tivoli. On the carousel. Dead. I'm almost positive the note I got in the restaurant was from him."

"But how was Homeless Guy connected to you, and us and the High Steppers? To Ruth and Bostick?"

"I don't know, Jay. I've thought and thought about it and I can't come up with any answers that make sense. I think now that he might not have been a homeless person at all and that the homeless thing was just a cover, but for what? For who? I'm convinced that the note the waiter gave me in the restaurant at Tivoli came from him. I think he wanted to meet me, talk with me, at the carousel but I was delayed and he was killed before I got there. I believe now that he followed me, followed us, around New York and halfway around the world. I just don't know why."

"What about Ruth and Bostick? Could they have had a connection with Homeless Guy?"

"I can't imagine how, unless they were involved in something without knowing it. But what? They both led pretty simple lives."

"Well, I guess, but we didn't know about their special relationship until Bostick told you, did we? Maybe they had other secrets, too."

"Oh, please. An occasional boodle on the Jersey shore in no way compares with whatever's going on here. This is heavy stuff."

"It all goes back to the High Steppers, though, Sidney. There's something going on with the High Steppers and that missing red bag. The other passengers on the Rapture don't seem to be involved, just us. We think we know this bunch pretty well, but do we? How much do we really know about them as individuals? What if one of them is a Lizzie Borden? A Son of Sam? We need to take a harder look at the High Steppers. You're always Googling people. Have you thought to Google the High Steppers?"

"Uh, no. Have you?"

"Yes, of course. That's how I spend my weekends. Are you kidding me? No. It never occurred to me to Google the High Steppers. But that's definitely what we need to do now. I can't believe you haven't already thought of it, Nancy Drew. Don't do it on the ship, though, where people are watching. You know how little privacy there is in the computer room. Wait until we dock tomorrow in Stockholm and check it out at an Internet café in port. I'll escort the group tour and cover for you. We don't want anyone to know what you are doing and anyway, it'll be cheaper off the ship. That bitch Diana would never authorize the expense and you will end up paying it. Meanwhile I'll babysit."

He looked at his watch.

"Hungry, Sidney? I am. Let's grab some pizza at the disco and just dance all this mess away. I feel like dancing, don't you?"

"You go ahead, Disco Queen, have fun. I'll check on the High Steppers before I turn in."

"Okay," he said, too quickly, letting me know that he needed some space, too. "Later, babe."

♓

"Buy you a drink, lady?"

The voice from the dimness of the Buccaneer Bar startled me out of my fog. I had been wandering aimlessly through the ship, ostensibly checking on the well-being of the High Steppers, but really just thinking in circles.

It was Fernando Ortiz, the only customer in the bar, now rising from a corner table. He pulled out a chair for me, signaling two with his fingers to the bartender. He was looking good tonight, his deep tan and long dark hair set off by his creamy linen shirt. The shirt was partially unbuttoned, revealing a muscular chest and a thin gold cross on a fine chain. It was surprising, because he seemed so sophisticated, and the open shirt/chain thing would never be my choice, but it looked pretty good on him.

"Two drinks? How did you know I would accept?" I asked, looking up at him as he seated me.

"I took a chance," he said, resuming his seat. He swallowed the remainder of his drink as the waiter set the new order down in front of us.

I asked myself why I gave this arrogant man the time of day, even as I watched him blow off the tip as he signed the tab for the drinks. I had no idea. He was not my type at all. Instinctively I knew I should stay far, far away from this ole boy, but still …

He leaned forward, smiling, clinking his glass with mine, and his intimate smile and sudden nearness made me catch my breath.

"You look worried, Sidney. You should stop worrying. Relax. There's nothing you can do that changes anything that has happened or will happen on this ship. Don't fret over those dreadful old people. What does it matter? Their lives are over. Their time is up."

"How can you say that, Fernando? That's a terrible thing to say, and it's not true. They are good people, and I can't help worrying about them. I'd love to stop thinking about them all the time but I'm afraid it's not so easy. I can't stop worrying until I get them safely home. They may not be young and have the same interests that you have, but they have lives, interesting lives, most of them. They are nice people and they are happy, Fernando, in their own way. How can you say that their lives are over?"

He shrugged elaborately and leaned closer.

"Whatever. Not your problem, my darling. Let it go. What's past is past."

"It's not just what's happened in the past on this trip that concerns me. I'm worried about the future, too."

He set his glass down on the table and, with a warm smile, took my hand in his. Turning it over, he traced the lines of my palm with his finger, and I had the wildest urge to just spill my guts to him right then, about everything. The man was a hypnotist.

"Do not worry about the future. I can read the future in your palm, beautiful Sidney. I see a torrid romance, very soon, perhaps tonight, with a dark, Latin stranger."

"I see you getting fired if you don't haul ass right now to the call center to speak with Diana, Sidney. It's her third call."

Jay's voice boomed through the room as he jerked my hand out of Fernando's and pulled me to my feet.

"Gotta go. Right now, Sidney, gotta go, really urgent."

Fernando leaned back in his chair, smiling at Jay with his mouth, but his eyes told another story.

"Ah, Mr. Wilson," he said, eyes darting from Jay to me, "How nice to see you. Won't you join us?" Then, with a smooth smile he said, "No? Well, then take her away if you must. Duty comes before pleasure, I suppose. Another time, Sidney."

I glanced back at him as I walked away from the table with Jay. He winked.

Jay looked back, too, and as he marched me out of the club he said, over his shoulder, "Adios, Zorro."

♓

"Dear God, Sidney! What were you thinking, fooling around with that guy? Just what in the hell were you thinking? If I hadn't wandered by when I did he would have had you out of that bar and down to his cabin before you could say 'empanada.' Is your brain on vacation, Sidney? What's wrong with you? Did that dirt bag mesmerize you?"

"All I did, Mommy, was have a drink with the man. What's wrong with that? Stop acting like my grandmother, Jay."

"Yeah, well, I know where that was headed, sweetie, and so do you. God. What a creep. Why would you even want to mess around with a slick SOB with a gold crucifix and tight pants? Leave him alone, Sidney. That guy is dangerous."

"You don't know that, Jay, you don't know that at all. He was sympathetic and kind tonight. Really nice. I think our first impression of him was wrong. You're just being judgmental."

"Look, Sidney. I know men. Believe me, I know men. You've got to give me that. And I'm telling you, that Fernando Ortiz is a bad one. Stay away from him, chica. As your best friend, I'm telling you, stay away. Now come on, let's go out on deck. I need some fresh air and so do you. Maybe it will clear your head."

"But what about the phone call, Jay, don't we need to call Diana?"

"Please. You *are* slipping."

He was right. I needed a lot of fresh air. I needed oxygen. If I can't even tell when Jay is lying, my brain is scrambled for sure.

23

Morning dawned bright and clear in Stockholm, the sun glinting off the pointed roofs. Eating my breakfast on the aft deck, at the Lido Café, I relished the sound of the ship docking, bells ringing, the shouts of the longshoremen, and the sound of the gangway being lowered. Even the diesel engines of the provisioners' trucks waiting to unload all those crates of fresh produce sounded good to me that morning.

I finished my eggs Benedict, savored one final perfect strawberry, sipped the last of my coffee, and went down to the cabin to get ready to go ashore as soon as the ship was cleared.

Everyone was restless after two nights and a day at sea. The shore excursions had sold out, and I expected even those who were not on a tour to head ashore.

Very few of the High Steppers had opted for the City Highlights Tour, with most preferring to venture out on their own. Jay was leading the city tour, leaving me with a whole day to myself in one of the world's loveliest cities. It also gave me time to complete a few necessary tasks, like checking out the High Steppers in private, without answering to anyone.

After the tours marched off the ship, I hurried down the

gangway to a bank of pay phones in the ship's terminal.

While waiting in line for a phone, I watched the commotion as a baggage cart was off-loaded from the gangway. I supposed it was Bostick's, but quickly realized that the luggage and high-end store boxes on it were far too deluxe for him. Another cart followed, also fully loaded with the same kind of fancy stuff.

When I saw the third cart, bearing several fur coats, a lot of designer shoe boxes, and a leopard-print garment bag with SK monogrammed on it in big, gold script, I had figured out what was happening.

Sylvia was leaving the ship. And from the looks of things, she had spent a ton of Abe's money on her way out.

The sailor in front of me in the phone line finished his conversation, and it was my turn. I dialed the access numbers. This was a personal call, so I had to make a collect call from the pay phone instead of using Itchy's calling card. Otherwise, Diana would have a hissy fit. A quick collect call using the access numbers would cost less than paying international roaming with my cell plan, too. I tried to use my cell only in emergencies, except for text messages, which were affordable.

The connection to Mississippi was crystal clear.

"Mamma, it's me, accept the call."

"Who?" My mother's sleepy, cross voice shrieked. "Oh, my goodness, yes, operator, yes! I'll accept the call. Sidney Lanier Marsh, are you alright?"

"Yes, Mamma, yes, only ..."

"Then what are you calling me for, long distance, from Lord knows where, in the middle of the ... Are you getting married?" Eternal hope swept shards of sleep aside.

"No, Mamma. I just needed to ask you something."

"Oh. Well, make it quick then, darlin'. This is costing me a fortune."

"Mamma, Do you remember those people who lived across the street from Aunt Pearl named Finkelstein? They lived in that squatty, red-brick house by the school. She was a checker at the Piggly Wiggly, and he worked for a beer distributor, I think."

"I sure do. Bill and Harriet Finkelstein. I'll never forget her. I fixed one of my hash brown potato casseroles and took it over there when her grandmother died and she never returned my good three-quart Pyrex. Didn't even get a thank you note. That's the kind of people they turned out to be. I kept thinking she would bring it back and I hated to ask, but one day they just up and moved away. She must have taken my good three-quart, Pyrex casserole dish with her. They owed money all over town."

"And their names were Bill and Harriet Finkelstein? Are you sure? And it was *her* grandmother who died, not his?"

"Yes, that's right. Her grandmother was a Mrs. Murphy, and they moved here from somewhere in Florida. Tallahassee, I think. Mrs. Murphy always had oranges delivered to them at Christmas. She had a stroke and died at the Midnight Madness Sale at the Sunshine Mall. The mall people sent Harriet the door busters because they felt so bad about it."

"When was this, Momma? Five or six years ago? Seems like I've been hearing about the Pyrex for about that long."

"No, honey, it was only three years ago, and you would still be talking about it, too, if it had been your good Pyrex!"

"Well, we better hang up now, Mamma, we're burning up your money. I'll pay you back for the call when you get the bill. Remember to let me know how much it is. Thanks, and you take care now. I'll call you when I get back to New York. Tell everybody I said hey."

"All right, darlin'. And you look around on that cruise ship. It's pretty big, and I bet you can find a nice man if you try."

"I will, Mamma, thanks again. Sorry I woke you up. Bye now."

I hung up the receiver and leaned against the wall, thinking.

Gladys Murphy was lying.

Why would Gladys Murphy make up that big old tale about

her mother-in-law? Of course, it was an extreme and amazing coincidence that I would have any connection to the Murphys or her story, or even remember those names unless you consider the strength and extent of the kudzu-like connections that grow all over the South, binding the people and families of each small town to all the others.

Anonymity doesn't exist in Dixie, where everyone minds everyone else's business. Perfect strangers ask you personal questions about the most intimate details of your life. No one considers such behavior to be nosy, but instead sort of noble, an expression of friendliness and concern, a kind and charitable duty. We keep up with each other. We care.

After several interminable meals with the Murphys, I had heard more than I ever wanted to know about their family.

My attention had, of course, wandered quite a bit during those long meals, but the one thing that had stuck with me was the impression that both the Murphys' parents were dead, and that their only family was Muriel and another daughter named Finkelstein, Harriet Finkelstein.

Harriet Finkelstein, according to Gladys, had once lived in Mississippi, actually in my hometown. That's a pretty amazing coincidence, when you consider the population of my little burg, but it happened.

Knowing that Gladys, shall we say, tends toward exaggeration, I had pretty much dismissed her narrative until I remembered my mother's old Pyrex story, and the names clicked in my brain. My phone call home has just confirmed Gladys' tale that Harriet Finkelstein and her husband really had lived way down in Dixie, but it also proved that Mother Murphy had cashed in her chips long, long ago.

Why would Gladys make up a story about her mother-in-law and Dr. Sledge's brother? Why tell something so far-fetched? What was the point?

I now believed the fact of the Finkelsteins living in my town because my phone call had confirmed that, but the whole mother-in-law, Dr. Sledge's brother thing was just a big, goofy lie. Dr. Sledge might not even have a brother. And Gladys had insisted to Gertrude that she had talked to her dead mother-in-law on the telephone. *Hello, heaven? Is Mom there?*

But why? Why tell that big tale? Why go there at all?

It didn't make sense. Unless she thought it provided cover for more than a passing acquaintance with Dr. Sledge.

I hung out for a while, hoping to tell Sylvia goodbye, but she didn't appear, and I decided not to waste anymore time waiting on her.

If Sylvia acted true to form, her departure would be dramatic, and could take the better part of the day. She was probably still in the salon, putting one last hairdo on Abe's tab.

24

The Internet café in the Gamla Stan, or Old Town, was packed, but as soon as a terminal opened up, I got busy. Thirty minutes and as many euros later, the search engines finally popped up some answers.

I gathered my notes, stuffed them in my bag and headed for the main square and coffee.

The streets were crowded with tourists and morning shoppers. Even a city as large as Stockholm becomes crowded in the tourist areas when a big ship is in port.

Sidewalk merchants displayed their wares on big carts. People strolled along, leisurely shopping, enjoying the lively scene, buying flowers, visiting with friends, and crowding around several street performers. The costumed and painted mimes stood stock still on painted boxes as the crowd surged around them, moving with a flourish only when someone dropped coins into their hats.

"Yoo hoo, Sidney!" Esther Levy was tugging at my arm. "Why aren't you with the group?"

"Why, hello, Esther. Hello, Marjorie. Today is my day off. Jay is with the group. And I might ask you the same thing! I thought you were going on the City Highlights tour."

"We intended to go on the bus," Marjorie said, "but we changed our plans when we learned of something much more important that we needed to do."

"Oh, really," I said, wondering what she meant, "what is that?"

"Well, you see," Esther explained, "Chet told us that there is a famous museum here dedicated to social justice and we decided that it is our moral duty to visit it, rather than just going on some silly tour with him and the others."

Marjorie chimed in. "We've been trying to locate it all morning, but no one seems to know where it is. Can you tell us?"

"No, I'm afraid I'm not familiar with it," I said, "but you might check with the Tourist Information Center. I try to keep current with the attractions in the ports we visit, but I've not heard of this museum. It may be new."

I bet it is new, I thought. Real new. In fact, I bet that slick old Chet just made it up this very morning to get rid of you both.

I said goodbye to them and off they marched in their sturdy shoes, dedicated to their quest, clucking, no doubt, over my ignorance.

In the shade of the buildings across from the Clock Tower, the air was chilly, but the open square in the sunshine was bright and beautiful. I dug in my bag for my sunglasses, chose an empty table at a sidewalk café, and ordered coffee and one of Stockholm's delightful specialties, delicate waffles with fresh strawberries, confectioner's sugar, and lots of whipped cream. Spreading my papers out on the table along with Vinny's manifest, I began to piece together the puzzle of The Strange Voyage of the High Steppers, as Jay called it.

A shadow fell across the page, and I looked up into Jerome Morgan's scowling face.

His broad, muscular shoulders under a white, pinpoint shirt

blocked the sun. He was not looking at me, but, instead, at my papers.

"You seem to be doing a little detective work on your own today, Miss Marsh. I'm afraid that must stop. Do you mind if I join you?"

"Not at all, Mr. Morgan," I said, hastily cramming the papers into my bag, "please, have a seat. Detective work? Don't be silly. I was just reading up on Stockholm, doing a little homework, that's all. Isn't this a lovely city? The flowers, the old buildings, and best of all—"

"Miss Marsh," he interrupted, a faint smile on his lips, reaching inside his jacket, "don't waste my time. We know what you are doing. We seem to have been working at cross-purposes for quite a while. Now I think it's time to have a little talk. Your snooping is beginning to cause me problems."

"What do you mean, detective work? I am a travel agent, Mr. Morgan, not a detective. Besides that, even if I was checking into a few things, what I do on my own time is my own affair. And how would you know what I have been doing or not doing? What business is it of yours?"

He produced a black leather wallet and flipped it open. I have to admit, I was impressed. You don't see a real badge like that very often, at least not in my neighborhood. That is, if it was real. At this point I wasn't sure of anything.

"Your group, Miss Marsh, our group, the High Steppers, and you, as well, have been under surveillance since before you left New York. We have reason to suspect that one or more of your party may not be the innocent tourist that he or she appears, but rather an agent of an international criminal organization dealing in the sale and smuggling of drugs, counterfeit currency, and documents. We believe they are using your group as a cover for criminal activity. You yourself were actually under suspicion in the beginning, but we have now realized that you could not possibly be involved. Therefore we would like, if we may, to enlist your help."

Man! What a shocker. I felt like I had just dropped onto the set of *Mission Impossible*. Maybe I could choose my own code phrase. "The blue dog barks at midnight." Wow! I had about a million questions, none of which, of course, got answered.

"All I can tell you right now, Miss Marsh, is that you must be very, very careful to report immediately anything at all unusual or out-of-the way that you observe either directly to me personally, or by calling one of the numbers that I will give you. That's how you can help."

He handed me a card, blank, except for three hand-printed telephone numbers.

"And no more acting on your own, please. We do not want you to take any action whatsoever without first checking with us. Working on your own could very dangerous for you, and it might jeopardize our investigation."

He looked around, glanced at his Rolex, and pushed his chair back from the table.

"Now, remember," he said, tapping on the table for emphasis, "if you find out anything, notice anything unusual, or have suspicions about anything or anyone, anyone at all, just report it to me at once in person, or call one of those numbers. Leave everything to us. And of course, you must not mention our conversation, or reveal my true identity to anyone, under any circumstances."

He looked at his watch before continuing.

"When we are all safely back in New York, Miss Marsh, you will be contacted further and some of your questions may be answered at that time. Or maybe they won't. But just remember, by cooperating with us, even in a minor role, you are serving your country. That's the important thing. And now I think I've stayed here quite long enough. Here comes your order. Enjoy your day off."

He stood as the waiter approached and strolled off into the crowded square, leaving me to wonder how long my mouth had been hanging open.

25

I had just finished the last crispy, buttery waffle and was dusting confectioner's sugar off of my black sweater when I spotted Captain Vargos standing on the steps of the cathedral. I hadn't noticed him before, but I was so blown away by Morgan's revelations that I probably wouldn't have noticed if Elvis had rolled up in his pink Cadillac.

What is Vargos doing here? I thought. Why isn't he on the ship where he's supposed to be? That's suspicious.

Even as the question formed in my head, he disappeared into the crowd milling about the entrance.

I paid my bill, gathered my things, and quickly crossed the square, skirting the balloon seller, two tour groups, and any number of children and dogs.

"Don't do anything on your own without contacting me first," Morgan had said. *To hell with that*, I thought. Badge or no badge, I wasn't sold on Morgan or his story. I don't know much about G-men, but I doubt that they wear big gold watches.

Entering the narthex, I had to wait for my eyes to adjust to the dimness. Candles flickered in the chapels on the sides of the vaulted sanctuary. Tour groups moved quietly across the worn stone floor, stopping now and then to hear their murmuring guides explain, in several languages, the significance of the architectural features of the cathedral and recount its history. They shuffled from chapel to chapel, whispering stories associated with the statues and monuments that memorialized the famous and near-famous Swedes and saints.

The hum of muted voices created a hollow, echoing sound in the vastness of the great room.

There was no sign of Vargos. His white uniform should have been noticeable in the dimness.

I moved quickly down the outside aisle, working my way through the crowd and peering into every chapel, then moved across to the other side, in front of the high altar, past the statue of St. George and the Dragon, and back up the opposite aisle. No white uniform. Where could he have gone? There was only one public entrance, only one exit. Had I missed him? I didn't think so.

The only two places left to look that the public could visit were the clock tower and the crypt. I don't do heights, so I chose the crypt, a decision I instantly regretted once the huge metal door clanged shut behind me. My clumsiness was embarrassing, especially because the loud, echoing noise was followed by the sound of laughter, presumably directed at me.

The mustiness of centuries filled my head.

Bad choice, really bad choice. Got to make this quick, I thought, as I hurried down the winding stone steps, the air growing steadily stuffier. I couldn't imagine our fastidious captain even setting foot in this dusty, creepy place. *Still, I am here now*, I thought, *so I might as well take a look.*

With each step, the light grew dimmer. The walls were lined with engraved stone tablets and alcoves filled with the marble statues and remains of long-dead priests. I tried not to think about free molecules.

Vargos was definitely not there, I decided. In fact, no one was in the crypt but me. No one living, that is.

That's it, I thought. R.I.P., folks, I'm outta here.

I ran quickly back up the steps—the only way out of that dismal place—and pushed hard on the heavy door, too ready for light and fresh air.

Nothing.

I hit the door with both hands, then my shoe, then put my shoulder hard against it, then finally kicked it, hard.

Still nothing.

Don't panic, Sidney Marsh, I told myself. That won't help. Yell.

So I yelled and yelled and yelled and no one came. I beat on the door some more but nothing happened. Then the walls themselves seemed to vibrate as the huge pipe organ in the vast chamber above began the first notes of the evensong.

For sure no one could hear me now. I sat down on the damp stone floor and rested my head on the wall.

After a long while, the organ stopped and then I stood and beat on the door with my shoe and yelled and yelled again and again and again until it wasn't a yell at all, only a croak. But no one came.

I sat on the steps and put my head on my knees and tried to think my way out. Deep down, I knew I was stuck.

Evensong was over, the church would soon be closing for the night, and the *Rapture* would sail without me.

My best hope was that a sexton would check the crypt before closing down for the night. More likely, I would have to stay right where I was with the saints until the crypt was opened for visitors in the morning. What had the sign said? Was the crypt open every day, or just on certain days? Was the church even open every day? I couldn't remember.

At the worst, well, I couldn't even think about the worst.

I looked at my watch, tilting it so that I could read it in the faint light. 7:55. I was sure the cathedral would close soon, if it wasn't closed already. No one was coming to release me. No one.

I went to the bottom of the steps, made a pillow of my purse, and stretched out on the cold stone floor. At least the air was a little better nearer the floor.

Five minutes later, when I thought the situation couldn't get any worse, it did.

What light there was went out, leaving me in total darkness.

26

When they found me, my hair hadn't turned white, and I wasn't babbling or chewing on a long-dead hand or anything, but I was dirty, exhausted, and scared.

I heard a scraping noise and a torrent of Swedish, then Jay's voice. I saw a blaze of light as the massive door swung open.

"There she is. Oh, my God, Sidney, are you all right?"

Then he picked me up in his great big arms and carried me out of that awful place.

♓

"I still don't understand how you found me."

I was sitting propped up on pillows in my bed on the *Rapture*, sipping a double or maybe a triple brandy Alexander.

"Hannah Weiss, Sidney. You have Hannah Weiss to thank, babe, and also the captain. Hannah saw you go into the crypt and she didn't see you after that, and when you didn't get back to the ship in time for the sailing, she called me and told me and wouldn't let up until we got Vargos. He freaked out and held the ship and sent out a search party to find you."

"Well, thank her I will, bless her little heart, first thing tomorrow. I just can't talk to anyone else tonight. And I'm really glad it's a sea day tomorrow. If it's okay with you, I'd like to sleep in a little in the morning."

"You got it, Sid. After that ordeal, you deserve a little pampering."

"I just feel so stupid, Jay. It's embarrassing for a tour leader to get herself in a jam like that. What kind of dumbass accidentally locks herself in a cathedral crypt and delays a sailing? Diana will fire me for sure, now."

"Sidney. I wasn't going to tell you this until tomorrow, but you might as well know it now. It wasn't an accident, Sid. Someone locked you in that crypt. The door was wedged shut, and a heavy trunk was pushed in front of it, along with the 'closed to visitors' sign. We had to move it to get you out."

"But why, Jay? Why? Who would do that to me?"

"I don't know, Sidney. I don't know who, but I sure can guess why. You are getting on someone's nerves, big-time, babe. Someone is trying to warn you off, telling you in a major way to stop meddling. Did anyone see you when you were on the computer in the Internet café, Sid? Brooke, Hannah, Ethel, Gertrude, the Johnsons and Chet Parker were with me the whole time, so it wasn't them. I don't know where the others were."

"Captain Vargos was somewhere in the church or the square, Jay; I saw him. Jerome Morgan was around, too, and I think he saw the print-outs."

And then I told him about Morgan and his warnings.

"That's bullshit, Sidney, pure bullshit. He's no more James Bond than I am. You stay away from that dude. Stay far, far away. Think about it, sweetie, think real hard. You've really got to watch your back from now on. We can't have you getting yourself killed. Or, more importantly, getting *me* killed. Keep your head totally down until we get home, okay? To hell with all this, Sid. Leave the heavy lifting up to Empress. Someone comes up behind you one of these nights and gives you a quick shove over the rail, and it's all over."

He probably had more to say along the same lines, but the phone rang. It was Gertrude, who thought she had seen a mouse in her cabin. Jay swore and left to check it out, but not before saying, "All I really want now, babe, is to get both our asses and what's left of the High Steppers back to New York as soon as possible—and not in a pine box in the cargo hold. Diana can fire both of us anytime she wants. I don't care. I'm too creative for this job, anyway."

♓

My entombment was a very effective deterrent. If someone had meant to scare me off, they had succeeded.

I decided that night that I was going to stop trying to be a hero and heed all the dire warnings people were hurling at me. Perhaps they did genuinely care about my safety, even Captain Vargos.

Moreover, I realized that I really owed that handsome gentleman an apology and my thanks for holding the ship and sending out the posse to find me. Delaying a sailing is a truly rare occurrence on Empress Lines. They don't want to pay one extra penny in port charges. They'd hold it for the Pope, maybe, but not for a lowly travel agent.

I threw back the covers, then showered and dressed, taking special care with my clothes and makeup. Then I turned off the lights, locked the cabin, and took the elevator up to the Sun Deck, hoping to find Captain Vargos on the flying bridge, watching the stars through his brass telescope. Now that I was far away from the cabin and out of Jay's space, I could spritz myself with a little perfume sample Helga had snared for me. My behavior had already upset Jay enough; no need to set off his allergies as well.

As I stepped out on deck, the wind gusted in from the east, billowing my skirt out and making my hair whirl around my head. I was really careful this time, watching my back, minding

Jay's advice, staying in the shadows. As I walked I listened for footsteps, ready to duck back inside at the slightest hint of anything wrong, but no one was on deck but me. Everyone else was in the Broadway Showroom for Comedy Night.

The flying bridge juts out from the ship just above the Sun Deck. As I reached the rail on the deck below it, the sky was sparkled with stars, and sure enough, when I looked up, the captain's brass telescope was there, gleaming in the moonlight. There was no sign of the captain. Very disappointing.

I was staring out at the waves, in the shadow of a stanchion, watching the white foam rush by in the dark sea, when a gleam of light from above caught my eye. Looking up, I saw Captain Vargos step out onto the flying bridge, and I was just about to call out and wave to him when he bent to adjust the telescope, adapting the height to better suit the beautiful young blonde who stood beside him.

Damn.

I slipped back into the shadows.

You missed your chance with him, Sidney, you fool, I thought, as I slipped silently away, and now he's moved on. You never ever get it right, dummy, do you?

I stomped back down to my room, not only sad and disappointed, but pretty steamed, too, mostly at myself for believing his compliments and swallowing all that garbage he had told me about being lonely and stuff.

Was he using those lines on Blondie, too, when he asked her to look at the stars?

27

We reached St. Petersburg in the late afternoon on Saturday.

Everyone was on the rail for the sail-in past the rusted hulks of the old Soviet sub base. The wind off the sea and the glorious light as we approached Peter's Window on the West helped clear away the cobwebs left in my brain by my awful experience in the church in Stockholm.

The fresh sea air and the loveliness of the sunset's golden glow on the stones of the magnificent old buildings also gave me new resolve: *Just enjoy the beauty around you. No more wasting time or energy on what might have been with Stephanos Vargos, Master of the M/S Rapture of the Deep.*

The last day at sea had been, thank God, uneventful. I slept late, had a pleasant lunch with Brooke, Hannah and Ethel, then sat in on the shore excursion talk and slide show. Meanwhile I seized the opportunity to chat up everyone I could find. I was all too ready to solve the mystery, turn my information over to the cops and just go home, back to New York, far, far away from dangerous killers and handsome, fickle captains.

I did not see Captain Vargos or his little blonde Barbie-doll all day.

Jay stayed in the cabin going over my notes and computer printouts. Later, he talked the purser into letting him use a computer in his private office. He was finally getting down to business.

My own search hadn't yielded a lot. There were no hits whatsoever on either Fernando Ortiz or Jerome Morgan. I thought that was odd—unless they really were G-men. We found no hard evidence that those two were even connected to each other, except that Fernando was apparently the only person Morgan ever spoke to, excluding, of course, his astonishing speech to me in Stockholm.

The jury was still out on Morgan, but with no evidence to the contrary on Fernando, I decided that he was in the clear. I liked him, and just because Jay didn't, I wasn't going to hang him out to dry.

Abe was a different story. Abe was all over the place. He had been the focus of any number of reported investigations, although as far as I could tell, he had never been convicted of anything. Either he was truly innocent or he had a lot of clever lawyers.

No one had seen much of Abe lately. He stayed in his cabin or by the pool most of the time, especially since Sylvia's sudden departure. I didn't have a clue what he did all day, but he sure wasn't playing shuffleboard with the High Steppers.

There was next to nothing on any of the others—a few harmless mentions—the exception being one shocking account of Muriel Murphy taking it all off in Grand Central Station before being arrested for public intoxication. No wonder her parents were trying to put the lid on her.

Most of the tours for St. Petersburg were fully booked; everyone was excited about visiting all the fabulous palaces, the Winter Palace, the Catherine Palace and Peterhof. I was excited too, and not just about the tours. Fernando Ortiz had called my cabin after lunch and invited me to dinner and the ballet at the famed Mariinsky Theatre.

Who knew what the Captain was up to? I decided I didn't care. I had plans of my own.

Besides, Fernando clearly liked me a lot, which is more than I could say for a certain captain. I hoped he would be watching through his stinking telescope as we rolled away from the dock in the shiny black limo.

Jay didn't like Fernando Ortiz at all and he had preached the Stay Away From Him sermon again to me that morning.

For once, though, Jay wouldn't object to my going out with Fernando, because I wasn't going to tell him.

Jay and Edgar had plans to skip dinner and go out drinking off the ship with a Russian pianist Edgar had known at Juilliard.

"I mean, I can't wait, Sidney," Jay said. "Vlad has this amazing apartment and Edgar says we are going to experience some of the best iced vodka ever. So don't expect me back anytime soon. You're on your own tonight. But be careful, love, because when I get back from my little adventure I will be in no condition to rescue you from any tombs."

"I'll be fine, Jay. Y'all go and have a good time; don't worry about me. I've got the High Steppers covered through dinner, and then I'm going to the ballet. Nothing bad can happen at the ballet."

After the port talk I had my chance to confront Pete Murphy about Gladys' tall tales.

"Why did Gladys lie like that, Pete? About Dr. Sledge being your mother's doctor? I found out that your mother passed away three years ago in Florida."

Pete's big face reddened. He shook his head.

"Because she was embarrassed, Sidney, that's why. About Muriel's drinking. We both are. Gladys tries to cover up everything about Muriel. See, Gladys has been talking to Dr. Sledge a lot lately about Muriel's drinking and mood swings and I guess she thought that dumb story about Dr. Sledge's brother would help hide it."

He took out a handkerchief and blew his big nose.

"I know it doesn't do any good, Sidney, but Gladys feels like she has to cover up for Muriel. She always has. I don't know why. Anyone can see she has a problem. Muriel is our youngest, you know. We thought maybe it would help if we took this trip, spent more time with her, just the three of us. We hoped this nice cruise would help her make some friends and bring us closer together as a family. We have all our meals together, and we've signed all three of us up for nearly every class and excursion they offer. Keep her busy, I said, get her interested in something besides her singing, because I know that ain't going nowhere, no matter what Gladys says. But with all the bars around, Muriel's just gotten worse. I'm looking for her now. We thought we could watch her, keep our eyes on her, but she's an escape artist. See ya later, Sidney. I gotta go. I hope you understand. Don't think too bad about Gladys."

I watched in pity as that poor, driven man shuffled off down the glittering arcade, peering into every shop, looking for his baby.

I strolled in the same direction, hoping to buy a small gift for Roz, my friend in the office. I always try to bring home a little something for her.

The ship was in full Russian theme. The shops were stuffed with Russian merchandise—fur hats, amber jewelry, vodka, and those painted-wood, nested dolls. Dr. Zhivago was playing in the movie theater that evening, and the dinner menu included Beef Stroganoff and Chicken Kiev.

Nearing the end of the row of shops, I thought I saw Captain Vargos approaching but soon realized it was only First Officer Avranos. I felt another brief pang of longing to be going to the ballet with the captain instead of Fernando. Get real, Sidney, I thought, Pack up the violins. I firmly shoved all thoughts of the captain aside and scooted downstairs to the beauty salon for my appointment. At the ballet, I would be looking good and having a marvelous time. Little czarina, that's me. I bought a manicure and pedicure, because you never know, do you?

I tried to glean more information about Sylvia and Abe from Monique, but she didn't add much to what I already knew.

Monique was indignant. "He is a bad man, zat one. Why she ever wants to be with 'im, I do not know. Sylvia is a beautiful girl, beautiful hair, beautiful skin, big bosoms. Many men desire 'er. Why she wants to sleep with zis old toad? Pff! For 'er, of course, from 'im, many gifts. Fur coats, jewelry, many, many gifts. She likes that. She loves gifts. For me, all ze gifts in the world would not suffice."

I fully agreed. No amount of luxurious gifts could convince me to hook up with a guy like Abe, either.

Of course, I had no basis for comparison. The best gift I get from my cheap dates is a rose from the deli on the corner and maybe a heart-shaped box of chocolates on Valentine's Day.

Jay was standing at the racks outside the photo gallery hunting for pictures of himself when I finally emerged from the beauty salon.

We walked together to our cabin. He commented on Monique's handiwork the entire way. For once, I passed.

"You really look terrific, Sidney. Very chic. I don't see why you don't splurge like this more often. Put a little fun in your life. Don't be so stingy!"

Have I mentioned that even though Jay has a great apartment and a closet full of designer clothes, he never has a dime? At the end of his pay periods he has to go to parties put on by travel vendors and people he barely knows just to eat.

"Just because I save enough to pay my bills, you call me stingy! If you would pay up what you owe me I might not have to be stingy!"

"I'll even things up next month, you know I will, but let's not talk about that now, okay? I didn't mean to start anything, Sidney, I just wanted to say that you look really good, very chichi!"

Jay unlocked the cabin door, and we were both stopped

in our tracks by the enormous vase of deep red roses on my bedside table.

"Oh, look! Someone sent me flowers!" Jay trilled. He made a grab for the card, but I snatched it out of his paw and opened it, turning my back to him.

The card inside was printed "With the Compliments of the Captain." Written below it in slashing black ink were the words,

> It would give me great pleasure if you would join me on the bridge at 8:00 tonight for dinner followed by stargazing in my private quarters.

> —*Stephanos Vargos,* Master, m/s Rapture of the Deep

Jay laughed as he read over my shoulder. "Good going, Sid. Roses from that handsome hunk. Are you going?"

"No, I'm not. It's too late. I already have plans for the evening. Remember the ballet?"

"Well, yeah, but who wants to go to the ballet with some old ladies when you could let our captain put stars in your eyes?"

"Stop pestering me, Jay, or I'm going to have you seeing stars!"

"Touchy, touchy, Miss Prickles. Why are you so supersensitive?"

I thought about Fernando and the ballet. Then I thought about the captain and the roses and the stars. And that reminded me of the beautiful blonde I had seen him with, looking at those same stars, less than twenty-four hours ago. Wonder if she received roses with her invitation, too?

I rang for Abdul, and when he came, gave him the flowers and five bucks.

"Abdul, would you please return these to Captain Vargos? Tell him that I said there must be some mistake, that they must have been delivered to the wrong girl. Will you do that?"

He nodded yes, and I thanked him, then reentered the cabin

and closed the door.

"I don't understand you, Sidney," Jay said, "and I think you must be nuts to turn down that invitation, but it's your choice, not mine. I think there is something I'm missing here. Now, show me your outfit for tonight and then I'll show you mine!"

Shelving all thoughts of Captain Vargos, I forced myself to open my disaster of a closet. Besides getting myself together for the evening, I really needed to spend part of the afternoon sorting and packing my stuff, although I sure didn't want to. I hate packing, but this was the last free day for a while.

After two days in St. Petersburg, the itinerary called for a day in Estonia, then back to Harwich for disembarkation and the flight home.

My stuff seemed to be in a bigger jumble than usual.

"Jay, have you been rummaging through my things again? This closet is a mess."

"Your stuff is always a mess, Sidney, unlike mine, which is always perfect."

True. Jay pitches a fit if his clothes are disturbed in any way, even slightly out of place. He wants his trousers all hanging neatly on special hangers covered in dry-cleaner plastic. He packs his suitcase with tissue paper—you know the type. No one would ever think of calling my motley collection of outfits a wardrobe.

I planned to wear my one really, really good dress, a black silk, to the ballet. The silver sandals that go with it had super-high heels. I thought my new pink pashmina would be great with the black silk dress, but the scarf wasn't where I had left it. I couldn't find it anywhere.

I looked in the closet and all through the drawers, then hauled my suitcase out from under the bed and dug through the dirty clothes, but I still couldn't find it. By then I was pretty sure someone had been going through my stuff, and the prime suspect was sitting right there, looking innocent.

"Okay, Jay, where is it?"

"Where is what?"

"My new pink pashmina, that's what. Where is it?"

"Don't glare at me like that. I didn't take it," Jay said. "I don't wear fake-minas, and it's the wrong color for me anyway. You don't need a shawl with that dress, Sidney. It's going to be warm outside tonight, and the boys at the ballet will like you better if you don't cover up your boobs."

He was right. The plunging neckline of the black silk dress would have Aunt Minnie clucking, but Fernando would probably think it was just fine.

I gave up looking for the scarf and chose instead an amethyst drop on a fine silver chain and matching earrings.

Neither Jay nor I had to babysit the High Steppers tonight. None of them were going ashore. A troupe of Russian folkloric dancers was performing after dinner in the Stardust Lounge, and all the old folks wanted to get to bed early because of Sunday's all-day shore excursions.

Instead of the regular bus trip, Brooke had hired a car and driver through the ship's concierge for the next day, inviting Hannah and Ethel to go along as her guests.

They were thrilled, of course, but Gertrude, who was not invited, was furious. At dinner, she sat with the Murphys and Marjorie and Esther Levy, glaring across at Brooke's table and making loud spiteful remarks about her throughout the entire meal.

"Just look at her," she said, giving Brooke venomous looks, "all that red hair and just dripping in diamonds! She thinks the bus isn't good enough for her. She can't sightsee with the likes of us. No, she has to have a private car and driver! I wouldn't go in the car with Miss Got Rocks if she begged me."

Gertrude, the Levys, the Johnsons, the Petrones, and Chet Parker had all booked the all-day bus tour, Palaces and Treasures of Imperial Russia, which was scheduled to leave from the pier at 8:00 a.m.

"Muriel Murphy was pretty vague about her family's plans,"

Chet Parker reported over eggs and caviar. "Either they haven't told her yet or she was too fuzzy to remember."

"I hope they go with you." I murmured. "You should have to sit between them and the Levys on the bus as payback for the dirty trick you played on the Levy sisters in Stockholm."

"But they don't know I did it," he smirked. "I was too smooth. They think the Institute of Social Justice really exists, and that everyone, including you, was just too stupid to point them in the right direction. But have mercy on me, Sidney. If you had to spend the time I've spent with those two, you'd be sending them on snipe hunts, too."

He had a point.

Chet is really not a bad guy. He's sort of appealing in a little lost boy kind of way. At least he was honest about his guest host duties, and he didn't appear to be trying to take advantage of any of the ladies he entertained. I wasn't going to pass judgment on Chet Parker. Plus, I wasn't totally sure of his orientation—not that it was any of my business. Jay says Chet is gay, and Jay probably knows.

Our captain was not at his table at dinner, and I wondered where he was dining, and with whom.

Jerome Morgan had gone ashore the second the ship was cleared, and no one had seen him since. That seemed to be his pattern whenever the ship reached a port. No one had a clue what Morgan's business was in St. Petersburg. But there was lots of High Stepper speculation.

"I heard in the beauty shop/ spa/ at breakfast/ last night for sure that Jerome Morgan is a drug dealer/ CIA agent/ evangelist/ smuggling Bibles to poor people/ a gun dealer/ a kidnapper, has run off with that little blond girl …" Their speculation covered most possibilities. Take your pick.

Angelo Petrone had the most solid information. "He eats at our table at dinner, see, not because he wants to, just because he has to, the way this set-up works. Most nights he don't show. My wife, she tried fishing around, you know, just being friendly, but he clammed up tight. She kept pestering him—she wants to know everything—but all he would say was that he is a "business associate" of Fernando Ortiz and Abe Klein. He tried to sound on the up-and-up, real official-like, but whatever he's selling, I ain't buying. I seen guys like him before. Smells like mob to me."

I wasn't sure either what Morgan's real story was, but I didn't care as long as he stayed away from me. I wasn't totally convinced that he was innocent in that crypt deal. Morgan had certainly been in the area when the doors slammed behind me.

Vargos had been, too, of course. His story was that he was visiting an old friend there—a priest at the cathedral. If his story was true, then he must have entered the church and then passed through the public area to the private area with his friend; that could explain why I didn't see him when I entered a few minutes later. *If* it were true.

There were so many possibilities, so many variables in this thing, that I had stopped counting. Not to mention, of course, the literally thousands of other passengers and crewmen. The culprit could have been anyone. It could have been someone in the church or the town, someone totally unrelated to this whole deal. It could have been a kid, playing a prank.

I was sick and tired of worrying about everything and everybody. This crazy cruise was making me crazy, and I decided that for once, Jay was absolutely right. I did need to cool my jets. Nothing really bad had happened to me in the church, but it sure could have. A night off relaxing at a beautiful ballet with a great-looking man was just what I needed. An evening with Fernando might also exorcise any lingering feelings I had for the captain. Fun! It would be fun! And for tonight, at least, no more Sherlock Holmes.

28

I have to admit that Jay had been right about something else, too.

The Mariinsky Theatre may have been the famed home of Pavlova, Nijiinsky and Barishnikov, but at the ballet that evening Fernando spent more time watching my neckline than he did watching the ballerinas.

At intermission he ordered a glass of champagne for me and an iced vodka for himself, and we stood on the same balcony where czars and princesses had stood, overlooking the moonlit square.

He raised his glass. "To you, Sidney. You are beautiful, you know, you really are, and especially tonight."

He kissed me then. Three more champagnes led to a lot more kisses. We stayed out in the moonlight long after the chimes signaled that intermission was over.

"You don't really want to see the rest of the performance, do you?" he asked.

Suddenly I felt woozy. I did want to see the rest of the performance, but I wasn't sure I could stay awake for it. I shook my head and we started down the steps toward the exit.

In front of the theater, Fernando whistled and a car instantly appeared. He helped me into the backseat.

I needed help. I don't know whether it was the booze or the man, but by that time I was more than a little wobbly. The car left the square and sped us away down a broad avenue.

He kissed me some more and then pulled a silver flask from his coat pocket, insisting that I have a drink. I don't like vodka, so I shook my head.

"Oh, come on, my darling, one drink. It will relax you. Take a little sip."

He held me tighter, put the flask to my mouth, and tried to pour some of the vodka between my lips, while at the same time unzipping the back of my dress. He said something to the driver in Russian; the driver laughed and the car accelerated.

I pushed the flask aside but he forced it right back up to my lips, spilling a few drops down the front of my dress. His grip on my arms tightened. Alarm bells were going off big time in my head, with the word *roofie* flashing neon in my brain. *Was the vodka drugged*? My magical evening was going to hell in a hurry.

To make matters worse, I suddenly realized that the car, which had been steadily accelerating, was heading *away* from the ship, not *toward* it.

He pulled me even closer, nuzzling my neck, and whispered into my ear, "Sidney, darling, where is the red bag?"

Those five little words scared me so badly that I almost wet my pants.

"Sidney Lanier Marsh," I told myself, "get your young ass out of here *now*."

I kissed Fernando hard on the mouth. "Fernando," I purred, breathing into his ear, gently prying his hand from its lock grip on my wrist and placing it squarely on my breast, "Can you get the driver to pull over real quick and tell him to take a walk? I just really, really want to be alone with you, and I don't think I can wait another minute."

Fernando shouted something to the driver, who immediately braked and swerved into a dark side street. Ortiz was so busy getting his pants down that he didn't realize for a minute that I had bailed.

I hit the ground running, cutting across the backyards of two houses so they couldn't chase me with the car.

Feet, I prayed, don't fail me now!

He was out of the car then, running down the alley behind me, screaming my name. His needing to pull his pants back up before he could chase me had given me a tiny head start, and I needed every second of it. I had kicked off the silver sandals before I jumped out or I would never have made it.

I cut through the back yards of some dilapidated apartment buildings, dodging clotheslines, rusted out cars and garbage bins, going as fast as I could without falling over anything. My feet were hurting, running barefoot through the night, but they could take the abuse if I didn't step on glass or anything. I'm a Southern girl and go barefoot all the time.

I ran silently, staying in the deep shadows and praying that no dogs would give me away.

Fernando swore and shouted to the driver, and the car's engine roared. Then a car door slammed and the black Mercedes began to cruise slowly up one street and down the next, lights on bright, searching for me.

The Neva River was in front of me then, and to go any farther I somehow had to get across it. The bridge was impossible—too exposed, too much traffic. I couldn't swim the river. Fernando and his pal were right behind me.

I crouched down in the shadows, desperate for an escape plan.

I was trapped, just as they had known I would be. My only option was to hide somewhere until they gave up looking for me.

Having grown up a tomboy in the rural South, I had no trouble shimmying up the first good tree I saw.

And there I sat, treed like a coon in the moonlight, being hunted down by a lying, sneaky, dangerous son of a bitch whom just one hour before I had found attractive.

I must have been out of my mind. Jay had been totally right about this dirtbag. What was I thinking? My mother is right. Like all my aunts, I clearly have no brains at all when it comes to men. The Marsh Curse strikes again!

29

When I finally decided it was safe to come down out of that tree, the eastern sky was starting to lighten.

Limping back toward the port, barefooted, exhausted, my good dress torn, my hair full of twigs and leaves, I didn't even feel sorry for myself. Before all of this mess, I had thought of myself as a sophisticated, street-smart, worldly-wise New Yorker. Not. I was a dumbass from the sticks.

I traded my silver necklace to a truck driver for a ride back to the ship. I think he stopped for me because he thought I was a hooker winding up a night's work, maybe willing to turn one last trick cut-rate. Maybe he just recognized me as a crazy American. He didn't have much English but I managed to communicate where I needed to go. "Tourist? Ship? Da!"

Whatever. His wife would love my necklace, and I was more than happy with the deal.

♓

The sun was just beginning to come up when the truck turned into the port. Its light illuminated the ship, and also police cars and an ambulance and Jay, in his polka dot pajamas.

Two burly policemen had him by the arms. Edgar was talking to the cops at the end of the pier. God knows what Jay and Edgar had done, I thought.

"Where the hell have you been, Sidney Marsh?" he screamed at me. "Just where the hell have you been?"

"Don't yell at me, Jay. I've had a rough night."

"Yeah, I can see that. You look like crap. Well, I've had a rough night, too, sweetie ... not that you care, of course. While you out having a blast with your Latin lover, I tried and tried to call you, but you wouldn't answer your phone. Then I heard your purse ringing in the closet. You left your cell in the cabin on purpose, didn't you Cinderella, so I couldn't call you when I needed you! Well, welcome back, Sidney, welcome back. I have a little bad news. There's been another emergency. And guess what? I'm being arrested. They think I did it."

Sylvia Klein hadn't left Abe and the ship in Stockholm, after all. She was still on the ship, floating naked in the hot tub in the red glow of the sunrise, my new pink scarf knotted securely around her throat.

♓

"Wait a minute," I said for the fourteenth time, to the Russian detective. "You can't arrest him. He had nothing to do with Mrs. Klein's death. How could you even think such a thing? There is no proof. This is ridiculous!"

"Not ridiculous at all, Miss Marsh. Mr. Wilson has not yet been charged, but we are taking him to headquarters for questioning and I must say that things look very bad for him. He was in the hot tub with Mrs. Klein just after midnight. He was the last person seen with her before she was found dead. And the scarf that was used to strangle her is yours; it came from the cabin where Mr. Wilson is residing. I have nothing further to say to you at this time. Call your employer. Call your embassy. They may be willing to intervene. Or they may not."

And then they stuffed Jay into the car and drove away,

leaving me absolutely powerless to help him.

Two of the High Steppers, Hannah and Ethel, along with about half the other passengers, had watched my walk of shame from the deck and then viewed the entire spectacle of Jay's arrest. With breakfast being served and the entertainment over for the moment, the crowd quickly dispersed, all except Hannah and Ethel. They remained standing silently along the rail, in their bathrobes and plastic hairnets, or rain bonnets, or whatever those things are, like a pair of marabou storks, staring as I made my way up the gangway.

Then they confronted me, interrupting each other as the words spilled out.

"Where were you all night, Sidney?"

"We were so worried. We have been looking for you."

"The most terrible thing has happened. Did they tell you about Sylvia?"

"Where is Jay going in his pajamas? Why is he leaving with those men?"

"You must come with us now to our cabin. We have something to show you."

"Yes, you must come right now. We need to talk with you right away. We've been waiting."

"Ladies," I said. "I'm very sorry to have caused you any more distress and I know how upsetting all of this is for you, but I can't come to your cabin now. I have to shower and change clothes so I can make some important phone calls and try to straighten things out. I'm dreadfully sorry, but this will have to wait until later, perhaps this evening."

They both shook their heads emphatically, gray curls bouncing inside the pink plastic rain-bonnets.

"No, no, no, Sidney, it can't wait. We've waited too long already. You must come. Promise us you will come, just as soon as you can. We need to speak with you in private."

High Steppers are always urgently needing to speak with me in private.

"Please," Hannah said.

That got to me. Hannah is one of my favorites and without her I might still have been in that crypt in Stockholm.

But Jay's freedom came first.

"Okay, ladies, okay. But just let me grab a shower first and make a few phone calls. I'll be there within the hour. I won't be able to stay more than a few minutes, but I'll be there. Later, I promise, later."

Through the walls of the glass elevator on my way to my cabin, I could see Russian officers all over the ship.

This time things would be very different. This time, we were not at sea. We were docked in a Russian port, and it was apparent that the Russian officials were fully in charge.

I headed to the cabin to shower and change. Then I was going to call Itchy and the embassy. Poor Sylvia! And poor Jay! And what had Sylvia even been doing on the ship in Russia? Her luggage had been unloaded in Sweden. Where had she been hiding all this time?

Finally clean, I resisted the urge to crawl into my bed and pull the covers over my head for the next couple of years. I swallowed two aspirin and chugged some water, pulled on a pair of black knit pants and a sweater, brushed my teeth, and swirled on some mascara and lipstick.

Hearing a loud, insistent knock on the cabin door, I threw the lock, snatched it open, and found Muriel Murphy standing there, hands nervously clutching her coat and pulling it tight around her.

"Good Lord, Muriel! What a knock! Is something wrong? Do you need anything? I was just on my way out."

She moved toward me into the room and was about to speak when Rahim rapped on the open door behind her, entered and said, "Miss Marsh, pardon for interruption. Captain says you must come, come now to bridge please."

A flash of annoyance crossed Muriel's face.

"I'm sorry, Muriel, but you heard Rahim. I must go now. We'll talk later."

"Samurai!" Rahim said, his eyes wide.

"What?"

"Samurai!" he repeated, pointing at Muriel.

She had a large steel knife in her hand.

"This is what I wanted to show you, Sidney," she said, giggling. I found it on one of the deck chairs by the hot tub, under the cushion." Her eyes were dancing, as if she had found the golden egg. "I think it's from the kitchen, like the ones we saw on the galley tour. And this, too!"

From the pocket of her coat, she pulled the top of a leopard print bikini, neatly sliced in two, strings dangling.

"Muriel! Where exactly did you find this—the bikini and the knife?"

"On the table in the lounge, Sidney, where they had the cooking demonstration."

"But you just said you found them on deck, near the hot tub. Two different places?" I paused, as the truth dawned on me. "You don't know where you got them, do you? You don't really remember, do you?"

She shook her head, smiling. "No. But it doesn't matter, does it? I get to keep them. They're mine now. I can keep them, can't I? Finders keepers."

"Muriel. You know you can't keep that knife. Even if you could, how would you get it home on the plane? Now, please, give those things to Rahim and he will take you and both the items to the Captain so you can tell him all about it."

Pouting, she gave the knife and the sliced-up bikini to Rahim. Her lower lip stuck out like a child's.

"Thank you very much, Muriel. You've been very helpful. Rahim, please tell the Captain that I will be there as soon as possible."

I walked them to the elevator and let Muriel push the button.

Then I waited until the door closed before bolting up the stairs to Hannah's cabin.

♓

Now everyone on the ship was clearly shaken up. Word that something was terribly wrong had spread, even to those who had never heard of the High Steppers, and who had been blissfully unaware of what was happening all along.

Passengers, stewards, and crew members stood in clusters, whispering, all over the ship, and the line at the guest relations desk was very long.

I knocked on Hannah's door. "Hello, Hannah, it's Sidney. I'm here."

I heard noises from the other side of the door and knew she was looking through the peephole. I smiled and waved.

She opened the door. "Oh, thank goodness, Sidney. Please, come in."

She pointed at the table and simply said, "Look."

And there it was, on the table.

The red train case.

Ruth Shadrach's missing bag.

Still bright red, but not as shiny as it had been when she brought it home from Macy's One Day Sale.

"Where did you find it?" I asked.

"We didn't find it. It found us," Ethel said. "Ruth gave it to Al Bostick and Al gave it to Sylvia and she gave it to Monique to keep for her. Monique hid it in the bottom of the hamper in the beauty salon where she keeps the smocks. Sylvia told Monique that the bag was her insurance, that she should keep it safe where no one could find it, and that if anything happened to her, then Monique was to give it to you."

"We had the first appointments this morning," Hannah said, "and when we got to the salon, Monique was crying. She gave us the bag to give to you and so here it is."

"Does anyone else know you have it?" I asked. "Did anyone see you with it?"

"No," Hannah said. "Monique wrapped it in a smock and warned us not to let anyone else see it. So we brought it straight here and locked it in the cabin, and then we went to find you."

"What do you think is in it?" Ethel asked.

I looked at the bag. "Did you open it?" I asked.

Ethel looked offended. "Why Sidney, we wouldn't ..."

"It was locked," Hannah said.

"Of course it is," I said. "It's Ruth's bag. It probably has two locks."

"Monique said that Sylvia had the key," Hannah said, "but I guess now that's ..."

"Gone." Ethel finished.

"Okay, ladies, come with me," I said, wrapping the smock back around the bag. "This bag is going to Captain Vargos, this very minute, before it disappears again. The Russians are on the bridge right now, and people from Empress and the embassy, and God knows who else. As much as I would like to break that lock and look inside, the only thing to do is to turn it into the authorities. They need to take charge of this puppy, not us. This bag has caused enough trouble. But we don't need to go parading through the ship with it. Somebody pretty ugly might be watching. Come on, you don't need your purses, let's go."

Going up to the bridge in the glass elevator, I was nervous. I guess it was silly, but after all that had happened, as I was carrying that bag, I felt as if every eye on the ship must be watching our little procession.

We didn't have much conversation. Even Hannah was subdued. I was lost in my own thoughts, and I'm sure Hannah and Ethel were, too.

At the bridge, I rapped on the door and told First Officer Avranos that we needed to see Captain Vargos immediately.

"Please, come in and have a seat, Miss Marsh, ladies. I'll tell him that you are here, but he is very busy and might not have time just now to see you. Are you sure that it is important?"

We all nodded.

"He sent for me," I said.

"Very well, then, I'll tell him you are here. Please be seated."

He quietly opened the door to the Captain's office and slipped inside. The office was crowded with people.

We waited.

Finally Avranos returned and motioned for us to enter.

Everyone stopped talking as we entered the room. The captain's blue gaze rested on me.

"Well, Miss Marsh, I'm very happy that you could join us, but perhaps the other ladies would wait with Officer Avranos while you ..."

His voice trailed off into silence as I placed the bag in the middle of his desk and removed the cover.

"It's Ruth Shadrach's missing bag, Captain," I said. "Sylvia had it in her possession. She gave it to Monique for safekeeping and told Monique that it was her insurance. It may hold some answers."

Everyone rushed the desk, claiming custody, but Vargos ordered them all to step back. After obtaining gloves and tools from Avranos, he broke the lock and lifted the lid.

None of Ruth's things were inside. Instead, the case was stuffed with cash, U.S. currency, computer USB drives, and passports, lots of passports.

30

It was well into the evening before all the High Steppers had been questioned, along with Monique and anyone who had had more than casual contact with Sylvia.

The computer drives in the bag held more than enough evidence to implicate Abe, Fernando, and that big phony Morgan in an international smuggling and money-laundering scheme.

Abe and Morgan were being questioned by the Russians, and the authorities were searching for Fernando and his driver, neither of whom had returned to the ship. More arrests would likely be forthcoming, we were told, on both sides of the Atlantic, as the data was analyzed. Abe, Fernando and Morgan were apparently only a small part of a very large operation.

But the Russians were adamant. They would not release Jay. "Not good enough, Miss Marsh, it is not good enough. We do not believe that Mr. Wilson was in any way involved in the smuggling ring, but he is not under suspicion for smuggling. He is being questioned in the death of Mrs. Klein. No evidence exists to absolve him. He is still the last person be seen with her before her body was found, and no witnesses can corroborate the story that he was asleep in his cabin under the influence of alcohol at the time of her death."

If I hadn't been ashore playing hide-and-seek with Fernando I could have been Jay's alibi. But no, where was I when my best friend needed me? Up a tree.

⊬

The fat cat from the embassy was no help.

"I'm afraid it's completely out of my hands at this point, Miss Marsh," he said, the wind barely moving his comb-over. "Be patient. These things take time."

That was easy for him to say. He wasn't poor Jay, enduring a Russian police interrogation.

⊬

I gathered the High Steppers in the Sunset Lounge.

"Jay was the last person seen with Sylvia on the night of her death, so he is now the prime suspect. We all know that he would never harm Sylvia or anyone else. But somehow we have to come up with concrete proof. If any of you saw or heard anything that might be helpful, please speak up now. This is no time to remain silent. Jay needs your help."

There was a long silence. No one said anything.

Then, finally, Hannah said, "Monique told us this morning, Sidney, that Sylvia has been on the ship all along, since Stockholm, staying in Fernando Ortiz' cabin, hiding from Abe. Maybe you should talk to Monique."

⊬

But Monique had nothing to add except a lot of venting about Abe. "Zis bad man. Why she lives with zis bad man? She was afraid of 'im and now 'e has killed 'er. I know it!"

"How do you know it, Monique? Do you have any proof that we could take to the police? Anything she told you or gave you other than the red bag? Anything that might prove that Jay was not the one who killed Sylvia and perhaps the others?"

"Proof! Pff! I do not need proof. My proof is 'ere, in my heart! In my heart I know Abe killed her! M'sieur Ortiz was working for Sylvia's husband and 'e saw her unhappiness. He saw her beauty. Her sweetness. So 'e made a plan. Such a clever plan! He arranged to have 'er things sent ashore in Stockholm so zis bad husband would think she was gone. But all the time she was here, in M'sieur Ortiz' cabin. Whether zey were lovers or not, I do not know, but it doesn't matter. But I do not think M. Ortiz would kill 'er, no?"

No. He hadn't killed her and I knew he hadn't because I had been with him, snuggled up like a sick kitten to a hot rock, or either running scared blue through the backyards of St. Petersburg at the time Sylvia was killed. Like it or not, I was Fernando's alibi, not Jay's. My face burned at the thought.

♓

"Proof," I thought, standing outside Abe's cabin, waiting for a chance to sneak inside for a once-over. "There must be some proof, somewhere."

Mustapha was the cabin steward for Abe's cabin.

I found him napping in the steward's closet. He woke, startled, when I knocked at the open door, and he immediately started apologizing.

"No, no, no, Mustapha," I said, "It's absolutely okay for you to grab a little sleep if you can. You must have had a long night."

"I did, Miss Marsh, I did, with all that was happening."

"Mustapha, could you let me in, just for a quick look, into Mr. Klein's cabin? He hasn't returned, has he?"

"He hasn't returned, Miss Marsh, and he won't be back. But his things are gone. They took them away. The cabin is empty and has already been cleaned."

"Has anyone besides you been in the cabin since it was cleaned, Mustapha?"

"I did not see anyone, and the cabin was locked."

"Oh. Well, thank you, Mustapha."

Another dead end and still no proof.

"Miss Marsh?" he said. I turned back to face him.

"The floor was wet early this morning outside the cabin. There was an empty bottle of champagne on the floor, and just outside the door, I found this."

He held up the other half of Sylvia's leopard string bikini.

♓

Edgar desperately wanted to help Jay out, but couldn't.

"I'm afraid I'm no help, Sidney, no help at all. Sylvia slipped into the hot tub with us about one a.m., wearing the leopard bikini, both bits. I left Sylvia and Jay there, in the water, when I retired at about two a.m. and was sleeping soundly, I'm afraid, when the alarm was raised.

"Jay told me that he left the deck shortly after I did, leaving Sylvia alone in the hot tub, but I cannot swear that to be true because I had already gone. I was just not there."

"Did you meet anyone on deck or in the passageway, Edgar? What about Abe?"

"I only saw the Murphy family returning from the Midnight Buffet. Abe was said to be in the Mariner's Bar alone most of the night, and the bartender is vouching for him, although that particular chap is known to accept, ahem, tips. Abe is also saying that he believed, along with the rest of us, that Sylvia left the ship in Stockholm."

I persisted. "But what if Abe suddenly discovered her, not in Stockholm at all, but on the ship, living in the cabin of another man? Or half-naked in the hot tub all alone? What then?"

"I hate to play devil's advocate, my darling. That is an excellent theory, but what *might* have occurred is of no use. You need solid proof."

Proof. I was back to that word again. Something that exonerated Jay. I needed proof.

♓

I went to my favorite spot on the Lido Deck to think.

From there I could see the guards standing on the pier by the gangway. The ship was sealed off. No one was being allowed to enter or exit without permission.

I could also see the hot tub, now cordoned off with police tape, off limits while the investigation was conducted. The sun was shining on the hot tub, the motor was switched off, and the still surface of the water in it was slick and slimy. A layer of oil floated on top.

I stared at the water.

Was it suntan oil? Why would anyone use suntan oil after dark?

I blasted down the outside stair to the hot tub and smelled it on the north wind even before I reached it.

Not suntan oil, bath wash. Giorgio. Sylvia's favorite perfume. Someone had dumped it in the water of the hot tub; the heavy fragrance was unmistakable.

And I knew at that moment that Jay was free.

Not only did he hate the heavy lush scent of the perfume; he would not, could not, be near it because of his allergy.

If Jay had been in the water with that oil he would be wheezing and all covered in a rash. And moreover, we could prove it.

Proof! Jay was in the clear. Either Sylvia had added the perfumed oil to the water after Jay left her or someone else had.

I searched all around the hot tub, and then plunged my arm into the nearest trashcan. Nasty. Drink cups. Wadded-up napkins. Paper plates with old scraps of food from the Midnight Buffet. Pizza crusts. And then, I saw it, the real golden egg. An empty tube of body wash, with the distinctive Giorgio label.

I didn't touch it, hoping that fingerprints on the tube might really seal the deal for Jay. Covering it back up with trash, I went for help.

31

Much later that evening Jay was released and returned to the *Rapture*.

Dr. Sledge confirmed Jay's perfume allergy, Helga produced a charge slip showing Abe's perfume purchase on the last night at sea, and Abe's fingerprints were found on the tube along with Sylvia's.

After Jay had left the hot tub, Abe, or perhaps even Sylvia, had apparently poured the perfumed oil into the water. As Sylvia relaxed in the warm, fragrant water, she had been throttled from behind with my missing pink scarf. Tiny cuts on her body marked the spots where her bikini had been sliced away with a knife, perhaps the very knife that Muriel said she had found on the deck.

I shivered in the cold night air as Jay and I stood by the rail on the Lido Deck and watched the police drive away with Abe and Morgan. Abe was still loudly protesting his innocence and proclaiming his love for Sylvia. Morgan said nothing.

The Russians didn't care what Abe or Morgan said or didn't say. They just stuffed them into the Tupelov and drove off.

Jay put his big arm around my shoulders. "That Morgan was

really rotten, Sidney," he said. "He is truly a killer, too. Vargos told me late this afternoon that the authorities said that the badge they found on Morgan was real, all right, the same one he flashed at you. It just didn't belong to him. It belonged to the dead guy on the carousel, the one you called Homeless Guy, who followed you in New York. He was the real spook, and Morgan is being charged with his murder. Morgan killed him at Tivoli. Homeless Guy was working on the ship, disguised as a crewman. He was following us. He may have even followed you into the park that night, Sid, to warn you. But he slipped up somehow, and Morgan wised up and killed him."

"So the note the waiter brought me in the restaurant that night must have been from Homeless Guy, Jay. I had a strange feeling, felt uneasy on the paths in the gardens, as if I was being followed. I feel certain now that Homeless Guy must have followed me off the ship to the park. I guess he wanted to warn me. He'd already tried twice before, remember?. Only this time, someone made sure he wouldn't succeed."

"All I know, Sidney, is that Morgan was no more a secret agent than your Aunt Minnie. As for your boy Fernando ..."

I looked up at him.

"Please. Let's just don't say anything more about him, okay? And he's not my boy."

My memory of my special evening at the ballet with Fernando Ortiz is burned into my brain as one of my top ten most embarrassing romantic experiences ever, and—as Jay will be happy to tell you if you've got a couple of hours—some of those were pretty dreadful.

When Jay's snickering finally subsided, I posed a question that had been bothering me since he told me the news about Morgan. "Jay, do you think I need to find somebody to tell about seeing Homeless Guy in New York?"

He shook his head, smiling. "No, Nancy Drew. They know that. They've got it all figured out. They know now that Homeless Guy was following you in New York and on the trip, even on the ship, hoping to catch the smugglers.

"How did Sylvia get the red bag, Jay? Do you think Al gave it to her?"

"No, I *know* he didn't. Sylvia took it out of his cabin the same night we were there. She found it while we were hiding. It was Sylvia who slipped in to search while we were in the closet."

"Sylvia! She would have been my last guess. I thought it was a man. The bag must have been in that cabinet. The one we heard open and close. And Sylvia had a knife? How could you know all this, Jay?"

"Monique told me. Monique and Sylvia were good friends. Sylvia told her everything, all her troubles, and Monique did all she could to help her. Sylvia carried the knife everywhere for protection after she left Abe because she was afraid of him. Monique got the knife for Sylvia from a guy she dates, one of the chefs."

He gave me a little hug.

"Now let it all go, Sid. It's time to pack it all in for the night. You've done enough for one little senior citizen's cruise, don't you think? Cool those jets, babe. We've solved the mystery, and thanks to you, I'm out of jail. It looks like this gig is finally over. Tomorrow we're out of here."

After a major consultation with the Russians, the cruise line, and the embassy, plus about a million calls to and from New York, we had finally gotten everyone to agree to fly us and the remaining High Steppers home the following afternoon.

The *Rapture of the Deep* would remain in St. Petersburg for another day while the investigation was wrapped up; then the ship, carrying the remaining passengers, would finally sail for England. By that time I should be back in my apartment in New York with this nightmare behind me.

"I still can't believe it, Jay. I mean, really, who would ever suspect a High Stepper?"

"Apparently that's what Abe and his boys thought, too, Sid. That's why they picked poor Ruth to act as their mule.

"One of the Interpol guys told me off the record that they believe that this was probably not the first time the High Steppers have been used as unwitting couriers by Abe's gang. He's traveled with us before, remember?"

"Yeah, and he never really fit the normal High Stepper profile, did he?"

"Sidney. Think about what you just said. *Is* there a *normal* High Stepper profile?"

"Um. No, I guess not."

"My guy also said that we, and particularly you, were also followed in New York by Fernando's driver, who, of course, was really part of the ring, too, and not just a driver."

"Back to Homeless Guy, Jay. Who did he work for?"

"They wouldn't tell me. They just said that he was on the other side, the good side, trying to catch Abe's gang. But he got too close to Morgan, so Morgan took him out at Tivoli."

"Jay."

"Yeah."

"Do they know for sure which one killed Ruth and Al and Sylvia?"

"Well, they don't have a confession yet. Abe's insisting he didn't kill any of them. And remember, they're still looking for Fernando. They haven't caught up with him yet, but they will. And when they do, he'll sing. I bet that the Russians will find out everything they want to know by the time they finish their interrogation. How would you like to spend the rest of your life in a Russian jail? I almost did. If it hadn't been for you I guess I'd be on my way to Siberia by now, if they still do that. A Russian prison camp would be really bad."

"That would be only a little worse than facing up to Diana, Jay. I can tell you, I'm not looking forward to hearing what she has to say when we get back to the office. She probably blames us for the whole thing."

Well, I think that witch should have the decency to apologize. We deserve a raise for what we went through."

"Yeah, right. Like that's going to happen."

"Try not to mention Tiger Woman anymore tonight, okay, Sidney? You'll spoil my evening. I'm going to karaoke. Want to come?"

"Not tonight, Jay. Thanks, you go ahead. We're leaving in the morning and I have to tie up a few loose ends. And you know what? I don't think anything can spoil this night. I mean, it feels pretty fantastic to have finally worked it all out and be headed home, doesn't it?"

"Yeah, babe, it does. It sure does."

♓

I was standing on the Sun Deck, watching the moon rise in the night sky, when I saw him step out, alone this time, onto the flying bridge, and bend to adjust his telescope.

"Hey, sailor," I called up to him. "How about showing me some stars?"

He stared down at me for a moment, and then, with a broad smile, unlatched the gate and pulled me up onto the flying bridge.

32

We loaded the bus with the High Steppers early Wednesday morning.

Stingy Diana and Itchy had handsomely sprung for a tiny little farewell tour of St. Petersburg between the airport and home, probably to try and head off the lawsuit that the Levy sisters were loudly advocating.

"How cheap is that?" Jay whispered, after we heard the arrangement. "I'll bet Itchy is going to have to cough up a lot more than this pitiful little shore excursion before it's all said and done."

Jay was doing the bag count, tagging each piece as it went in the compartment under the bus. I stood at the bus door, helping those who needed it up the steps. Things were pretty much back to normal. Well, normal for the High Steppers, I mean.

"Stop! Stop the bus!"

Gladys Murphy rushed down the gangway, wild-eyed, followed by her husband Pete, who looked exhausted.

"What's wrong now, Gladys?" Jay asked.

"We can't find Muriel," Gladys shrieked. "We've lost her.

What if something's happened to her?"

"Ain't nothing happened to Muriel unless she passed out dead drunk in some deckhand's bed," Angelo Petrone murmured to his wife. "But he'd have to be drunk, too, and blind."

"Now, now, Gladys," I said, "Calm down. Muriel's okay. We'll find her."

"Stop all that screeching, Gladys," Gertrude Fletcher snapped. "Nothing has happened to Muriel. I saw her not ten minutes ago outside the Sunset Lounge, drinking vodka out of her purse."

"My baby, my baby," sobbed Gladys.

Great. Just great. Now I'll have to go and find her, I thought. We couldn't hold the bus a minute longer and still have enough time for a shore excursion.

"Get on the bus," I said to the Murphys. "I'll go back for Muriel and bring her to the airport in a cab. She'll have to miss her tour, but you shouldn't have to miss yours. Enjoy your tour and don't worry. It'll be fine. Just get on the bus. I'll bring her."

Jay rolled his eyes and whispered to me as he climbed aboard, "Very noble, Miss Marsh, quite a sacrifice, missing the last shore excursion with the High Steppers to round up a stray. I'm not sure yet who is getting the better deal here. You might owe me."

"Well, we don't have much choice, do we, Jay? We can't just leave Muriel on the ship and it's not fair to make the others miss any more of St. Petersburg. Depending on the shape she's in, we might catch up with you at the Hermitage, or I might just have to take her straight to the airport. I don't know."

"You know, Sid," he said, handing me Muriel's passport and air ticket, "I'm really glad you have this overdeveloped sense of duty."

"Yeah, right," I told him. "Me, too. You be sure and thank my grandmother for that the next time you see her."

"Okay, High Steppers!" he shouted, bounding up the steps

and grabbing the mic. "Let's roll! And just wait 'til I tell you all about Ivan the Terrible!"

The doors whooshed shut and the bus pulled away from the pier. I waved goodbye until it was out of sight; then I turned and headed back up the gangway to look for that ridiculous Muriel. It was just like Gladys to ride blithely off on the bus, leaving Muriel to me. Now where could she be? We had already paged her repeatedly on the loudspeaker.

Wonderful, I thought. I will just have to search all eleven decks of the *Rapture* until I find her.

33

I started on the top of the ship at the Sunset Lounge where Gertrude had reported last seeing Muriel.

Mario was mopping the dance floor.

"Yeah, she was here earlier, but she's gone now. You'll find her soon, I bet. She was hitting the bottle pretty hard. I don't think she could make it too far on her own."

I got pretty much the same answer from workers and remaining passengers in all the lounges, restrooms and public areas on the top three decks.

Deck Eight was all suites, but none of the cabin stewards I talked to there had seen her. She could have hidden in an empty stateroom, I thought, but not for long, because the staff was all over the place, preparing the ship to depart for England. I asked everyone I saw to page me if they spotted her.

Because we were in port, the shops and casino on Deck Seven were closed, but on the Promenade Deck, I got lucky. I ran into Dr. Sledge. Gladys had alerted him, and he was looking for her, too.

"Muriel has been quite a challenge for us all, hasn't she, Miss Marsh? Let's divide and conquer, shall we? You search the port side and I'll take the starboard."

He looked up and down the corridor and then lowered his voice. "I must say that I will be very glad to see Muriel Murphy headed home, and I am sure you will as well. I have advised both Muriel and her parents of her need for professional help. This spotty guard dog approach that her parents have been taking doesn't work very well, what?"

"It sure doesn't, Dr. Sledge," I said.

And neither do you, I thought, considering his inept, unprofessional, and spineless performance in all that had happened on this voyage.

Where did they get these people?

34

I found Muriel huddled in a corner of the library, which should have been closed and locked at that hour, but wasn't.

She was sipping vodka out of a pint in her purse and singing softly, curled up in a leather chair like a little child, with magazines and candy wrappers scattered all around her on the floor. She was hammered.

"Muriel! There you are! I've been looking all over for you. Let's go, dear. It's time to leave the ship. The bus has already left."

"Do we haaaaaaaaaave to go, Mish Marsh? I loooove it here. I don' wanna go home."

She peered at me over her glasses, trying to focus. Then she tried to stand, wobbled for a moment and crashed back down into the chair. She obviously couldn't walk by herself, and she was no lightweight.

Great, just great. Now I've got to haul her out of that chair, get her off the ship by myself, pour her into a cab, and sober her up enough to be allowed onto the plane.

They don't pay me enough. They don't pay me enough. They don't pay me enough. My new mantra.

I thought about going for assistance, but all the ship's crew was really busy, and besides that, if I left her to get help, she might stumble away and hide again. I was through playing that game.

"Muriel. Give me your hand. I'm going to help you up, and then we're going to take the elevator down to B deck and leave the ship. Okay? A cab will take us to the airport to meet the others. Wouldn't you like that? The bars on the ship are all closed now, Muriel. The cruise is over. The airport is really nice; you'll like it. Now just hold on to me, that's it, and try to stand. That's great. Good girl. Steady now. Hold onto me. Now let's try to walk."

I put my arm around her and heaved her up out of the chair.

They don't teach you this stuff in travel agent school, but they should. Muriel was certainly not the first problem drinker I had dealt with on tour. Drunks are an occupational hazard on package tours.

We stumbled toward the glass elevator. I held Muriel up against the wall while I pushed the down button, talking to her all the time.

When the doors opened, I muscled her into the elevator, propped her in the corner against the back wall, and punched the B Deck button. She had stopped mumbling and was humming instead, the same snatch of tune over and over and over.

Itchy's really got to up my pay after all this, I thought.

The elevator started down.

Through the glass wall I could see the taxi line. Most of them had left, but a few remained. The suitcases that had been lined up outside the customs shed were almost gone. The elevator stopped on Continental Deck, but no one was there waiting.

The doors closed again and we continued downward. I waved at Captain Vargos, who was standing, tall and handsome, at the purser's desk. When he saw me waving he didn't wave back, but instead said something to the purser and pointed at me; then he headed rapidly toward the stairs without another glance in my direction.

What's wrong with him? I wondered. I thought we were okay now. More than okay. In fact, last night was pretty great.

"Whee!" Muriel said, her green-grape eyes glowing as we whooshed through the atrium of the main lobby then into the enclosed shaft that passed through the lower passenger decks.

While Muriel hummed behind me, I watched the lighted numbers change above the door. We stopped on B Deck, where the entrance to the main gangway was located.

The doors were opening for B Deck when the cord went around my neck.

Somehow, somehow I managed to get a few fingers under that cord bare seconds before I was down on the floor, fighting for my life.

Muriel shouted out that maniacal cackle that had haunted my days and nights since my macabre performance in the Broadway Showroom. She pulled the cord tighter against my fingers, around my neck.

Muriel was incredibly strong. Incredibly sober. And mad, completely mad.

"Don't struggle against me, Sidney, don't fight me. It won't help. I'm much stronger that you, you know. Just take your punishment. You can't win. There now, just relax, you little trollop, and it will soon be all over. Relax!"

I clawed against the cord as hard as I could, trying to bite her, kick her, buck her off my back, but it was no use. She not only outweighed me, she was so strong, so incredibly strong. I couldn't take my hands away from under the cord to try to hit her. I couldn't risk it.

"It was me, Sidney." She giggled in my ear. "Did you know, did you know, did you know? It was me all along. All along. All along. And you never guessed, did you, did you, did you? No, no, no. No one suspected. No one guessed. Hee hee! Poor drunk fat Muriel punished them all. One by one. By one. By one. Snippy Ruth, sleeping with her nasty Mr. Bostick, and silly Sylvia and you! Harlots, both of you, screwing, screwing, screwing my beautiful Fernando. Don't say you didn't. I know you did. Because he didn't want me, you know. He said so. He laughed at poor Muriel, all because he only wanted you. He could only see you. But when you are gone; then he will want Muriel. Yes, yes, yes. Beautiful, beautiful Muriel. And if he doesn't, why then Muriel will punish him too, dear, when she catches him. Yes, she will. Muriel will punish him, too."

She had me pinned face down on the floor of the elevator, slowly twisting the cord tighter against my fingers and neck, her horrible, hateful voice whispering in my ear.

I kicked the wall of the elevator, over and over, kicked it, trying to buck her off, trying to turn over, but it did no good. She paid no attention, just kept up the relentless pressure on my neck.

I fought her as hard as I could for as long as I could, but in the end, her massive weight and manic strength in the enclosed space were too much for me.

I couldn't breathe. She sat on the middle of my back, crushing me against the floor, riding me into oblivion. I was weaker now, and weaker still, unable to push her off my back, unable to breathe, and the cord was tightening. I could no longer feel my fingers. She was huge, she was relentless, and her strength was amazing.

I could barely hear her hideous voice. I was losing consciousness, no longer able to fight, going down, down, down into darkness.

This is it, I thought at the last, this is really it. What a stinking way to go.

35

When I heard the shouts I thought it was the angels. They shout when you get to heaven, right? And they were all dressed in white.

The biggest angel picked me up in his arms and rocked me gently, like a child, like a baby, kissing my hair, saying my name over and over. "Sidney. Sidney, darling. Oh, my darling Sidney. Open your eyes, Sidney. Wake up, my dearest, my love. It's all over now, Sidney. You are safe, Sidney, my precious girl. You're safe."

✻

The big angel turned out to be Captain Vargos, of course, in his whites, and the other angels were the security guards who had pulled Muriel off of me right before I checked out for good.

Vargos knew that the final shore excursion bus had already left. After he saw us pass through the atrium in the elevator, he had realized from the wild look on Muriel's face that something must be terribly wrong. That's why he started down the stairs to help me with her. Then the security guards heard the sound of my kicks in the elevator.

I didn't make the flight home with the High Steppers. Jay got them all back safely, except, of course, for the ones who were already dead or in jail.

It turned out that there truly was no Mrs. Vargos or any little Vargoses waiting back in Athens. Zoe was definitely wrong about that. And I finally met that beautiful blonde I thought was my big competition. She is the Captain's niece, Helen, who is completing an Empress Line internship in the purser's office.

I sailed back to England, without the High Steppers, on the Rapture of the Deep, recuperating in the big bed in the captain's cabin.

"But will you still have a job if you go back to New York?" he asked, nuzzling my shoulder, kissing the bruises that, after a few days, were beginning to fade from my neck.

"I don't know," I said, turning over, "and right now, I just really don't care."

♓

I guess now you're waiting for me to tell you all about the big wedding on the ship, with the ship's horn blasting, and the pastry chef's seven tier cake, and my designer gown, and all the white doves and balloons being released from the Sun Deck, but I can't, because it didn't happen that way.

Instead, when we reached Harwich, Devon, the High Steppers' faithful driver, picked me up at the dock to take me back to Heathrow for my flight home to New York.

It wasn't that things didn't work out for Stephanos Vargos and me. Things are great. He is a very sweet man, a pretty special guy. It's just that his job comes first, and I don't think any woman can ever compete with it, whether he realizes it or not. He said so himself; his first love is the sea. But we'll be together again soon when he comes to New York for a visit, and maybe, just maybe, I'll change my mind about learning to make spanakopeta. Can't you just see me, Jay and Stephanos drinking ouzo and breaking plates at the wedding? *Oom-pah!*

But even if I never see my Captain again, I will have a smile on my face for a very long time.

It was only that, leaving the North Sea and nearing England, standing on the flying bridge in the mist, I finally thought it all through and realized that I couldn't picture myself bouncing babies and making baklava in Athens while Stephanos sails around the world without me.

At the dock, Devon put my bags in the car and then insisted over my protests that I ride in the back seat. Devon is a very proper guy.

As we rolled away from the pier with Captain Stephanos Vargos—his white uniform silhouetted against the sky— watching us from that flying bridge, it was with more than a little regret that I watched the twin stacks of the Rapture of the Deep grow smaller and smaller, then finally disappear from view in the rear window.

Devon accelerated onto the A10.

"Sidney?" Devon said.

"Yes, Devon?"

"Remember the red bag?"

Do I? I thought, *How could I possibly forget it?* But what I said was, "Yes, Devon, yes, I do."

"And remember those two cheery chaps who stopped to help us with the bus accident?"

I nodded. His warm, brown eyes watched me in the mirror.

"Well, it turns out that they weren't such good lads, after all. I picked them out of a lineup at the Yard yesterday morning. There was a third chap, too, the driver of the lorry that clipped us. The inspector explained that bit to me."

He paused for a moment, as he passed a large truck, then continued. "The lads we thought were our friends after the accident were actually the ones who switched Miss Shadrach's red bag in New York for the one with all the treasure. One of them tried to grab it back at Heathrow, but she snatched it away from him, so they followed us on the road to have another go. After the first chap hit us and drove away, the other two stopped and pretended to help. While one of them was talking to Jay, the other one was trying to steal the bag from the bus, but he couldn't because I was right there. He fooled me. I thought the bugger was being helpful, checking the boot for damage. Miss Shadrach must have been on to them. I think she saw him out the window, mucking about with the luggage. He saw her spot him, and that did it for her, what?"

"No, Devon, I don't think so. Those men didn't kill Ruth. Muriel Murphy did. Muriel killed Ruth, Al, and Sylvia out of jealousy or for her own strange reasons. That it was Ruth's bag that was involved with the smuggling ring had nothing to do with Muriel or any of the High Steppers' murders. The fact that the gang picked Ruth's bag instead of one of the others was completely coincidental. One of the guys who was following us in New York before the cruise saw her buy that bag at Macy's; so he went back, bought one just like it and loaded it up with all the goodies. Then they followed us to make the switch. We were all apparently leading a parade around New York without knowing it. Any one of the High Steppers' bags would have done, not just Ruth's. All the gang really needed was a bag that might go through customs without suspicion. A group like ours was perfect. The whole scheme was working pretty well for them, until Muriel came along."

"She is mad, then, Muriel, is she?" he said.

"As a hatter."

"Right-o," he said. "So are you happy to be headed home, Sidney, with everything all finally solved? I mean the mystery and everything."

"Yes, Devon, I am. I certainly am."

"Well," he smiled, "now that this trip is all wrapped up, might I just mention that Diana rang me this morning and said to tell you that she hopes you enjoyed your little holiday, and that she has you booked to go out again on Sunday?"

I won't tell you what I said in reply.

Not you, or my grandmother, and especially not my Aunt Minnie.

Photograph by Chad Mellon

Marie Moore is a native Mississippian. She graduated from Ole Miss, married a lawyer in her hometown, taught junior high science, raised a family, and worked for a small weekly newspaper—first as a writer and later as Managing Editor. She wrote hard news, features and a weekly column, sold ads, did interviews, took photos, and won a couple of MS Press Association awards for her stories.

In 1985, Marie left the newspaper to open a retail travel agency, and for the next fifteen years, she managed the agency, sold travel, escorted group tours, sailed on nineteen cruises, and visited over sixty countries. Much of *Shore Excursion* was inspired by those experiences.

Marie also did location scouting and worked as the local contact for several feature films, including *Heart of Dixie*, *The Gun in Betty Lou's Handbag*, and Robert Altman's *Cookie's Fortune*.

In mid-1999, because of her husband's work, Marie sold her travel agency and moved to Jackson, MS, then New York City, Anna Maria Island, FL, and Arlington, VA. She and her husband now live in Memphis, TN, and Holly Springs, MS.

Shore Excursion is Marie's first novel, and the first book in a new series featuring amateur sleuth Sidney Marsh. You can find more information online at

www.MarieMooreMysteries.com.

Made in the USA
Charleston, SC
25 April 2013